The Chatelaine of Montaillou

Susan E Kaberry

Published in 2017 by FeedARead.com Publishing

A CIP catalogue record for this title is available from the British Library.

Chapter 1
The First Interrogation, 26th July 1320

It is a half-day's walk from Dalou to Pamiers. The road is mainly straight and flat, running through the countryside of the lowlands. Vineyards and cultivated fields line each side of the well-worn track, with here and there a solitary farmer working. Trees of fig, sweet chestnut and oak dot the landscape and offer occasional shade as the sun warms the day. The mountains of the Pyrenees stand solidly in the near distance, quiet witnesses to the three figures.

They leave Dalou early in the morning. Béatrice de Lagleize is walking at speed as if she can outpace the conflict that rages within her. She is going to face the Inquisition, although her better judgement screams at her not to. The two clerics are stout and middle-aged and they struggle to keep up with her pace. But their red-faced, puffing presences give her some comfort, even though she knows that they do not understand her situation. That may be for the best, the less they know the better.

The sun is growing hotter, the air is humid and they are all sweating. The water they carry grows warm and stale. Their bread and cheese lose their freshness. But Béatrice has had little appetite since she received the summons two days ago. Her first instinct was to run as far away as possible from Bishop Fournier's jurisdiction, for he is the face of the Inquisition, a man with a fearsome reputation. She has asked herself many times during these two days why she didn't follow her instincts. She knows of course that she is following the advice of the churchmen she consulted. And she listened to them and trusted them. Or did she?

"Fearsome, yes, but also fair and just," they said. "Besides you aren't guilty of anything, are you?"

This is the crux of it. She doesn't feel guilty, but would Bishop Fournier see things the same way?

"As a noblewoman you will be treated properly, Madame," said the Rector. "He simply wants to question you about other people," he added. "I have the Archdeacon of Majorca visiting me at the moment and we will both accompany you to speak on your behalf."

Since the summons came, Béatrice, pacing her home by day, and tossing and turning in her bed at night, has puzzled and worried over and over again as to why Jacques Fournier has sent for her now. Since he became Bishop in 1317 he has created his own Episcopal Inquisition in his diocese. It is very clear that he is determined to eradicate the last vestiges of the heresy that remain in the area. He has put bounties on the heads of well-known Cathars, those who were Perfects, and those who sheltered and helped them. There has been wave after wave of arrests, interrogations, imprisonments and burnings. There can't be many heretics left alive or free. The Bishop must have gathered a great deal of information, so what does he want with her? What is specific to her? She pushes away a disturbing thought. No, the Rector must be right. Bishop Fournier wants to verify what he already knows and question her about others who were there at that time.

The closer they come to Pamiers, where the Episcopal Palace is situated, the more anxious Béatrice becomes. It seems all wrong to be walking towards the Inquisition. It's like walking towards the gates of hell. As they enter the outskirts of Pamiers, she tries to lick her lips, but her mouth is dry. Her guts are rumbling, fermenting the fear inside her into terror. She stops and looks at the two men.

"I'm not going to the Palace, I can't." She wrings her perspiring palms together. "I'm going to find a horse or donkey for hire and I'll ride straight back to Dalou."

The men look at each other.

"Madame," they say together.

The Archdeacon continues. "If you flee now you will look guilty – besides, the Bishop's men will easily outride you. The best way is to go and meet him."

"That must be so," agrees the Rector. "It will not bode well for you if you run, and he will soon find you."

What they say has a ring of truth to it. She puts her hands up to her face.

"I don't know what to do," she says. Tears well up and fall down her cheeks. She rubs them away. She has left it too late; she should have fled as soon as the summons arrived.

"Trust us, Madame, he is questioning everyone who lived in Montaillou in those days," says the Rector. As he speaks, she wonders if the Rector remembers the many times she has not been in his church on Sundays. But now overwhelmed with conflicting feelings and physically exhausted, she cannot find the strength to defy them and turn and flee, so she continues towards Pamiers. They are close now. Buildings and houses built of stone with wooden upper storeys line their route. A few carts pulled by donkeys rumble past them laden with bags of wheat or flour. Pedestrians and men on horseback are alongside them as they make their way into the centre of the town.

The Bishopric is in the heart of the city, on one side of the large main square where a market is in progress. The sweet smell of ripe fruit is mixed with the

7

pungent stench of animal droppings. The market traders shout to them as they walk past but they do not respond. The Rector brushes a pestering pedlar to one side. Even the strident sound of a honking mule does not claim their attention as they walk towards the entrance of the Bishopric.

The tall cathedral, built of slim terracotta bricks, is flanked by the buildings of the Palace and other outbuildings, around a courtyard. They are met at the entrance gates by a monk who is expecting them. He ushers them into the Palace through a small reception hall and into a larger room, where they are told to sit at the table, which is on the far side of the room and wait for the Bishop. The light filters in through high window openings creating a shadowy effect. Thankfully there is fresh water on the large oak table for them and it is cooler within these stone walls. Is this to be her fate? What God wants for her? That is, if there is a God. This old unspeakable thought comes into her mind. It must be the Devil in her that causes her to think like this. Get thee behind me, Satan. She pushes the thought away – there must be no thoughts of the Devil when she meets the Bishop. There is so much to lose – her life, even. She must present herself as best she can. But there are dark sweat stains on her kirtle and her face must be dusty and grimy from the journey. Tears prick, she blinks them away. Should she take out the little mirror that she carries in her bag and check her appearance? Perhaps not… the meaning of a mirror could be misconstrued. She pats at her hair and her head-dress, pushing stray strands of dark chestnut hair off her face. Her head is bowed and her hands are agitating in her lap as she searches within herself for strength to face Bishop Fournier. There is nothing further she can do to change things. She takes another sip of water and looks around the room. There is a high carved wooden ceiling and, on one of the walls, a tapestry depicting Christ carrying the cross. A massive fireplace covers most of another wall. A great crucifix is directly opposite her. She looks at Jesus suffering on the cross, His crown of thorns and the drops of blood running down His face, His bowed head, His poor bleeding hands and feet with nails driven through them. What does He think about this? She prays silently. A Pater Noster and an Ave Maria.

A door opens and the three of them turn to see the Bishop entering with two monks. Béatrice gathers herself together and as the Bishop and the monks approach them, the three of them at the table stand up and bow their heads. They prepare themselves to kiss his hand but he wafts past them, leaving a musty whiff of incense and dust behind him. The smell of piety and Inquisition.

"Please be seated," says the Bishop as he moves to the other side of the table. He sits down to face them. The monks in their grey habits seem to crouch and settle at either end of the table like two rats at a banquet, relishing the prospect of what lies before them. Why are they there? Béatrice and the two clerics are still standing and she finds herself shaking as the Bishop speaks.

"Madame de Lagleize, Rector, Archdeacon." He nods to each of them as he says their names. "Please be seated. I intend to interrogate Madame de Lagleize today. Brother Mathieu and Brother Jean are our scribes and witnesses." He gestures to them to sit.

There is a short pause as the Bishop looks at Béatrice. His eyes linger on her face, slide down over her body then flicker towards the Archdeacon.

9

"Archdeacon, Madame de Lagleize is here as she has been accused of serious crimes. I believe you wish to speak on her behalf. What is it you wish to say? Archdeacon?" He does not look at them as he speaks and there is an impatient note in his voice.

The Archdeacon glances at the Rector. "My Lord Bishop, with all due respect, we… that is, the Rector and I believe that there has been a mistake, Madame de Lagleize is Roman, she attends church."

"According to information I have been given, Madame de Lagleize is strongly suspected of heresy," says Bishop Fournier.

"My Lord Bishop," says the Rector. "I have known Madame de Lagleize for a number of years. She attends church, her children have been brought up in the Roman faith. I beg you, my Lord Bishop, to reconsider. There are no heretics in our midst in Dalou. Madame de Lagleize has had no contact with heretics. My Lord Bishop, I beseech you to let us take her home."

The Bishop puts up his hand. "Madame de Lagleize will be given a fair hearing. This is a preliminary meeting. She will most likely be free to return to Dalou after we have spoken. You may wait for Madame de Lagleize in the outer hall if you wish. I shall interrogate her alone." He stands. "Please show the Rector and the Archdeacon out, Brother Mathieu." Almost as an afterthought he gives the sign of the cross and says, "God's blessings upon you."

The two men stand up. They look at each other. There is nothing more they can do. They are ushered out by Brother Mathieu. The Bishop turns his attention to Béatrice. He leans his arms on the table between them and looks at her.

"Madame, you are accused of very serious offences." She flinches under his gaze. "Blasphemy, witchcraft and heresy." He intones the words slowly. "I have witnesses who have given evidence of these crimes. However, I do not require you to take an oath today, but I caution you that you must speak the truth purely and completely about yourself and others."

She looks up at the crucifix behind the Bishop on the wall. The dusty painted figure of Christ fascinates her as she notices the muscles of His limbs are so perfectly carved, and His skin is so naturally shaded. She sees the wound in His side, the crimson drips of blood on His pale body. The stained loin-cloth He wears. His terrible suffering. She silently appeals to Him. "Help me, please."

"Madame, do you have anything to say?"

"I have nothing to say except to deny the charges. There has been a mistake."
The Bishop's eyes are on her body. He licks his lips.

"Think carefully, Madame. I want to know if you have ever questioned whether the sacrament on the altar is the true body of Christ?"

She is transfixed by the crucifix and wonders if Jesus is here watching them, and although she hears him speak, she does not reply. Bishop Fournier speaks again.

"Have you ever said, that even if Christ's body were as big as a mountain it would long ago have been consumed by the priests alone?"

"No, my Lord."

"Have you ever seen or received into your home, or visited at any time, Pierre, Jacques or Guillaume Authier or any other heretic?"

"I knew Pierre Authier, when as a notary he dealt with the sale of items from my first husband's estate. At the time he was not known as a heretic. Both he and his brother, Guillaume Authier, came to my first wedding. I have not met nor received Jacques Authier."

"During the time you lived in Montaillou, did you encounter any heretics or hear any heretical discourse?"

"I may have heard some people talking about the heresy and the heretics at that time, but I can't recall their names."

"Have you ever seen or received into your home the late Madame Gaillarde Cuq of Dalou, who was known as a sorcerer and diviner of evil spells?"

"I was received one evening at her house, but I did not hear her speak of sorcery nor did I see any evil spells cast by her."

"You are the daughter of Philippe de Planisolles, a known heretic, who was required to wear the yellow crosses?"

She puts her hand up to her face then down into her lap. Her hands are shaking. She looks down. She knew it, she knew he would bring that up. Will she never escape that damned curse? A flash of anger sparks in her. She lifts her head and looks directly at him.

"You know who I am."

He frowns and purses his lips and she feels his eyes boring into her. He waits for a moment then quotes Saint Matthew's Gospel to her. His voice is quiet and menacing.

"Every good tree bringeth forth good fruit; but an evil tree bringeth forth evil fruit."

She shivers. It is hopeless, as she knew it would be. He has made up his mind already. She should not have listened to the Rector. There is nothing she can say or do to change Bishop Fournier's mind. She sits in silence.

"Madame, I will give you time to think about my questions and prepare yourself. I will see you here again on Tuesday, when you will be required to answer my questions under oath. I expect that you will have remembered more about the heretics of Montaillou by then."

Their eyes meet. He clenches his fist and slowly bangs it on the table top as she stammers out her promise as firmly as she can that she will be there, fully prepared to speak under oath on the following Tuesday.

"These things must be done in God's name," he mutters.

She stares at him. He looks about ten years younger than her, in his mid-thirties. He is a large man, tall and bulky with a big, coarse-featured face; an unattractive man. He is fully attired in his Bishop's robes made of heavy, embroidered fabric. The mitre upon his massive head increases his height, and authority and power emanate from him. But does his whispered utterance hint at complexity, at an internal struggle? He must believe that he is on the side of God and righteousness, and there is plenty of evidence to show that he will not flinch from doing his duty in respect of that faith. But perhaps he is not without compassion and does not relish the terrible sentences he is required to inflict on people. She sees too that like most of the men she has known he has been affected by her presence, the way his gaze lingered over her body at times, a certain look in his eyes. Could she appeal to this side of his nature in some way? She sits in silence.

"I will excuse you then, until Tuesday," he is saying. "In Nomine Patris et Filii et Spiritus Sancti. Amen." He makes the sign of the cross.

"Amen," she says and remembers to cross herself. She knows what she must do.

She inclines her head a fraction and, rising from her seat, she leaves.

Chapter 2
Childhood

I cannot say when I first became aware of the atmosphere of secrecy that pervaded my childhood. How does a child know these things? As a small child, I must have been barely conscious of it… it was like the mists that hang over Montaillou, dense and heavy, taken for granted as part of life; it was in the air that I breathed and the ground that I walked on. But as I grew older, I noticed the conversations that ceased when I entered a room, the false light-heartedness and forced smiles of my mother; it was always my mother who tried to disguise the atmosphere. I heard snatches of comments from strangers and name-calling that I didn't understand from other children. Later there were moments when the mist lifted and I caught glimpses… of things that made no sense to me. As more tangible evidence accrued, I worried about it. What was so bad that it had to be kept hidden? It grew into a monster in my mind.

There was no church in Caussou, our home village, so every Sunday we walked to Unac. The journey over the mountain tracks could take one or two hours, depending on the weather conditions and the speed of my little sisters, Gentille and Ava. And that depended on whether one or the other of them was carried by Philippe, my father, or one of my older brothers, Philippe and Bernard.

As we left Caussou, the wooded hillsides of the mountains rose up above us on one side, with rich pastureland on the other side and the valley below. In winter, we wore sheepskins or woollen, fur-lined mantles to keep out the freezing cold as we plodded through silent snow, taking care not to slip. In summer we would saunter in the shade of a canopy of deciduous leaves, away from the searing heat of the sun. At any season, storms of thunder, torrential rain and low, dangerous lightning could prevent us from making the journey.

The toll of the church bell reminded us of our purpose as we neared Unac. I always felt a flutter of gentle excitement in anticipation of going through the great wooden doors of the church, which seemed like stepping into another world. The candles illuminating the frescoes with flickering light, the smell of ancient dust overlaid with incense, and the rich stink of many unwashed bodies created a warm and familiar fug. I was thrilled by the mysteries and dramas of religion – the power of the magic at the altar when the bread and wine became the body and blood of Christ fascinated me. The dusty statues with their sad eyes, in particular the statue of the Virgin Mary with Baby Jesus – her beautiful, kind face and her heavenly blue gown – were a source of wonder to me. I would stare at the statue for many a long time hoping to see some movement in the features of the Virgin, or a tear fall down her cheek, some kind of a miracle – as if by willing it, I could make it happen. The rhythms of the rituals and prayers, the presence of my family and neighbours comforted me then.

On that Sunday – I must have been about six years old – I wandered out of the church with my family. The congregation were milling around enquiring after each other's health, babies were crying and children were running around glad to be free. The priest, standing nearby with a frown on his face, grabbed hold of my father's arm as he passed and spoke into my father's ear. My father pulled away and his voice, fierce and angry, rose to a shout. Everyone around us fell silent and stared. My father turned and marched off at such speed back to Caussou that we could not keep up. My mother, Esclarmonde, with her head down and avoiding everyone's eyes, gathered us all together and we walked back in silence. None of us dared to speak as we neared Caussou – none except me. I just had to ask my mother what the matter was. The reply she gave me was to become a familiar one over the years.

"You're too young to understand."

After this I noticed that my father wore his tunic with the large yellow crosses sewn onto it, front and back, when we went to church. I had seen him and others wearing these crosses before. I thought that they were a sign that the wearer was more religious than other people. I puzzled over this after the incident with the priest; surely a priest wouldn't be angry with someone who was more religious? I had an instinctive understanding that this was connected in some way to the secret but it made no sense to me.

It was a common thing on Sunday mornings to hear my parents' fierce whisperings behind the closed door of their bedroom. On occasions the whispers would become louder and a tense atmosphere could persist for hours, sometimes days. The pall of heaviness surrounded us and affected the whole household. No one dared speak to my father when he was in one of these moods. My mother gave up trying to pretend it wasn't happening after a day or so, and she plodded on, doing whatever she had to do in a quiet, sad sort of way. Whenever I could, I escaped all this by playing with the village children. It was through them that I caught another glimpse of something that I did not comprehend but that I knew was part of the secret.

As the only noble family in Caussou, we lived in the manor house in the centre of the small village. In front of our house, in the village square, stood the water source. The water flowed down from the mountains over the rocks and along a small channel into a large stone trough. There was a low stone wall and shady trees on either side of it, and when the women came to fill their pots they sat for a while and caught up with the gossip. They often brought their children with them and I would slip outside to find playmates there.

I went out one morning carrying a doll with me that had been given to me the week before. My grandmother had made the doll and had dressed her in pieces of fine silk and brocade. She had golden hair made from threads and her embroidered facial features were fine and beautiful. My mother had said she was not a doll to be played with outside; she was really more of an ornament. But I had sneaked her out, I called her Stéphanie, a noblewoman's name. I held her behind my back.

The women were picking up their pots and placing them on cushions on their heads ready to carry home. They gathered up the little children, leaving behind a couple of sisters, the daughters of one of the poorest and roughest families in the village. These two girls were a year or two older than me and I was wary of them. The family had a reputation for violence and bullying.

"What have you got there, Béatrice?" said Guillemette. She came up close to me. The rank smell of her, her ragged clothes and her greasy hair wafted into my nostrils – it was the stench of poverty. She stood next to me, towering over me, her hands resting on her big hips. I felt a twinge of fear as she put her face near mine, even though she was smiling.

18

"Nothing," I said. "I'm going in now."

"Just a minute." Guillemette moved to block my way. "You have got something there, I can see it."

"It's a doll, but I'm not supposed to bring her out," I said looking around to make sure my mother wasn't watching. "I'd better take her back in." I started to walk around Guillemette to go towards the house.

"Show us," said Raymonde, who jumped in to support her sister.

"I can't show you here, I don't want Maman to see," I said. "Let me go in now, I'll show you another time." Guillemette who had been skirting around me, jumped at me and grabbed the doll out my hands.

"I've got her, I've got her," she sang.

"Give her back, your hands are dirty," I said.

Guillemette threw the doll to Raymonde, who caught her and threw her back to Guillemette, who threw her back to Raymonde. They continued this game and I ran to and fro between them trying to intercept and retrieve my doll as they laughed. I was smaller than them and my fruitless efforts made them laugh all the more. My frustrations boiled over and tears raged down my face.

"Give her to me," I shouted.

Guillemette took Stéphanie to the stone trough that the water dripped into and dropped her into the puddle of mud beside it.

"Oops," she said putting her hand up to her mouth in pretend shock. "She's very dirty now, my Lady Béatrice."

Raymonde picked Stéphanie up and looked at her.

"We'd better give her a wash," she said and dropped her into the trough of water.

I watched in horror. Stéphanie would be damaged and I would be in trouble if Maman found out.

19

"You've ruined her, you're so mean, you're just jealous," I said between my sobs.

"What are you going to do about it?" said Raymonde. "You can't run to your mother, can you?" Her eyes glittered in amusement as she laughed. She fished Stéphanie out of the trough. They both ran off into the village and I chased after them. Raymonde stopped, threw Stéphanie on the ground and shouted at me.

"Here's your fancy doll, take her with you when you go to hell for heresy!"

"Your father's a heretic, heretic, heretic!"

I ran back towards home clutching the ruined Stéphanie. Philippe and Bernard were in the square in front of our house.

"Béatrice, what's the matter?" said Philippe. Only the other day they had both been teasing me with the same doll, throwing her around like Guillemette and Raymonde, to the point of making me cry, but I knew they would always run to my defence if anyone else upset me.

"It's Guillemette and Raymonde, they threw Stéphanie in the water trough and they said Papa was a heretic," I said, wiping my snotty face on my sleeve. "They shouted after me: 'Heretic!'"

"We'll go and find them," said Philippe. "That family needs to know who's in charge round here."

"We'll teach them a lesson," said Bernard. "They've had it coming for a long time."

"What's a heretic?" I said.

The boys looked at each other.

"It means Papa doesn't believe in God," said Bernard. "That's why he wears the yellow crosses."

"But Papa comes to church," I said.

"Yes, but… well, it's different," said Philippe.

"How is it different?"

"Different… you won't understand because you're a girl," said Bernard. "I'm bored with this, come on, Philippe."

"But…"

"Ask Maman," shouted Philippe as they ran off.

I went to ask my mother, even though I was sure she wouldn't tell me anything. I left Stéphanie to dry in the sun on the front porch. Maman was sitting in a small room next to the kitchen, which we used as a family when there were no guests. She was sewing, mending a tear in my old mantle, which had been passed down to Gentille.

"Béatrice, whatever is the matter?" she said putting her arm round me.

"Maman," I said. "Is it true that Papa doesn't believe in God?"

"No, that's not true at all, whatever made you think that?" said Maman.

"Philippe and Bernard said that's why he wears the yellow crosses."

"Papa does believe in God, but he disagreed… once, about… some… well, some of the Church's ideas," said Maman. "So yes, the crosses are because of that."

"Is that why Papa shouted at the priest?"

"Well, in a way… it's complicated Béatrice, and you will only be able to understand when you are older."

And I had to be content with that. Except that I was not content with that. I knew it made me vulnerable, I didn't know what could happen next. Why would nobody explain it to me?

When I was eleven I was taken to the annual fair at Foix with my parents and older brothers. Gentille and

21

Ava were left behind with our servants. The fair was held on 13th October, the feast of Saint Géraud. It required two days of walking in the autumn rain to Celles, a village not far from Foix, where we were to stay with my aunt, who was my father's sister, and my cousins. My excitement about this overruled the discomforts and tediousness of the journey, and I didn't care about my damp clothes and my squelching, sodden boots. I had never been so far from home in my life and I had never met my cousins before. Most of all I was longing to meet Montagne, who was three years older than me.

A welcoming party of Aunt, Uncle and cousins greeted us from their front door as we arrived at their manor house on the edge of Celles. I picked Montagne out immediately. I knew she was the eldest, and she looked so beautiful to me – her oval face with sparkling brown eyes, her pretty lips and her fine skin framed with thick brown hair – so grown-up.

"Look at Béatrice, she's going to be a beauty all right," said my aunt, embracing me. "I thought you might like to sleep with Montagne, Béatrice."

Montagne gave me a gracious smile. "I'll take you to my room, Béatrice," she said. "And you can change your clothes and wash off the mud from the journey."

Montagne's room was at the top of the manor house, which had three floors. It was large and furnished simply, rather like my own room at home except she didn't share it with any little sisters.

"My two little sisters are just babies still and they sleep in the nursery with their nursemaid. The others are boys, so I'm lucky, I have my own room," said Montagne. "But I'm pleased to share with you, Béatrice."

I looked around. A log fire burned in the fireplace, and shutters and tapestries kept out the worst of the weather. There were sheepskins on the floor, a small table with a basin of water and a bed. My mother appeared with some dry clothes for me.

"You can change in front of the fire," said Montagne. "Come down when you're ready, I think we'll be eating soon."

That night we hardly slept as we talked non-stop. She told me about her monthly bleeding which had started last year, and what her mother had told her about a wife's duties. I was not naïve, I'd lived around animals all my life and played with the village children who informed each other with relish about any new facts they discovered. My earliest knowledge came from Brune, my friend in the village, who told me that the newly born kittens that were in the barn had come out of their mother's bottom. Brune knew this because she had seen them born and she also knew that that was where babies came from – your mother's bottom. My brother Philippe enlightened me further when we came across two dogs copulating in the square outside our house.

"They're mating," he said. "Fucking – that's what people do to make babies."

"What, like that?" I pointed to the dogs that were now stuck together.

"Yes, except people don't get stuck," said Philippe.

"That means Papa did that with Maman?"

"Yes," said Philippe. "Five times, as there are five of us."

By the time we made the visit to Montagne and her family, I knew the basic facts from my own observations of watching the animals give birth, to

23

friends informing me of the special place in a woman's body where babies were born from. So when Montagne told me she would soon be betrothed and what her fears were, I had some understanding and sympathy with her.

"They're looking for someone suitable for me," she said. "He must be a nobleman, rich and not too old or ugly. I told Mother that if he's old and ugly, I wouldn't let him do it to me. Mother said I would have to do what every wife has to do, whatever her husband is like." Montagne pulled a face of disgust. "I couldn't do it with some ancient old donkey, can you imagine?" We giggled at the thought of this but I knew it would not be so long before I had to prepare myself for the same fate.

We rose early the next morning to make our way from Celles to Foix. The rain had stopped and the sun was shining. The track gradually widened, becoming crowded with people and animals as we approached Foix. The smells of the animals and the perfume of fruit hit us as we entered the crowded town. There was so much to see. There seemed to be donkeys everywhere, with the dark cross of Christ on their backs, carrying baskets of oranges and lemons from Aragon. Pale, ungainly mules pulling carts with piles of turnips and cabbages, wooden implements and bales of fabric plodded steadily through the hordes of people. So many people, many more than at the market in Ax, peasants in their coarse working tunics, priests and monks in cassocks and robes, as well as better-dressed nobility like my own family. People came from all over the county of Foix and beyond. Stallholders shouted to us, "juicy oranges? Come and feel them," accompanied by a wink in Montagne's direction. Above the cacophony of braying donkeys, honking mules and shouting people, I heard people speaking – at first I

24

didn't know what – then I realised it was another tongue. My own tongue was spoken strangely here too by some with an accent that I found hard to follow.

As I looked around at all these people and their animals I noticed that people were staring in our direction. I thought at first that they were staring at Montagne, who had told me that men were always staring at her and she had difficulty fending them all off. But I realised that they were staring at my father. I had noticed he wore his yellow crosses when we set out, and as always it was not spoken of. The people at the fair did not disguise their reactions at all, they looked, they pointed, and they moved away, crossing over to the other side of the road, as if to be near would contaminate them. It was as if my father was part of the entertainment, a nobleman wearing the yellow crosses, another freak to stare and point at, like the dwarf who was juggling some balls nearby, all part of the fun of the fair. My father just walked on as if he hadn't noticed what was happening. Mother tried to distract me by drawing my attention to the dwarf who was now performing acrobatics. Near the animal pens, a group of shepherds were more subtle, not staring quite so much, talking in whispers behind their hands, but it was obvious nevertheless. I was unnerved by it. I resolved to ask Montagne about it when we alone together that night. It was Montagne who gave me the opportunity by asking if I noticed how the men at the fair were staring at her.

"I saw a lot of people staring…" I said. "I think some of them were staring at my father's… at the…err, yellow crosses."

"Oh, those," said Montagne.

"Yes, those, I wish that someone would tell me."

"What?"

"About them, I've asked my mother so many times and she just says I'm too young."

"Oh," said Montagne with an air of authority. "It's punishment – the yellow crosses – for having different beliefs."

"Do you know anything about it?" At last someone who would talk about the heresy.

"They think that the Devil made the world, don't they? The heretics?"

"Oh, is that all?"

"They don't believe in the sacrament at the altar, the transubstantiation of bread and wine into the body and blood of Christ either."

"That must be why the Pope punishes them," I said. "But why do people stare and move away from my father here? No-one does that in Ax when we go there, or in the church at Unac."

"It's the Inquisition, they have spies here." Montagne dropped her voice and looked around the room. "The people in Foix make a big scene about moving away, so if any spies are watching, they won't think they're heretics."

"What about you then? And your family?"

"Umm," said Montagne. "We're not heretics… anyway, we're a noble family like yours, so it doesn't matter so much."

"I saw a few beggars wearing the crosses in Foix," I said.

"That's what happens to them," said Montagne. "No-one will give them work."

I had never been able to see the point of the crosses. But the talk with Montagne caused a wave of understanding to flood my mind. It made sense. My father was a nobleman. Our family home and estate

26

high up in the village of Caussou was well away from Foix and Pamiers, and my father could carry on his life without wearing them. It was possible to forget they existed, especially if he missed attending church for a few weeks. But the priest would come to see him if he missed church too often. They could never be entirely forgotten.

Chapter 3
The Second Interrogation

"The Bishop has allowed you home, Madame?" says the Archdeacon as Béatrice joins them in the Palace's entrance hall.

"Yes, but I must return on Tuesday," she replies.

"We will accompany you back to Dalou, Madame," says the Rector.

"No," she says. "Thank you, but I need to be alone, you go on ahead."

They exchange looks. "Are you quite sure, Madame?" says the Archdeacon. "You look pale, you should not be alone."

"I've had a shock, that's all, I need time to think, so please leave me," she says. "And thank you, thank you for coming here to speak for me."

"Well, if you're sure…" says the Archdeacon, looking concerned.

She manages to smile; they have done their best. "Well, perhaps I'll walk through the town with you… and then I'll find somewhere to sit and rest for a while, and you can go on without me." After all, she feels better now she is out of that room, away from the terrifying Bishop Fournier.

They walk on together in silence. There are fewer houses lining the track now and they are soon in open countryside. They arrive at a shady spot where a clump of trees grows at one side of the track, and she stops.

"I shall rest here, please…" she puts her hand up to stop them speaking as they both open their mouths. "Please leave me. I shall follow you soon."

They nod and move away muttering to each other. Béatrice sinks down beside an oak tree and leans back on its broad trunk, watching as the two men waddle along the track. She sighs and brushes strands of hair out of her eyes. One thing is very clear to her. Never, ever, will she go back there. Jacques Fournier has decided she is guilty. It was when he mentioned her father – that was when she knew that she could never escape the legacy of her father's punishment. When Bishop Fournier allowed her to go, she was surprised. But he has handed her an opportunity and she is determined to take it, to use this chance wisely. Where can she go? Somewhere well away from him, where he will never find her. When all this has blown over and he has forgotten all about her, she will go back home, quietly and safely. He's been questioning so many people, surely he will give up on her soon enough.

Her four daughters are waiting at her home. They crowd round her when she arrives back.

"Maman, how are you? We've been so worried about you," Esclarmonde, the eldest, says through tears. "The Rector told us that the Bishop would not listen to him, and that the Bishop said that nothing would stop him from doing his duty."

"He's right, the Bishop is a terrible man," says Béatrice.

"The Rector said he has heard since that Lorda Bayard has been arrested again, and her husband is second only to the Count of Foix in this region, isn't he?" says Condors. "It seems no-one is immune."

"What will you do, Maman?" says Ava, wiping her eyes.

"I don't know yet," says Béatrice. "But I've nothing to fear, I've done nothing wrong. Dry your tears now, all of you. I'll just go and talk to Bishop Fournier again and he'll see that I am guilty of nothing and it will all be over in no time." She gives them all a forced smile. "Now, Condors and Esclarmonde, go back to your families, and I'll stay here tonight and prepare myself for next week."

It's later that same day when Pons Bole, Béatrice's notary, who had been the one to first alert her that she might be summoned by Bishop Fournier, visits her again. Ava and Philippa, her two youngest daughters, are asleep and the servants are in their beds. Béatrice has been pacing around her room unable to sleep and she hears him knocking. She opens the door to him.

"Madame, I have important news for you," he says. They stand facing each other in the hall and he blurts it out straight away. "They have arrested several more people from the villages around here. I think you are in grave danger. You must leave. Go over the mountain passes, as many others have done from Montaillou and Ax. Go well away from Pamiers into Aragon, where the Inquisition will not follow. Whether you are guilty of anything or not, you are guilty by association. And you know, they'll make you confess to anything through… well, through… certain things, some terrible things are said." He looks very grave. "I must not stay as I could implicate myself, but I wanted to warn you, Madame. This is my best advice to you."

"Yes, you're right, I'll go… somewhere, and you must go now – don't put yourself in any danger," says Béatrice.

"Is there anything I can do to help you?" he asks.

"Could you arrange for a muleteer to be here at first light to carry my clothes? Someone you can trust not to speak? I'll pay well."

"I'll see to it, Madame."

She packs up into a bundle the things she wants to take with her. She lies on her bed and tries to sleep. Her mind will not be still and she falls into a restless half-sleep – she's being chased and her legs will not move – she wakes, sweating and frightened; she's had that dream before. She sits wrapped in a blanket until a finger of dawn light pokes through the shutters. She awakens her maid to tell her that she is going away for a while. She wakes Ava and Philippa, and tells them she is taking them to stay with Esclarmonde, as she has decided to go back to Pamiers. The girls are sulky, not fully awake and they walk in silence the short distance to Esclarmonde's home.

"I'm sorry to wake you so early," says Béatrice, to a surprised and sleepy Esclarmonde. "But I've decided I will go back to see the Bishop. I shall stay in Pamiers and wait until he sees me again, and then I'll come back home and it will be over and done with."

"But Maman, are you sure this is wise? You said he was a dreadful man," says Esclarmonde.

"He is, that's true, but I really have nothing to fear. I told you, I'm not guilty of anything. He just wants to know what I know about others. Everyone is being called in for questioning. It's really nothing to be frightened of. I was upset yesterday because it was such a shock."

"Well, if you're sure it's the right thing to do, Maman…" Esclarmonde sounds doubtful.

"Yes, I'm sure," says Béatrice.

"Then yes, of course Ava and Philippa can stay here with me. I'll tell Condors as well," says

31

Esclarmonde. "Please take care, Maman." She kisses Béatrice and puts her arms around her.

Béatrice goes back home, where the muleteer Pons Bole has arranged is waiting with her bundle of clothes on his mule.

"Good morning, Madame," he says. "Where are we going?"

"We're going to Belpech," says Béatrice.

Belpech is a full two days walk from Dalou. They make slow progress, only reaching the outskirts of Pamiers towards the end of the first day. The heat is fierce and oppressive, and they need to rest at midday for a couple of hours to avoid the worst of it. Their sweat and the mule's attracts hordes of flies and they are constantly batting them away as they walk. The muleteer wants to rest for the night just outside Pamiers, but Béatrice insists that they push on away from Pamiers, into the countryside. She cannot risk being spotted by any of the spies that the Inquisition are said to have everywhere. They walk on until dusk through the vineyards, fields and woods of the plain. Béatrice has money and when they seek sanctuary in a remote hamlet, a farmer and his wife are glad to feed and house them for the night. They rise early and make better progress in the cooler morning air. They reach Belpech in the late afternoon.

"I want to find lodgings away from the centre, if I can," Béatrice says to the muleteer, but this proves impossible and she has to settle for a place not far from the castle. The muleteer drops off her baggage and goes on his way. Béatrice asks for a messenger to go to find Barthélemy Amilhat, the priest in Mézerville, about an hour's walk away.

"Who shall I say sent the message?" says the boy.

"Just say it's from a friend, and tell him that I want him to come and meet me here, in this house, in Belpech."

There is nothing more she can do and feeling very tired she retires to her room in the lodgings to wait for Barthélemy. She cannot sleep and alternately paces the room and lies on the bed, worrying that he will not come. She knows he is busy; at least that's what he always says on the rare occasions they have met over the last few years. But he knows she was going to see Bishop Fournier a few days ago, so he will understand – she hopes he will understand that this is connected to her interrogation. Perhaps though she should have stressed this more to the messenger: "Tell him it's important, it's his wife who needs him." But she didn't, so now she must wait.

It's dusk when she hears him being shown into the house and his footsteps on the stairs. She opens the door before he can knock. "Oh Barthélemy, thank God you're here, you must help me. I'm in a terrible situation. Pons Bole has told me to flee. Jacques Fournier was a dreadful man. I'm so frightened." Her words tumble over each other and tears fall down her face.

"Hush, Béatrice, hush," says Barthélemy, pushing her gently into the room. "Before you speak of these things, we must move from here, it's far too public, everyone in Belpech will know you're here. I know a place where we can go. I have a friend here, Guillaume Mole, he's a parchment-maker, we buy our parchment from him. I think he will help us. We'll go there, then you can tell me the whole story." He looks at the large bundle she has with her. "Where are you thinking of going with all that?" he says.

33

"I'm going to Limoux, to stay with Gentille," says Béatrice. "No-one will know I'm there. I told Esclarmonde I was going back to Pamiers to face Jacques Fournier. Pons Boles thinks I'm going over the mountain passes to Aragon. Barthélemy, I have no-one else to turn to, there's only you, you are my husband, after all, even if we do live apart." She starts to cry again. He puts his arms around her.

"Come Béatrice, we'll talk some more at Guillaume's. We can stay the night there and then we can decide what to do. You can tell me everything that happened with Jacques Fournier."

Guillaume Mole's house is on the edge of Belpech. The two men embrace and smile at each other. Barthélemy simply asks if they can stay the night and Guillaume Mole agrees without asking any questions. He shows them a room with a bed, a small table and two chairs. He offers them food, cold chicken and bread. He brings this to their room with a pitcher of wine, places it on the table and leaves them. As they eat, Béatrice tells Barthélemy everything that Jacques Fournier said and what Pons Bole advised her to do.

"To me, it looks as if you are guilty if you flee, you should go back and explain everything to the Bishop, just tell him the truth of what happened all those years ago in Montaillou; from what you've told me, I think it was just those men trying to get into your bed," he says. "The Bishop will see that too, I'm sure. He's known for being fair and just."

"I'm not going back there. He terrified me, nothing will persuade me to go back there," says Béatrice. "He's already decided I'm guilty, I just... I just cannot go back."

"Béatrice, I think you're wrong, he's not interested in you, it's the people you knew in Montaillou…"

"I'm not going back there," says Béatrice.

"I see your mind is made up…" he says. "But I wish I could persuade you otherwise… I think you're wrong."

"Barthélemy, I'm going to Limoux and I want you to come with me."

"Go to Limoux with you? Béatrice, I can't, I've got so much work to do. It's the Invention of St Stephen on Sunday, you know, the third of August. That's the feast of the altar at Mézerville, I have to be there. Perhaps after that," he says. He doesn't sound convincing.

"But where can I go in the meantime?" says Béatrice. "I don't know what to do or where to go."

"Why don't you go to Mas-Vieux, where we've met before – the old monastery," says Barthélemy. "Brother Michel will look after you for a few days. He's there alone most of the time and he won't ask any questions. You can wait there until I'm free. It's off the beaten track, they won't think of looking for you there. What do you think?"

"I can't go back that way, towards Pamiers, it feels too dangerous," says Béatrice. "I want to go to Limoux, I'll feel much safer there. Can't you come a little way with me in the morning?"

"I thought you would enjoy going to Mas-Vieux, it's a beautiful place." As she starts to protest, he puts his hand up. "Yes, I know, you don't want to, you want to go to Limoux. I'll… well… I'll do what I can, perhaps first thing in the morning I'll go to find a mule to carry your bundle," he says. "But for now, let's try to get some sleep, Béatrice."

Béatrice nods and they prepare to go to bed together. It's some time since they have lived as man and wife and their meetings are infrequent. In bed, he turns away from her. She curves her body into his familiar body and places her arm around his chest. He moves himself closer to her and they stay in this position for a few minutes, warm and comfortable until he turns to face her. She responds to his kiss and his caressing hand as it roams over her breasts and her body. He is hard against her. She touches him and his hand moves down between her legs.

"You're ready for me," he whispers in her ear. His breath is warm and soft.

"Yes," she whispers.

In the morning she wakes to an empty space beside her. She sits up in a moment of panic but she lies back trusting he will help her. He soon returns saying there are no beasts to be hired in Belpech, but he has found a man who will carry her bundle. Barthélemy pays the parchment-maker for their bed and food, and they set off towards Limoux.

And so, on Tuesday 29th July 1320, the very day on which she has promised to return to Pamiers for questioning by Jacques Fournier, Béatrice, Barthélemy and a man carrying Béatrice's bundle, are all making their way along a dusty lane bordered on either side by vineyards. The rows of vines firmly rooted in the pale, stony earth stretch into the distance to meet the grey-green mountains beyond. It is late morning, nearly noon and the sun is high in the sky. All is quiet except for a lone cicada rubbing out its rhythmic sound.

They are walking from Belpech, in an easterly direction towards Limoux, away from Pamiers. As they round a bend in the road, they see they have reached a place where there is a turning to the left a little way ahead. Barthélemy stops.

"Béatrice, this is the turning to Mézerville, I must leave you here."

"Please stay with me, Barthélemy," she says. "Please."

They face each other and he puts his hands on her shoulders.

"Béatrice, I can't go to Limoux with you, I've told you, I must be at the church on Sunday. If you don't wish to travel from here to Limoux alone, why don't you go to Mas-Saintes-Puelles and stay at Mas-Vieux, like I suggested, until I can join you next week? You will be safe there – Brother Gaillard will look after you, no harm can possibly befall you."

Béatrice cries. The man carrying the bundle unfastens the straps that hold the load on his back and sits down under the shade of large sweet chestnut tree. He wipes the sweat off his brow with the sleeve of his tunic.

"I cannot go on alone," she says through her tears. "I'm terrified."

Barthélemy puts his arms around her. She lays her head on his shoulder.

"I'll go to Mas-Vieux, if you will come with me," she says. "Just take me there. You're right, once I'm there I'll feel safe, well away from Jacques Fournier. Then you can go back to Mézerville and I'll wait for you until you are free to join me."

She wipes her tears away with her hands and pulls back a little from him. She looks into his dark eyes, his familiar face.

"I expect that Jacques Fournier will give up looking for me when he can't easily find me. Then, you can come for me at Mas-Vieux, and we'll go to Limoux

37

together and stay with Gentille there for a while. You know I have no-one else to turn to for help. Don't leave me here alone, please."

He sighs. "I'm sure there is nothing to fear, Béatrice, but I'll come with you to Mas-Saintes-Puelles if you wish."

She takes a piece of linen out of the bag she is carrying and pats at her face and blows her nose. He kisses her on the lips and takes hold of her hand. They turn and start to walk back from where they have just come. Their luggage-carrier rises to his feet, sighs, straps on his bundle and follows them. More cicadas strike up, sounding like a group of minstrels serenading them. The noise is so loud that it causes them to smile. But they have only gone a short distance when they hear another sound in the distance. A thudding, pounding sound. They stop to listen and look at each other.

"Horses!" she says.

"The Bishop's men!"

"We must hide!"

They look around at the flat vineyards on either side of the path. There are only one or two scrubby bushes and trees in the landscape, nowhere to provide cover enough to hide them, only the vines.

"Into the vineyard and we'll lie on the earth!" He grabs her hand. But they are too late. In a flurry of dust and dirt, and pounding hooves, the horses appear from around the bend in the road and are quickly upon them. A shout goes up. "They're here! They're here!"

The sight of the five riders, one of whom is wearing a tunic with an official-looking insignia on it, the noise of the horses snorting and shaking their heads, the sharp smell of sweating horseflesh, and the shouting, impacts all at once onto Béatrice and

Barthélemy, who are standing at the edge of the vineyard, with the man carrying the bundle close by. Béatrice starts to shake, and she clings onto Barthélemy and drops her bag.

"Don't move! Madame de Lagleize and Barthélemy Amilhat!" shouts the man wearing the tunic with the insignia on it, as he draws close to them and reins in his horse. Three of the men jump down from their horses. They are all big men with rough, hard-looking faces.

"Who are you?" asks Barthélemy.

"I'm the Sergeant of the Bishop's Court from Pamiers," replies the man, waving a scroll in his hand. His horse skitters near to Béatrice. "I've orders to arrest you for contempt of court!"

"No," she says, taking a step back. "This is a mistake."

The Sergeant motions with his hand to one of the men who moves towards Béatrice, grabs her arms and ties her hands behind her back. He picks up the bag she has dropped and throws it to the Sergeant on horseback. Another of the men is tying Barthélemy's hands together. Barthélemy struggles.

"No, no, you don't want me, I'm a priest and Madame de Lagleize is a noblewoman. You can't treat us like common criminals."

"Even beautiful noblewomen and priests can be heretics." The man thrusts his face close to Béatrice's. "She's not bad for her age, is she?"

She smells his breath, sour from stale alcohol and bad teeth. Terror churns her guts and she retches. She moves her head to one side away from his grinning face. The Sergeant laughs.

"Been enjoying yourselves, you two?" He laughs again as Barthélemy continues to struggle.

"What about me?" says the man with the bundle. "I've not been paid yet."

No-one pays him any attention.

The Sergeant shouts, "Get moving, we're going to Pamiers."

Béatrice looks at Barthélemy, his even-featured face, which so readily breaks into a warm smile, looks distraught. She feels the hopelessness of their situation as she looks at him and sees her own despair mirrored in his face.

"This is nothing to do with him," she says. "Take me, but leave him."

The Sergeant dismounts and comes over to her. His face is close to hers as he speaks, "You would do well to obey orders, Madame, otherwise it will be the worse for you." The stink of his sweat and filth wafts into her nostrils and she turns aside at the same time as he hits out at her with his palm, across her face. The pain and the shock of it takes her breath away. She stumbles and falls.

The Sergeant shouts at her. "Get up you old heretic whore! Or there's more where that came from."

"Leave her alone," Barthélemy shouts back and starts another hopeless struggle to try and free himself. He receives a kick from one of the mounted men. The quivering muscles of the horse's flanks are level with his shoulders.

"Mind your own business, Priest," says the Sergeant as he mounts his horse. "Enough of this, let's move."

Béatrice and Barthélemy have no choice but to walk alongside the horses and their riders. The baking vineyards on each side of the track offer no shade and, in desperation, Béatrice asks for water. They ignore her.

"Just keep moving," says the Sergeant.

Béatrice and Barthélemy stumble and fall again but are dragged up and pushed forward. Barthélemy asks if they can stop, he needs to empty his bladder. A guard takes him behind a tree, then he is pushed on. They learn not to speak. Just to keep moving. She concentrates on putting one foot in front of another. Although she notices little of their surroundings, she becomes conscious of people on the road staring at them as they approach Pamiers. Soon she will be in there, in front of Bishop Fournier, in hell again.

It is late afternoon when they reach the town and, finally, the Bishopric, in the centre. The Sergeant dismounts and speaks to the guard at the gatehouse. He pushes Béatrice roughly towards the guard.

"You, go with him," he says and pushes Barthélemy away from her. "You, Priest, come with us."

He mounts his horse, and Barthélemy and the horsemen leave Béatrice standing with the guard at the entrance to the Bishopric. She stares after them with a feeling of utter desolation.

"I'm sorry, Barthélemy, so sorry," she says to Barthélemy's retreating back. He doesn't turn to look at her. The Guard points across the courtyard of the Bishopric. "This way."

"Where are they going?" She asks.

"Just move," says the guard. He pushes her hard.

Her hands are still tied behind her back and the guard is behind her as they cross the courtyard bordered by stone cloisters on three sides. The entrance to the main part of the building is opposite the gatehouse and he pushes her again in that direction. There are guards at each corner of the courtyard and one each side of the main entrance, all wearing the Bishop's insignia on

41

their tunics. They stare at Béatrice and her guard in silence. There is no-one else to be seen and everywhere is quiet. He pushes her towards a grand stone staircase with an intricately carved wooden bannister which sweeps around the stairs. She stumbles over her skirts as she climbs. Her hands are still tied.

"I can't climb the stairs," she tells him. He sees the difficulty, unties them and then shoves her forward. She loses her balance but somehow avoids tripping up the stairs and at the top of they proceed along a corridor with a polished wooden floor. Then, he pushes her again, up a steep and narrow enclosed wooden stairway into the loft of the Bishopric. His hand is on her back again when they reach the top.

"Down here," he points down another corridor with a door at the end of it. This upper storey has patches of flaking plaster on the walls and the flooring is rough planking. It looks as if it has not been swept in years.

"What is this?" she asks.

Her voice comes out small and hoarse, terrified. He does not reply, and just pushes her again towards a door at the end of the corridor. He opens the door and shoves her into the room with such force that she ends up sprawled on the floor in the dust and dirt. She hears the key being turned in the lock. She is a prisoner. She lies in the dirt where she has landed and sobs. Her back is bruised with all the shoving and pushing, and her face and head are throbbing with pain. She sobs for that. She sobs for the indignity of being pushed onto the floor. She sobs for finding herself a prisoner in this attic room, and for the loss of Barthélemy. She sobs for the injustice of being questioned by the Inquisition. She sobs and sobs for all this and much more besides.

Eventually she calms and quietens. She gets up, turns to the door and rattles the handle. "Let me out!" she shouts. "Let me out!" but no-one comes. "There's been a mistake." The sentence tails off to a whisper. She sighs, turns round and leans against the door, sliding her back down it and into a sitting position.

She lifts her head and looks around at the room. There is a rough pallet bed covered with filthy sacking, and a small table beside it. An opening, high up in the wall, provides a little light and air, although it is not enough to rid the atmosphere of a stench like something rotting, putrid and foul. In the far corner a wooden bucket has some fat flies lazily buzzing around it. The plaster and wood walls are grey and cracked, and the wooden floor has a thick layer of dust and dirt. A decoration of cobwebs festoons the ceiling and the corners of the small room. She puts her head in her hands and sits there.

She hears movement in the corridor. She jumps up and faces the door. The key turns in the lock and a man enters. This is not the same man who brought her. This is an older man wearing a simple, rustic peasant's tunic and he has the brown, lined face of someone who has spent his life working outdoors. He has a pleasant, amiable look on his rugged features. He carries a wooden platter with bread and cheese upon it and a flask of water which he places on the table. He walks with a limp. Her instinct is to try and push past him and run, but clearly there is no point.

"Madame," he says with a little bow of his head. At last, someone is treating her with respect. She bows her head slightly in response, as a noblewoman to a servant.

"Why am I here?" she asks. "Can you tell me?"

43

"This is the place where noble prisoners such as yourself are kept, Madame," he replies.

"But surely I'm not to be kept here for long?" she says.

"I'm sorry, Madame. I don't know."

"When will the Bishop see me?"

"I don't know anything. I just bring your food and water."

She turns away from him. The man is a fool. Bishop Fournier is bound to see her tomorrow if not today, now, very soon. Then she can go home and forget all about this dreadful experience. That is why she is here, in the Bishopric. If he wanted to imprison her, he could have thrown her into a dungeon in Alleman's Gaol, or the Wall of Carcassonne. It's more convenient here. He will see her and then he will release her.

"Please, tell him I am ready to see him," she says.

He looks at her uncomprehending. "I'll do my best, Madame," he says.

The man leaves, locking the door behind him. She drinks most of the water all at once, realising that she is very thirsty. She tries to eat the bread, but it is hard and stale, and sticks in her throat. She bites into the cheese, which is soft, and she manages to swallow some. But she has no appetite and gives up on the food. She sits on the edge of the pallet loathe to be in contact with the filthy sacking. She needs to empty her bladder and goes to squat over the container in the corner, brushing away the flies that hover around. The corpse of a dead rat alive with maggots lies behind the bucket. She shivers.

Footsteps are approaching the loft again. It sounds as if there is more than one person. Béatrice sits up. It is the same older man who unlocks the door and enters the room, accompanied by a woman dressed in a plain kirtle covered with a linen tunic. Her dark brown hair is tied back under a small head-dress. Her bright, dark eyes illuminate her round, pretty face. Stockily built, she looks like the kind of capable, sensible peasant woman that Béatrice has encountered many times before. Béatrice glimpses a fleeting shadow of hope in the presence of this homely looking woman. The man and the woman look at each other. It is the woman who speaks, "Madame, the Bishop has ordered that…." She coughs and stops.

"He's ordered what?" Béatrice speaks sharply. The man and woman exchange glances again. "Come on," says Béatrice. "Spit it out, this situation is no place for small talk. Tell me."

"He's ordered that we cut your hair off, shave it off in fact." The woman speaks quickly.

"What?" Béatrice stands up. "Oh no, no, you can't do that, stay away from me."

She moves to the end of the pallet and puts her hand up to stop them moving any closer to her.

"Madame, all prisoners have their heads shaved. It's to stop the lice spreading everywhere. It has to be done for everyone as soon as they arrive, otherwise the Bishop won't see you. He's asking if you are ready to see him, so we must do it right away," says the woman. Her discomfort is obvious.

"I won't let you near me," says Béatrice. "And no man is touching me, any part of me, not even my hair."

"I think you should wait outside." The woman says to the man.

He leaves the room closing the door behind him. Béatrice and the woman look at each other. The woman moves a little towards Béatrice.

45

"Stop, don't come any nearer," says Béatrice as she leans back into the wall and puts her hand up again.

"Madame, I don't want to shave your hair," says the woman. "But I know that if this isn't done it will be the worse for me, for the guards and most of all for you."

"What do you mean?" Béatrice still has her hand up.

"You must have heard the stories of what goes on here, down in the dungeons below the building?" says the woman. Béatrice stares at her.

"Well, I'll tell you what they do down there. I'm only saying this, Madame, so that you know exactly what you're up against. You are in great danger here, you must be very careful. In the dungeon, there's a room where the walls are all covered in black linen and they have the instruments of torture in there. The torturers are dressed in black with hoods over their heads so no-one knows who they are. They hang people up on ropes, drop them down suddenly and then wrench them up again. It causes their limbs to be disjointed and it's extremely painful. I've seen and heard the poor wretches that have had that treatment. There are other things too…"

"That's enough, I've heard of such things, but surely…" says Béatrice.

"Madame, no-one is immune from this. Believe me, if you don't let me shave your head then Bishop Fournier will send some of those rough guards up to hold you down and do it. They may mistreat you further at the same time." She looks at Béatrice. "You know what I mean?" Béatrice nods. She knows.

"If you don't co-operate, you will be punished one way or another. If you complain to him, even if what you say is true, he will say that the truth needs to be tested, and God will show whether a person is telling the truth by using the instruments of torture in the dungeon. Madame, they are respecters of no-one, noblemen or women, whoever. Believe me, you should quietly let me cut your hair."

"I see I have no choice in the matter," says Béatrice retrieving some dignity. "But I will not have him in the room whilst you do it."

"You are very wise, Madame. I'll just tell him to remain outside."

Béatrice sits on the edge of the pallet and the woman, whose name is Alamande, cuts her hair shorter than she has ever worn it in her life. As the long chestnut strands float to the floor Béatrice puts up her hand to feel it. There is now only a short layer of hair all over her scalp with one or two odd tufts of longer hair standing out like clumps of coarse grass.

"I must shave it now, Madame."

"Ouch," says Béatrice as the blade slips and nicks her head.

"I beg your pardon, Madame."

Alamande brushes Béatrice's clothes down with a small brush she has brought with her, then goes to the door and speaks to the guard. She brings in a broom and sweeps the room clean of Béatrice's long auburn hair including some of the dirt and cobwebs at the same time.

"I'll see if I can get something decent for you to eat and drink," Alamande says. She leaves and returns later with a bowl of soup and some bread.

"That's my homemade soup and bread, Madame," she says.

"Thank you," says Béatrice.

"There's nothing more I can do," says Alamande.

Béatrice nods. The only way to survive here is to obey the rules. She touches her head, runs her fingers over her bald head. It feels naked, strange, and must look even stranger. She cannot see her shorn head, her mirror is in her bag and the Bishop has that. She will ask for it back, the contents could be misunderstood. It's so shameful and humiliating, to have to appear before him in this naked state. She sighs and turns her attention to the food. The soup and the bread taste like the best soup and bread she has ever had, and she eats it all. Ignoring the filth, she curls up on the pallet. The sky in the high opening darkens and the room cools as night falls.

She is exhausted, but her mind will not rest. The interrogation of the previous week plays over and over. The question about her father was the one that caused her to attempt to flee, to leave the area and go to a place where Bishop Fournier would never find her. Her father's punishment for his heretical leanings, those yellow crosses have lain dormant for long periods of time, in a shadowy heap in a corner. Then something would bring them to life and they would dance madly before her, their vivid yellow presence mocking her, taunting her. Now, in this godforsaken place as she waits to be interrogated by the Bishop, an Inquisitor known for his pedantic and tenacious questioning of his prisoners, she knows they have played a part in this.

There are no sounds in the corridor, no-one is coming to take her to see the Bishop tonight. She will have to sleep on this disgusting pallet. Sleep does not come easily; she is restless, sleeping on and off, waking several times to see darkness at the window, then falling into a sleep disturbed by dreams of men dressed in black chasing her, desiring her, raping her, torturing her. She wakes up screaming.

48

At dawn, she paces around the small space, she cannot keep still. When will he send for her? She must get word out to the world outside this place – her children – Pierre Clergue, the priest at Montaillou, could he help her? The padding of footsteps approaching along the corridor catches her attention. The key turns in the lock and the attendant enters with bread and water.

"Good morning, Madame."

"When will I be seen by the Bishop?" she asks.

"I'm sorry, I don't know, Madame," he replies.

"What's your name?"

"Belmas, Jean Belmas."

"Well, Monsieur Belmas, I want to see a priest – surely the Bishop cannot refuse this?"

"No, Madame," he says.

"Make sure you ask for a priest. My family, too, I want to see my family as well."

"Yes, Madame," he says.

She lies on the pallet. She paces around the small space, she lies down again. She thinks of her family, her daughters, grown women now – apart from Philippa, the youngest – they are married with children of their own. Philippa will be missing her; she still needs her mother. Tears form in her eyes and run down her cheeks. She longs to see them, to explain, and to enlist their help. They could help her get out of here. They could arrange something. She has never told them about her past, about her time in Montaillou. There are things that a mother doesn't tell her daughters. And she has kept the yellow crosses and all that they stand for out of their lives.

A different, much younger guard brings stale bread and grey soup at midday. He is little more than a boy, but he doesn't speak and his small, sly eyes seem to glitter with amusement as they move over her naked head.

"When will the Bishop see me, do you know?" She tries to be the noble lady she has almost forgotten she is.

"I don't know," he says and shrugs. She turns away from him in despair. It's pointless to ask him anything, she doesn't trust that he could or would do anything to help her. As she tries to swallow the foul soup, she hears footsteps again. It's the young guard again, his eyes linger on her naked head and she turns away from his humiliating gaze. Has he come back to gloat?

"The Bishop will see you now."

"Now?" she says, standing up.

"Yes, now."

She pats and brushes with her hands at her dusty clothes. "I'm ready," she says.

He takes her down through the Palace. What more can she tell the Bishop? Has someone spoken about her? There are things she has done that could be misinterpreted, that could make her seem less of a loyal Roman. There are things she is ashamed of, mistakes she has made, but she must tell the Bishop as much as she can so he knows she is being honest. She and the young guard traverse the stone floors of the Palace and pass through its arches. They cross the courtyard. There are a few guards standing by doorways, staring openly at her and her naked head as she passes by. Béatrice lifts her head up and stares back.

She is led to a different room off the cloistered courtyard. A small, plain room with a heavy wooden ceiling. As in the large hall, a single crucifix dominates the wall behind the Bishop. Béatrice looks at it as she sits where she is shown, facing the Bishop. He is seated on a raised platform. There is a small table between them. He looks down at Béatrice from on high. He reminds her of a fresco in the church at Dalou, of God at the Last Judgement. A sudden spasm of fear grips her guts. She swallows hard so she will not vomit. A scribe sits at the side of the Bishop. He looks at her and studies her shorn head, then starts to write. She thinks she sees a flicker of amusement cross his face. Their eyes meet. That is surely a glint of supercilious laughter in his.

Her bag is lying on the table between them, its contents spread out on the table. Bishop Fournier casts his gaze over her head before looking directly at her. Their eyes meet. He speaks quietly and there is not a hint of warmth in his voice or his face.

"Madame, because of these objects found in your bag and because of your flight from this court, I have strong suspicions about your Catholic faith. I therefore now require you to take an oath that you will tell the truth, the entire truth, pure and simple, both about yourself and about others, whether living or dead, and all questions concerning the Roman Catholic faith. Repeat after me."

Béatrice repeats each phrase as he speaks them to her.

"I, Béatrice, appearing before you, Reverend Father in Christ, my Lord Jacques, by the Grace of God, Bishop of Pamiers, promise that I will tell the entire truth, pure and simple about myself and others, whether living or dead, and about all questions concerning the Holy Roman Church."

God, forgive me, she silently adds and looks at the crucifix. There is no sign that He has heard. She shivers; she feels no compassion in this place.

51

"There were two umbilical cords in your bag, pieces of cambric stained with what seems to be menstrual blood, a seed of rocket, grains of partially burned frankincense, and a small mirror. There was also a knife wrapped in linen and a grain of another plant wrapped in silk. There were some pieces of dried bread and more pieces of linen. Are these objects yours?"

"Yes," she replies. "My Lord Bishop, I can explain…"

He cuts her short. "I will question you about these objects later. First I must ask you now directly, are you guilty of heresy?"

"No, I am not."

"Have you had any relationships or intimacy with the heretics Pierre, Guillaume or Jacques Authier, or any other heretics? Did you give them anything or send anything to them, or favour them in any way?"

"No," she replies. "Except for what I already told you about them."

"Answer the question fully, Madame, you are under oath."

She repeats what she told him the first time.

"Do you know of any other persons alive or dead, who had any kind of intimacy or relations with heretics, or who committed anything in life, or when dying related to this crime of heresy?"

"My Lord Bishop… It all happened a long time ago… but, I can recall when I was a child, staying in Celles, about five or six years before my marriage to Bérenger de Rocquefort, we were going one day to the church there. An old man sitting outside his house started to talk to us as we passed and he asked us if we were going to church to take the body of Christ. When we said we were, he said there's no need to hurry because even if Christ's body were as big as a

52

mountain, as big as the Pech de Bugarach, it would have already been eaten many times over. I sometimes heard these words repeated… indeed, it's possible I may have repeated them myself as…"

"To whom and where?"

"I no longer recall." She looks down. This was the first thing that entered her head, she is trying to avoid mentioning names and she is tripping herself up. She must be careful. There is silence.

"Madame," he says, "I put it to you that you are lying, dissembling, and avoiding the truth. I see that you need time to reflect. You will be taken back to the loft now."

"No!" she says. "No!" She stands up. "I'll answer your questions now, I can tell you more of what you want to know, listen to me now."

He ignores her pleas and continues speaking in his quiet, cold voice.

"Madame, I ask you now to bow your head and be silent whilst I pray to God to give us strength to do what must be done in His name. In Nomine Patris et Filii et Spiritus Sancti, Amen."

She sees that he will keep her here until he has finished with her. She has no choice but to comply. The slightest thing that can be construed as non-compliance, avoidance or defiance will do her no good. He will punish her by keeping her here. She stands with her head bowed as he makes the sign of the cross.

She can only echo, "Amen."

Chapter 4
Marriage

It was just before my sixteenth birthday and I was in the barn standing next to Michel, the son of my father's steward and my childhood friend. We were watching some newly born puppies penned up in a corner. The pups were latched onto their mother's teats, sucking and pulling at her as she lay there on the fresh straw. Michel put his arm round my waist. He was at least a head taller than me by then and his shoulders had broadened out. His arm felt strong around my slim body. I counted the pups as I continued to watch them, they were so tiny and adorable.

"There are ten," I said.

"Are you sure – I thought there were nine," he said. We counted together. "Ten," we both said and laughed.

"Shall we go down to the riverbank, for old times' sake?" he said.

"Why not?" I replied. After all, Michel was an old friend, we had played together regularly until about five or six years ago. He was a couple of years older than me and he had grown out of childish play. He worked now, helping his father and mine on the estate. He had become a man, but I did not think of him as one of the men of the village that my mother had warned me to stay well away from – he was my friend. We admired the butterflies in the summer meadows and he tried to catch a swallowtail but it escaped. He picked a bunch of buttercups for me and when he gave them to me he took hold of my hand. When we reached the riverbank, he stopped.

"Let's sit here and watch the river," he said.

I sat beside him and we watched the water flowing over the stones, enjoying the way it rippled and whirled where it deepened into a pool and we could see little fish swimming there. Michel turned to me and touched my cheek. He kissed me gently on my lips and we lay down together. He kissed me again and caressed my body. The arousal, which had started in me as we meandered along hand in hand, intensified as our bodies touched and he hugged me close. His hand was on my bare leg moving upwards. I wanted so much to go where he was taking me to. I wanted to surrender myself to him. With a great effort, I pushed his hand away.

"Oh Michel, no please stop. I can't, I can't, you know…" I tore myself away from him. He sighed and looked away. I rearranged my clothes and we walked back together in an awkward silence. After this I avoided him. I was frightened of my own feelings.

It was only the week after this incident that I was once again in the barn watching the puppies when Mother appeared in the doorway.

"There you are, Béatrice," she said. "I've been looking for you. I wish to speak with you – not here – let's walk down to the river."

Mother's mouth was set in a severe line. She looked angry and seemed preoccupied. She couldn't possibly know what had happened the week before, or could she? I put my hand up to my hair, thank God I had braided it that morning.

"The puppies look healthy," said Mother as we walked. "There are a lot of them."

"Yes, ten, I love watching them."

"Yes indeed."

We picked our way across the farmyard and away from the farm buildings into the meadow, where the grass had been recently cut and the hay was piled up in stacks. There was a strong scent of new-mown hay and herbs. The insects working in the untrimmed hedges of the field, where flowers had survived the mowing, created a constant hum. An occasional loud buzz sounded in my ear as one flew close. The mountains, whose rocky peaks reared up on all sides, seemed to me to be closing in on us as we walked together towards the river. We carried on in silence until we came to the riverbank where the water meandered in its lazy summer state.

"Let's sit down here," said Mother. We sat down on the area of brown, dry grass near the river, just near where I had been with Michel, Mother still quiet. Fear prickled in my guts. Mother seemed so serious. Perhaps I should explain to her that nothing had happened between me and Michel.

"Maman…" I said.

"Béatrice," she said. "There is something…"

"Oh?"

"Well, it's just… I have something to tell you," she said. "Papa and I have noticed how grown-up you are now, you will be sixteen at the end of this month." She turned to me with a smile that looked unnatural, forced. "And so, well… we've been thinking, your father and I… We think that it's time to consider, you know we have talked about… when you are married, and so Papa and I, well, we think it's time you were betrothed." This last part of the sentence came out in a rush. My neck and face burned red hot. I stared at Mother. She continued, "And, in fact someone has asked about you."

"Someone has asked for me! Oh! Who? Tell me who it is!"

56

"It's Bérenger de Rocquefort, the Châtelain of Montaillou."

"Oh no!" I could hardly believe what Mother was saying. I could only shake my head and say, "No, no, no."

"He is a nobleman, Béatrice."

"But he's so old!"

"He is older than you, it's true…"

I interrupted her, this was intolerable. "He is a lot older than me. He must be the same age as Papa. No, no, no. I can't, Maman. How could you… how could you think that…?"

"Age doesn't matter you know." My mother continued in a calm, controlled voice. "And as you get to know him more, you'll forget about any age difference and as you yourself age..."

I could not listen to her. I cried. I said I wanted someone younger, more handsome. My mother carried on trying to explain the reasons why it would be a good thing for me to marry Bérenger de Rocquefort. I lay down on the warm earth with my back towards my mother who continued talking on and on. I wondered how this could be, if this was what God wanted for me and why He never seemed to answer my prayers. I had always known what was in store for me, but this, this was not what I imagined would happen – what I had prayed to God for – this could not be right. I must reason with Mother. I sat up and spoke to my mother in as grown-up a way as I could.

"Maman, please, please… don't say any more about this... this… idea. I cannot marry Bérenger de Rocquefort." I spat out his name as if it was poison. But my mother persisted.

"Béatrice, many girls are betrothed in childhood to form alliances with other families that are needed for… well… all kinds of reasons. We spared you that, but now the time has come for you to do what is in everyone's best interests, including your own."

"In everyone's best interests?" I said. "What do you mean?"

"There are certain… difficulties that we have as a family which mean that our choices in this matter are limited," said Mother, looking down.

"What difficulties?"

"Well…" Mother took in a deep breath. "It's to do with the yellow crosses." Her face looked strained. "Something I've had to live with and now it affects you, Béatrice."

"I don't know anything about that, you would never tell me… anyway what has that got to do with who I marry?"

"Some people will not associate with us for fear of being thought heretics themselves," said my mother.

"But why does that matter now? I thought that all happened a long time ago."

"It does matter now, the Inquisition is still watching and there are spies everywhere, you don't know who you can trust. We've tried to bring you and your brothers and sisters up as far away from the heresy as we could. That's why we've never talked about it. You can be judged guilty by association. You must stay well away from it."

"By marrying Bérenger de Rocquefort?"

"Béatrice, Papa and I are trying to help you by considering this marriage to Bérenger de Rocquefort. His family conform to the Roman Church. You can leave behind the curse of your father's punishment. They are a noble family, but they are not the wealthiest of families, they have only a small estate near Carcassonne, and that limits his choices. But you would

58

live comfortably in a château, and you and your children would be cared for by the de Rocqueforts."

"Why hasn't he married before? And why does he want to marry me now?"

"His father died recently and there are no male heirs to inherit the estate. He needs to marry now."

I could hardly believe what she said. They were using me to put right things that happened a long time ago. How could they do this to me?

"I've asked you about the yellow crosses so many times in the past," I said. "You wouldn't tell me, now this…"

"I know, Béatrice, but I didn't want you to worry about these things when you were a child. I tried to protect you from… from the implications."

"But I did worry, although Bernard and Philippe told me some things."

"I thought you may have heard something about it all from others but I didn't want to even mention it to you for fear of incriminating you. Perhaps I was wrong but we are always on our guard. I didn't want that for you." Mother stood up. "Come, Béatrice, a decision does not have to be made immediately. We'll talk more with your father."

But Father had made up his mind and no amount of talking, pleading or crying would change it. He did not listen to any of my more reasoned objections to the marriage. So I raged at him. Mother had some sympathy for me, and I heard them arguing about it. Father was adamant and listened to no-one. He threatened that he would never agree to me marrying anyone else. It was de Rocquefort or no-one. Now or never. If I didn't marry him, I could stay at home and help my mother run the household, and he would offer Gentille to de Rocquefort. I raged at him again. Finally, he said he would put me in a nunnery to teach me obedience and humility, the lessons he thought I needed to learn. For good measure, he slapped me hard and locked me in my room, telling me to think carefully about it. He left me there for a full day and night, crying, sleeping, thinking and crying some more. Should I run away when he lets me out? I could go quietly in the night. But where would I go? Any relatives I might run to would only hand me straight back to Father. I had no way to support myself. As a girl alone, I would be vulnerable to dangers of all kinds. There was no way out. I had no choice but to surrender. When Father opened the bedroom door and asked me if I had learned my lesson, I had to say yes.

I was still hoping that I would find a way of avoiding this marriage as I watched the plans for my wedding unfold. I could think of nothing. It was like being in a dream – one where the dreamer, me, sees events going on around her, but has no part in it and is unable to influence the action. I was paralysed and helpless. There was no point in protesting any more; it would all go ahead anyway. This wedding, my wedding, would be an important event in the social calendar of the county of Foix, but it felt as if it had nothing to do with me – it was all for the benefit of others.

A few days before the wedding, I set out with my mother for Montaillou. I struggled to keep the tears at bay as we bid a subdued farewell to our family and servants. They would follow us to the château just before the wedding, but this was good-bye to my life in Caussou, good-bye to my childhood. A mule, a muleteer and a servant, all laden with my belongings and my dowry, accompanied us on the day-long journey. The way over the densely wooded Col de

Marmare was steep and strenuous in parts, and we spoke little. The clopping of the mule's hooves as it negotiated the stony pathway and our breathing were the only sounds apart from the occasional crashing of wild boars way up in the forest, or the rustle of some smaller creature nearby in the undergrowth. The sharp autumn air smelled fresh with a hint of pine resin, which had dripped from the cones in the heat of summer. All around us were the high peaks of the mountains. We stopped to rest and eat our bread and cheese at midday, sitting beside the track on some convenient rocks. I couldn't eat anything, my stomach was in knots and I felt sick. I fed a robin with my bread as the muleteer told us a long story about where he had bought the bony mule and how much it cost him. My mother responded politely. We didn't speak of Bérenger; there was nothing more to be said.

In the afternoon, as we came nearer to Montaillou, my stomach churned. It was getting closer, this step of tying myself to a man I hardly knew, for life. It was in front of me now, facing me and whichever way I turned it was there, head on. I thought again of running away but all the reasons why I knew it was pointless still prevailed. I tried to think of any good that this marriage might provide for me. There would be a roof over my head and food on the table. As for Bérenger, well, what kind of a husband he would turn out to be was unknown. We had spent no time alone together. He seemed serious whenever we met, polite, but distant and formal. Beneath that façade could be anything. Everyone knew that there were women in Caussou who were regularly beaten by their husbands. It was no-one else's business. It was between husband and wife. My own father was regularly violent with Philippe and Bernard, and I had felt the back of his

61

hand a few times. I would be at Bérenger de Rocquefort's mercy, required to obey him. The knowledge that my father had known him for a long time was a small comfort, but friendship with another man was a different thing to marriage to a woman. To me. Then there was the… intimacy. I did not want to think about that.

As we approached Montaillou through the surrounding meadows, we had a good view of the château. It was built on the highest rocky point of the village and was visible from a distance. It rose up between the mountain peaks surrounding it as if it was part of the rocks itself. I had been to Montaillou a few times before and I knew that the château served the small community as a fortress and a prison. Its purpose was never more evident to me than on that day. Its tall, oblong construction, one round tower and arrow-slit openings in the stone walls, looked severe. The afternoon sunshine mellowed its grey harshness a little, but my spirits sank further as we drew closer. The village clung to the slopes beneath the château on one side and a small plateau lay on the other on which stood outbuildings, barns, stables and one or two dwellings for estate workers, all arranged around the courtyard of the château.

We climbed the steep path to the entrance and Bérenger de Rocquefort came out to meet us. He was a stocky and strong-looking man wearing a plain tunic and hose. His shoulder-length grey hair hung in thin strands. He took my mother's hand first and said, "Madame de Planisolles." I could hardly repress a shudder as he took my hand and said, "Mademoiselle de Planisolles, welcome."

I found the courage to look into his eyes for a moment. There had never been the opportunity to do more than glance at his face before. His eyes were very dark, shiny and lively looking. His strong nose, his trimmed grey beard and his habitual serious expression gave his face a distinguished air, I had to admit, and he carried himself in an upright and confident way as a man of substance, a man of character. But to me he looked so old, so far away from me and my experience of life. I couldn't work out whether I was frightened of him or just of the whole situation I was in. Either way, I was terrified.

He took us through the small entrance hall and into the main reception room of the château, a large, high room with intricate, painted patterns adorning the walls.

"May I introduce my steward, Raymond Roussel, to you both."

"Enchanted, Madame, Mademoiselle," said Raymond, bowing his head. "Let me arrange for your belongings to be taken up to your rooms."

"Yes, and some refreshment. You must be ready for something after your journey," said Bérenger. He gestured around the large room. "This is where we will have the wedding breakfast."

My mother nodded. "It seems much bigger than I remember from when I was last here."

"When was that?"

"It was quite some time ago, I think, about ten years, I'd say."

"I wonder… was that the time when the Count of Foix came…?"

"Yes, I think it was..."

I stopped listening and looked around at the room and all the activity that was taking place. Bérenger and Mother continued talking about the wedding arrangements whilst I wandered around the room gazing at the painted patterns on the walls of dusty blue, burgundy and white. The ceiling had a repeating pattern of squares and stars. In the great stone fireplace, a pile of logs smouldered.

There were a number of people preparing for the wedding. They looked at me as I wandered around the room. The men hefted furniture into new positions, and struggled with great baskets of logs. Women ran up and down the stairs with armfuls of linen, blankets and sheepskins. A man cursed as he dropped a basket of logs and the logs rolled out over the stone floor. Two women laughed together. My wedding was a joyful event to them, a celebration, and they were happy preparing for it. I thought I might cry if I stayed much longer in the hall. I looked at Raymond, who was talking to one of the servants. Raymond was a slim black-haired man with green eyes, probably about the same age as my future husband. He felt my gaze on him and he turned and smiled. The smile on his good-looking face seemed kind. I thought he could see my misery, I was near to tears. He came over to me.

"I can take you up to your room, Mademoiselle," he said. "And I will bring Sybille, your maid, to meet you there."

Raymond took me up the spiral stone steps to the tower. I swallowed back my tears as I followed him and managed a smile as he left. I was alone in my room. I looked around. The room with its circular wall and arrow-slit windows covered by shutters and heavy tapestries seemed large and comfortable to me, used as I was to sharing with two little sisters. Sheepskin rugs lay in front of the fireplace where a fire burned and lit the room with its glow. Two large chests, a bench and a bed furnished it. It looked comfortable. As Châtelaine, I was entitled to my own room and my own maid. Maybe marriage had some compensations.

In the late afternoon, I went down to the church with Mother and Bérenger to meet the priest. We walked down the steep hill from the château to the church, passing the village water source, the font canal, where some women were gathered, gossiping and collecting water. They exchanged greetings with us and as we continued down the track towards the church, I turned round to see the women making their way back to their homes with the heavy pots full of water carried on cushions on their heads. Down, down we went, past the village square on our left and towards the pastures below the village. The small church of Sainte Marie de Carnesses, round and grey, crouched like a large rabbit in the meadow just beyond the village.

"Do you know the story behind the church? You know, the reason why it's down there in the meadow instead of in the heart of the village?" Bérenger asked me as we approached it.

How could I respond to him? My mind was so occupied with my fear and distress that I could not think. Did I know the story or not? It seemed so pointless this chatter, and I shook my head. I averted my face from his as he talked to me. I could not bear it. He was so old and serious, and I would be wedded to him tomorrow – this was all I that could think about. Once again, I had to fight back the tears that came and pricked my eyes with this thought. He didn't seem to notice. He just carried on talking about the church.

"The story is that earlier in the century a young shepherdess was down there minding her sheep, when she saw a shining vision of the Virgin Mary, standing on a rock surrounded by animals." He pointed down to where the church stood. "When the child's vision receded, the footprints of both the Virgin and the animals were left behind, to be permanently visible as evidence, on the rock where they had stood. It's a special holy place – people come on pilgrimage to see the rocks and the church. We are blessed to be married here, I think." We walked towards the rock where we silently looked at the footprints and then made our way to the church where we met the priest and they all talked to each other whilst I remained in my silent dream-state.

On the eve of the wedding the château was full of people, my family, Bérenger's. His mother, Madame de Rocquefort, who was very old and frail, had travelled from Carcassonne with her eldest son, Jacques, and his childless wife. She had ridden on a cart pulled by a horse for most of the way, but no wheeled vehicle could go over the steep and rocky pathways around Montaillou. She walked very slowly with help and then, the old woman tiny, shrunken, and as light as a little bird, had been carried by two local men around Montaillou. When she was introduced to me, she looked me up and down and said, "She looks young and healthy enough."

I wanted to say, "I wish I could say the same for you," as I looked at the deeply furrowed face of this very old woman. Madame de Rocquefort was well over seventy years old, Bérenger had said, but her eyes, pale and milky with age, nevertheless had the gleam of life in them. Madame de Rocquefort, Bérenger and Jacques, and my parents talked together during the meal on the evening before the wedding. I heard Madame de Rocquefort saying to my mother, "It's a good thing to introduce new blood into a family."

"Yes," Mother replied. "It ensures healthy offspring."

"Umm." Madame de Rocquefort looked at her childless elder son. "Let's hope so."

"We've never had any problems of that nature in my family," said my mother.

I sat watching and listening, I didn't belong anywhere, detached from the adult conversation but no longer part of the children's group. I was a breeding bitch, it was my body they wanted. I half expected them to subject me to an examination of the relevant parts to see if they were in good working order. This thought made me smile as I pictured Mother showing them my body: "Look at this here." Of course, I knew the arrangement well enough; it was the usual one amongst the nobility. My dowry, money and goods settled on the marriage, but most of all my fertility, in exchange for his protection of me and my children. I didn't doubt that I could fulfil my side of the bargain, why not? I was young and healthy, as Madame de Rocquefort had said. I imagined that children would provide some comfort – that was one thing I did want, to be a mother. They continued to talk about me whilst ignoring me, until Bérenger noticed me. He asked if I liked my room.

"I love it," I was able to say truthfully. "I've always shared with my sisters before."

I clutched at this small kindness, although I was still full of anxiety about my future with him. It was a glimmer of hope in a desolate landscape. After the meal, we all walked down to the church again to make our confessions. We had to be prepared for the nuptial mass early the next morning. Madame de Rocquefort made us all laugh and Bérenger shook his head when she said she had nothing to confess and was going to bed with a clear conscience.

I shared my new room with my sisters for one last time. We found it difficult to sleep with all the excitement and, on my part, anxiety about the following day, and we talked for a long time before falling asleep. They knew my feelings on the marriage; they'd heard all the arguments.

"I think you'll look beautiful tomorrow in those new clothes," said Gentille, as she removed her own clothes in preparation for bed. I knew that Gentille, more compliant and accepting than me, would always try to say the right thing. I was going to miss her.

"Yes, the silk is beautiful," I said sitting on the edge of my bed in my shift. Tears came to my eyes. Gentille moved to sit next to me and put her arm around me.

"I'm sure it will all work out well," she said. "You're bound to be nervous, it's such a big wedding and… well, Bérenger always seems… to be a gentleman."

"I don't know whether he's a gentleman or not, no-one does really, do they?" I sniffed and wiped my tears away with the back of my hand.

"That's true, I suppose, but we've never heard anything bad about him, have we?" said Gentille.

I shook my head. "No, I suppose not."

"And we would have done, you know if there was anything. You can be sure one of the servants or the farm labourers would have found a way to pass on any gossip about him."

"He's just so old, I don't know what to say to him and well, you know…" I said. I looked across at little Ava who was five years younger and then back to Gentille.

"Yes, I know." Gentille looked at Ava too.

Ava said, "What's the matter? Are you worried about kissing him?" This made us laugh. "You'll just have to close your eyes and pretend it's someone else."

"That's probably good advice," said Gentille.

"I wonder who I'll marry," Ava came round and snuggled up to me.

"I'm next, I wonder who they'll find for me," said Gentille.

"There won't be anyone decent left for me," said Ava pulling a face.

"Come on, you two," I said. "We must go to bed and get some sleep, otherwise I'll look like Madame de Rocquefort tomorrow."

"You will be Madame de Rocquefort tomorrow," said Gentille and we all giggled hysterically at that.

It was early in the morning when my mother came to wake us. They all helped to dress me. My mother secured a small gold coronet in my hair, a family heirloom from her father's side. My dress of embroidered blue silk from Paris had been made by a woman in Pamiers, who made clothes for the Count of Foix. All the family had new clothes and my mother fussed around us until we looked as she wanted us to look. Finally they arranged a new green wool mantle lined with fur around my shoulders. My mother looked at me.

"Try not to look so miserable, Béatrice, he is a good man."

We set out on foot. A dense mist surrounded us as we descended from the heights of the château to the village. We could hear the tolling of the lone bell, summoning us down to the church and me to my fate. We trod carefully on the steep, rocky pathway putting one foot after the other, concentrating on not tripping on a stone or slipping on the mud. There was no-one about and the enveloping mist was cold. I shivered under my mantle. Montaillou was a dismal, inhospitable place.

"Be careful how you go," said my mother. "I don't want any of you to slip and get your clothes dirty."

I was told what to wear, how to arrange my face, what to say and what to do. I was lost in this adult world towards which I was being thrust. I was anxious now that I would forget the vows I had been taught by the priest at Unac. I would soon be a married woman but I felt more like a frightened child. The thought of my family leaving me and going back to Caussou filled me with dread.

Bérenger and the priest were waiting in the entrance. I had to stay in the doorway for the first part of the ceremony. My mother and sisters walked on into the church and a feeling of abandonment washed over me as I watched their backs move away. I blinked away my tears and gazed into the church where a great many candles flickered. The beams in the roof had fronds of evergreen attached to them, in which late-flowering lilies and roses were intertwined. Their thick perfume wafted into the doorway where I stood. The church was full of people standing to watch the ceremony. Bérenger came to stand next to me. He was wearing an embroidered silk brocade tunic in dark greens and blues. His beard had been shaved and his hair looked clean and neat. I noticed how his broad shoulders were emphasised by the cut of his tunic. He smiled at me and I tried to smile back. It was a shaky, little smile. The priest spoke to us.

"Bérenger de Rocquefort and Béatrice de Planisolles, have you come here freely and without reservation to give yourselves to each other in marriage?"

70

The priest looked at both of us in turn as he spoke and we each answered. "Yes."

My voice came out sounding low and hoarse. I cleared my throat. Here I was, speaking untruths in front of God. Doing the right thing can be complicated. God, forgive me if I am doing wrong.

"Will you honour each other as man and wife for the rest of your lives?"

He looked again at both of us in turn and we each answered, "I will."

"Will you accept children lovingly from God, and bring them up according to the law of Christ and his Church?"

We both replied, "I will."

"We are gathered here in the sight of God to join together this man and this woman in holy matrimony, which is an honourable estate, instituted of God in Paradise and into which these two persons present come now to be joined. Therefore if any man can show any just cause why they may not be joined together let him now speak or hereafter for ever hold his peace."

Silence. A small panic bubbled inside me. Will somebody say something? Do I want someone to stop it? Should I say what I think? I didn't, of course, and neither did anyone else.

"I require and charge you both as you will answer at the dreadful Day of Judgement when the secrets of all hearts shall be disclosed, that if either of you know of any impediment why you may not be joined together in matrimony that you confess it now. For you be well assured that so many as be coupled together otherwise than God's word doth allow, are not joined together by God, neither is their matrimony lawful."

I bowed my head at this wondering if this was God's word, what is right and what is wrong? And how can anyone know?

"Bérenger de Rocquefort, wilt thou have this woman to be thy wedded wife, to live together after God's ordinance in the holy estate of matrimony? Wilt thou love her, comfort her, honour and keep her in sickness and in health, and forsaking all others keep thee only onto her, so long as ye both shall live?"

"I will," replied Bérenger.

To the same questions I replied, "I will." My voice sounded quiet and flat. The panic was subsiding and being replaced by resignation.

We followed the priest into the church and walked along the aisle to the altar where the priest turned to the people and asked, "Who giveth this woman to be married to this man?"

My father stepped forward. "I do."

My father took hold of my right hand and gave it to the priest who in turn gave my right hand to Bérenger's right hand. Bérenger turned so that he was facing me directly and looking into my eyes, he spoke.

"I, Bérenger de Rocquefort, take thee, Béatrice de Planisolles to my wedded wife. To have and to hold from this day forward, for better for worse, for richer, for poorer, for fairer or fouler, in sickness and in health, to love and to cherish 'til death do us part, according to God's holy ordinance, and thereto I plight thee my troth."

I looked at him as he spoke without a stumble or a stutter. His eyes looked warm and his voice gave meaning to the words. He sounded sincere. I thought I must try to sound the same.

It was done. Now was the time to adjust myself to what was required and to push to one side my worries about the intimacy that must come soon. I caught my mother's eye as we walked back down the aisle as husband and wife. My mother was laughing and crying all at the same time. Everyone else merged into a blur of faces and greenery, the heavy scent of the roses and lilies enveloping everything.

We climbed back up the main track of the village towards the château. The mountains were still shrouded at their tops by mist but the village was clear of mist now and the autumn sun warmed the air. Many villagers lined the path, waving and smiling, wishing us well. It was heart-warming and I found I could wave and smile back. We concentrated on the climb up the last steep part of the track until we reached the top. The dark grey château, so high above the village, loomed over us through the mist, which still clung to its walls. When we stopped at the entrance, Bérenger turned to me.

"Madame de Rocquefort, welcome to your new home," he said and took my hand as we entered through the great doors together.

Together we received the guests into the main hall of the château. The feast which was spread out on the tables looked like an array of jewels, succulent and shining in the candlelight. Pâtés, dried meats and river trout to start the meal were followed by roast wild boar and lamb. A selection of local cheeses was arranged on vine leaves. Desserts made with figs, sweet chestnuts, apples, pears and perfumed quinces were all taken with wine from Tarascon in the lowlands, where the best wine in the region was made. The scents of candles and wood smoke mingling with the aromas of roasted meats and fresh fruits made a warm and welcoming atmosphere. There was music too. Minstrels played on lutes and tambourines, and after everyone had finished eating, a space was cleared for dancing. The log fire burning in the massive fireplace and the many candles cast a glowing light on the stone walls of the château. Our wedding breakfast was attended by so many people, the noblemen and their families who lived in the region, friends and neighbours, and others in the service of the Count of Foix, like Bérenger. My father wore a new, plain tunic. I knew of course of the wedding plans but I had not expected anything like this. So many people there to wish us well, it was overwhelming but heart-warming too. Even ancient Madame de Rocquefort sitting in a prominent position at the table cracked her wrinkled old face with a smile. The tumult of mixed feelings I had experienced during the service began to calm. I forgot my anxieties for a while and took pleasure in watching my friends and neighbours eating, dancing and enjoying themselves.

How strange it seemed when the festivities were over and everyone had gone. The château did not feel like home to me then and in spite of all my mother's preparation I was lost again. Bérenger took me to the door of my room.

"Sybille will come for you when dinner is served," he said.

I took off the coronet and the jewelled belt and flopped down on the bed. In spite of my concern about what was to come, I was so tired that I immediately fell asleep. I was woken up by a knock on the door.

"It's Sybille, Madame."

"Come in, Sybille."

"Madame, I'm sorry to disturb you," said Sybille.

"What is it?"

"The meal has been served in your husband's room."

74

"Thank you," I said.

"Do you want anything else, Madame?" Sybille stood inside the door.

I had been so busy with the wedding that there had been no time to talk to Sybille. She was a young woman not much older than myself, perhaps in her early twenties. Her hair was covered by her head-dress and she was wearing a plain kirtle over which she wore a tabard. There was something sensible and open about her attractive face, her smile and her large dark eyes.

"Are you married, Sybille?"

"No, Madame, I'm not."

"You were brought up in my husband's household in Carcassonne, I believe?"

"Yes, I was. My mother was a maid there and Madame de Rocquefort allowed my mother to keep me there. I… I never knew my father." Sybille blushed as she spoke. "They are a good family, Madame."

There was a small silence during which we looked at each other. Then Sybille said, "Madame, I think... err… no, perhaps it's not for me to say…" she stopped.

"Tell me please, what is it?"

"Well, it's just, I don't know… but I think you will grow to like it here."

I walked up to Sybille then and put my arms round her.

"Thank you, Sybille."

We stood together for a moment and then Sybille left and I prepared to meet my husband. I patted my hair in place and put on the jewelled belt. Now the time had come to be alone with him. I did not know what to expect. My mother had said that the first time may be difficult and that it may take a while… I stopped myself. Thinking too much served no purpose.

It would be whatever it would be and I just had to accept it. I expected that he would lead me and I could only hope that it was not painful or difficult in some way. Pleasure was not likely to come into it.

He opened the door and I went into his room. The only light was from the log fire and a single candle on a table. It was a large room, similarly furnished to my own with a bed and sheepskin rugs on the wooden floor. A tapestry covered the arrow-slit window and a table in one corner had a few scrolls and manuscripts on it. On a wooden shelf a few books, rare and expensive items, were laid neatly together. A table, set for two, stood in front of the fireplace with platters of food on it.

He gestured towards the table of food.

"Would you like to eat?" he asked.

"Yes, I didn't eat much today. I was too nervous."

We sat down facing each other. "Did you enjoy it? The day, our wedding, I mean," he asked. He sounded anxious. It had not occurred to me that he might also be worried.

"The church was beautiful," I said. Then I thought I should say more, so I added, "I liked seeing all my friends and family together, especially as they were there to wish us well."

"Yes, there were many well-wishers." He poured some wine.

Apart from when we had taken our vows, I had never been able to really look at him, eye to eye, face to face. I never asked him how old he was but he must have been at least forty. I thought his eyes were his best feature; they shone in the firelight and looked very dark. You wouldn't say he was conventionally handsome, but I experienced a real sense of his masculinity in his strong features and broad shoulders.

He was still wearing his wedding tunic which, with his composure and bearing made him look exactly what he was: a nobleman.

I lowered my eyes, fearing that my staring would look too bold. I looked at the food. It was the remains of the wedding feast. Cold meats, wild boar and lamb in slices, cheese and fruit. I took some meat and tried to think of what to say to him.

"I think others enjoyed it too," I said. "I noticed Guillaume Authier dancing with his wife."

"You know him?"

"Yes, I've been to his home in Ax with my father when Monsieur Authier drew up the document for my dowry."

"Ah yes, that reminds me that we should go to see him soon now that we are married, to sign documents relating to our wills." He sipped his wine.

"Oh, I hadn't thought of that."

I took some bread and put a piece of cold lamb in my mouth. The taste of the herbs it had been prepared with seemed to have deepened with standing. It was tender and delicious, and I savoured it.

"You never know what life can bring and it makes things easier if we have the inheritance documents clear and legal."

I nodded, realising that what he said was right. I sipped my wine. It had a mellow fruity flavour.

"The wine is good."

"It's what your father bought." He took a sip, swilled it around in his mouth for a minute, and nodded his agreement.

We ate and drank in silence for a few minutes and then we caught each other's eyes. I popped a chunk of the ewe's milk cheese into my mouth with a piece of bread.

"Mmm," I said.

"Good?" he asked.

I nodded and put my hand over my mouth and signalled by chewing vigorously that I couldn't speak – my mouth was full of cheese and bread – I widened my eyes at him.

"Would you like some more wine to go with that?" he asked laughing.

I shook my head.

"More meat or cheese?"

"No," I swallowed, "I've had enough, thank you." I drained the last of my wine.

"Me too."

We sat still gazing at each other, then still holding my eyes he rose from his chair and walked round to me. He took hold of my hands and bent to kiss my lips. He pulled me up onto my feet. I closed my eyes remembering what little Ava had said, to close my eyes when I kissed him. Immediately I noticed the scent of his skin, an earthy, animal smell, the male essence of him. The impact upon me was powerful and I began to respond to him. He kissed me then again. And to my surprise these lips belonging to this older man were as soft, moist and sensual as those belonging to Michel, the only other male I had kissed in this way. He kissed me then more firmly. I found I enjoyed the sensation of his mouth on mine. It was a mixture of softness and strength. And he tasted of that delicious wine. He put his arms around me and pulled me close to him. The feel of his strong arms around my body made me feel safe and the warm frisson of arousal between my legs intensified.

"We must disrobe if we are to progress further," he whispered in my ear and kissed my neck. It tickled and I laughed.

78

"How does this come off?" he touched my kirtle.

"Unlace it at the back," I said. He helped me remove the expensive blue silk and then he said, "Take the rest off, Madame." He gave me a sideways look and a smile and stepped back to look at me. I felt self-conscious at first, but then I felt more aroused by his admiring gaze.

"You are perfect," he said. "I knew you would be."

He cupped my breasts in his hands and then traced around my nipples with his fingers. His hand moved down my stomach to between my legs.

He bent and kissed my body down to my navel and then caressed my buttocks pulling me in towards him. I surrendered to the sensations caused by his kisses and caresses. I let go of the polite façade that had been in place all day; what a relief I felt.

"Your skin is so soft," he whispered in my ear. I moved slightly away from him and put my head on one side and gave him a sideways look.

"I think, Sire, if we are to progress any further, that you too must disrobe."

"Oh, I see how this is now, Madame." He narrowed his eyes. "I expected, 'Oh no, Sire, no', and some modesty from my little lady, but I see now that you are no lady."

"Is that so?" I laughed and watched as he removed his clothes. His body was muscular and strong looking. I wanted to stare at his erect penis arising from its nest of black hair but felt that I shouldn't.

He noticed and said, "What do you think?" And my serious husband did a little dance and his penis swayed about in its erect state as he moved. I couldn't help but laugh at him. "Madame," he said mock seriously. "You should not laugh. You should admire."

"I'm sorry, Sire." I made a pretence of a curtsey to him. "I can't help it, you're making me laugh."

He drew me to him and closed his eyes. "Give me your hand, touch me," he said and I fondled him as he showed me what he wanted.

He moved to the bed and led me by the hand with him. "Come, lie with me, Béatrice." He lay on the bed and patted the space next to him. I lay next to him and we arranged ourselves comfortably. He kissed me and his hand went down between my legs. I opened my legs for him. He stroked the inside of my thighs and then explored me, his hand gently touching me, finding his way inside me. I had a fleeting thought about him knowing exactly what to do, and wondered where he learned that, but it did not linger, it was what I had expected. I moved my body up to meet him. I wanted him. I was wet and ready.

"Are you ready for me?" he whispered. "I believe it may hurt you a little this first time, but after that, I hope you will enjoy it."

I bent my knees for him, moving my legs further apart as he moved on top of me.

"Help to guide me in."

He pushed gently and I responded. Slowly he pushed in and out through the tightness of me until he was properly inside me. "It's not hurting you?" he whispered.

"No, it's fine."

Afterwards he kissed me on my cheek and lay back. "You know, Béatrice, I think we're going to get on very well together," he said.

I lay awake for a while thinking about what had happened between us. It was so much better than I had imagined. I stayed in his room that night, and the following morning we both woke early. He brought me some water to drink.

"We must go to church this morning," he said. "But before we go I think there might just be time..."

Chapter 5
In the Bishopric

Béatrice stumbles into the room as she is pushed from behind and the door is locked. She tries the door handle in a futile gesture and turns round into the room in despair. She paces up and down the small room thinking. She must try to be more co-operative now and speak more fully about the past. There must be no excuse for him to keep her here. But compliance has never come easily to her – men, her father and her brothers, husbands and lovers, all have tried to control her life and have been angry with her in the past for her lack of obedience. She must swallow her pride if she is to get out of this place. More than anything, she wants to see her family, her home. This thought brings on tears of sadness and frustration.

"Let me go! Let me go!" she cries out, knowing that no-one will respond.

She calms herself down, hysterics are not helpful; she must think about the Bishop's questions. They were again about events that occurred years ago. There were a number of heretics in Montaillou at that time and Béatrice remembers spending many hours arguing about and discussing religion as well as giving goods for the Cathar holy men, the Perfects, when friends who were Cathars asked for help. As for her own beliefs, she still does not know what is right, what is God's true spiritual path, and there have been occasions when that most forbidden of thoughts flutters into her mind and out again. Is there a God? This radical idea lurks near her at times, ready to move to the forefront whenever the topic of religion rears its head. Her trouble is that she has never been able to blindly believe in anything. She always questions. This is the difficulty, of course, she sees that, because, if she cannot have faith, He will never answer her prayers anyway, that is if He exists. This is how her thoughts go round in circles. She doesn't know what is right and true – will she ever? She feels alone with these thoughts. Everyone else it seems accepts and believes, their differences are about the details of their beliefs. She must think about what to tell the Bishop. What she told him about the Pech de Bugarach was a common enough joke amongst the people, not just heretics. Many others, peasants and noblemen alike, questioned the transubstantiation of bread and wine into the body and blood of Christ. But when she gets out of here, she will not listen or join in with this kind of talk, she must be more careful because it's clear that people will say things when they are frightened or tortured. She shivers. Someone has betrayed her, someone has repeated only what many say, and they have twisted it so she looks guilty. She will concentrate on giving the Bishop what he wants now and when she is released she will go to church on Sundays, she will say all the right words, make the sign of the cross. She will genuflect, she will pray and she will take the sacrament at the altar. She will keep her mouth shut and trust no-one. But no-one can control her thoughts, not even Bishop Fournier.

The terrible possibility of torture or being burned alive seems closer the longer she stays in this place. People say that God won't let a believer suffer if they burn for their beliefs. That's another thing she doesn't believe. The thought of being tied to a stake and the flames flickering around her as if she were a suckling pig, a live piece of roasting meat, is unbearable. She's heard that first the sacrificial garments and the hair are burnt off by the flames; the body is then exposed for the gawping and blood-thirsty crowd to see. Then the flames devour the skin. She shivers, every word must be weighed with the utmost care. If she must lie, she will, but it must be done in such a way that the Bishop believes her. She will take her chances with God when her time comes, and hope and pray that her soul will be saved. Or perhaps her soul will die with her – the thought of hell… she shivers again.

No food and water is brought to her that evening. Bishop Fournier is a clever man. By giving her time to think, he hopes she will remember more and be desperate to tell him so that she can leave this hell-hole. He's right. The time has come to remember more, to get her thoughts in order so that she is prepared. She will try to tease out what he wants to know, what is important, and, most important of all, what will save her life. Her head must be clear so she can be as clever as he is. Calmer now, her mind drifts and her eyes close.

A pale blue dawn appears in the window and Béatrice stirs from the troubled, half-sleep state in which she has spent the night. Two flies are buzzing around her face and she bats them away ineffectively. She turns on her side and covers her face with her hands. Will the Bishop send for her this morning or will she be left lying here, waiting and wondering if she has been forgotten? She has never spent so much time alone before and longs for someone to talk to.

Although she grew to love and respect her husband Bérenger, Raymond Roussel was the one she talked to. Then it was Pierre Clergue, they never stopped talking together and he is the one she wants now – in spite of all he has done, he may be able to help her. It's a vain and ridiculous hope, but, small as it is, it sustains her.

84

He knows how the Church thinks and works. They will listen to him – he is one of them, a priest.

She loved Othon, her second husband too, once she understood what was required of her. He too was a husband with no time to talk, like Bérenger. Both marriages she sees now caused her to fall back on her own resources as both men were busy with their work and their lives. She is thankful for that, it strengthened her. Then there was Barthélemy. Thinking of him now causes her spirits to sink as she pictures his retreating back as he was taken away by the Bishop's men. What a heavy weight of responsibility she carries for bringing him down with her. If it wasn't for her, he would never have been in this dangerous mess.

There are footsteps in the corridor and by the sound of them there is more than one person. Quicker and firmer than usual. The key turns in the lock, and the door bursts open and slams against the wall. Two guards wearing the Bishop's insignia on their tunics stride towards her and she has time only to sit up as they approach her, drag her off the pallet and tie her hands together behind her back.

"No, no," she screams. "Leave me!"

"Co-operate and you won't be hurt," one of them speaks close to her ear. The animal stench of his breath turns her stomach and she retches. She is half lying on the edge of the pallet and half on the floor on her side.

"Stand up, you're going for a walk," says the other one, at the same time dragging her up by her arm. He stinks of alcohol. He grins and his red-rimmed eyes leer at her. She stumbles up on her feet as the other one pulls at her. They both have hold of her arms now.

"Where are you taking me?" Her voice quavers with shock and fear.

"You're going for a little walk, nice day for it."

She is fast learning the rules of this place, that they will tell you only what they want you to know and that asking just provokes more trouble, so she remains quiet.

"Move!" they shout and, pulling her arms, they propel her along, out of the room and down two flights of stairs, along a corridor and then down a further flight of stairs that leads down beneath ground level. It all happens at such speed that she doesn't at first understand where they are taking her and why there are two of them manhandling her. Then she knows. They are taking her down to the dungeons. She struggles and screams, "No! No! Take me back! Have mercy!"

One of them – the one who seems sober – stops, faces her. A sharp cut of pain hits her head and sets her head spinning. She gasps and screams.

"Shut up or it'll be the worse for you," he shouts.

They drag her down the last few steps. They are below ground in the dungeon of the Bishopric. Béatrice is held up between the men, her head is spinning and hurting, her stomach is sick, and she faints. When she comes to, she is in darkness. She blinks and as her eyes adjust she can make out that this is a small room, what looks like an ante-room with two doors opposite each other and nothing in it apart from herself lying on a bench against the wall. Her hands are still tied and her head pounds with the worst headache she has ever known. A small movement sets the room spinning round.

One of the doors opens and through the gloom two figures emerge. One of them carries a candle and what she sees causes her to shake and scream. "Oh no, please no."

The figures are entirely robed in black linen garments, hoods over their heads, covering their faces and necks, and with holes for their eyes. No part of them can be seen, except for their eyes which glisten when the candlelight catches them. They look like the Devil himself. The candle is put down in a corner and they move towards her, take hold of her arms and drag her through the door from which they have just come. Her head is still spinning and the pain on one side of her face and head is excruciating. A wave of nausea hits her, and she retches. She cannot find her feet to place them on the ground and as they pull her through the door, her shins and feet are painfully grazed. They are still for a moment and she manages to gain some equilibrium, she stands on her feet shaking and trying to calm her sobs. One figure retrieves the candle and closes the door behind them. She sees that they are in a larger chamber which contains a strange-looking machine. The walls are covered in black linen, just as Alamande described. She catches her breath and a deep sob surfaces. This unholy place is the torture chamber.

The two figures move her close to one of the machines. She screams again and struggles, but wait, he is showing her something. He doesn't speak but the figure is demonstrating how the machine works. He uses his hands as if to invite her to lie on the narrow wooden frame which has thick ropes going across from side to side which she sees would tie a body down. Then he attaches the ropes to a pulley and turns the handle. The ropes tighten and she sees what will happen. The ropes will cut into flesh and bone if tightened. She turns away but her head is turned back to see that the frame is adjustable and can be lengthened to pull limbs out of their joints.

"No, don't do that," she sobs. "I'll tell you whatever you want to know, spare me, I beg you."

Unbelievably, they move away and momentarily she feels relief until they take her through another door on the far side of the room, into another black walled chamber, and she sees in here in the centre another arrangement of ropes and pulleys, this time attached to a wooden frame which reaches up to vaulted roof. One of the black-robed figures demonstrates the mechanism. He shows her the rope which goes under the arms and round the body to then hoist a person up with heavy weights attached to the feet. Then he demonstrates how the rope is let go and the body is dropped down. This is done over and over as he shows her. This time, she is overcome by shock and sickness, dizziness and pain, and she falls down.

She wakes up back in the loft. Her head feels like it's been split in two. She sits up and the room spins around. She lies back. She has been spared, but she is under no illusions now as to what they will do to her if she does not co-operate. Did she really experience all that or did she dream the whole thing? The throbbing headache and the blood from a wound on her face which has dripped onto her kirtle is evidence that she experienced it. And she knows in her heart that she was there, that she saw the torture chambers under the Bishopric. Under the house of God.

Of what time of day it is or how many days have passed since she was last lying on this pallet, she cannot tell. It seems like late afternoon by the heat in the room, and the sky in the window opening is a deep blue. Her mouth is dry, she is very thirsty, but there is nothing on the table. Unable to move, she lies still and sleeps again.

Béatrice awakes at dawn. She must have slept for some time and deeply, as there is bread and cheese, and water on the table. Vivid dreams of death and terror, nightmares and being chased are still in her mind, broken, fractured images of pain and torture. Her head still aches and she is light-headed, but she is no longer dizzy and sick. She sips at the water. It tastes good although it is warm and not fresh. She nibbles on the hard bread. When was it that she last ate and drank? The bread and water find their way round her system and the light-headed feeling eases. She stands carefully, stretching each of her limbs in turn. She feels weak, but there appears to be no physical damage done except some scrapes on her shins and feet, leaving raw but superficial wounds. She knows now that the dangers here are real and deadly. It's terrifying. She must get word to her family – they must know she's here and they must try for her release. Monsieur Belmas is her only hope. It's early evening when he arrives with the bread, cheese and water.

"What news do you have for me?" she says. He looks bewildered.

"Can I see my family or a priest?" She must be patient.

"I'm sorry, Madame, but no visitors are allowed," he says.

"Surely there is another way. No-one else needs to know." Tears of frustration and despair start in her eyes. He looks doubtful.

"I will pay you well when I leave here."

"I'm sorry, Madame, I don't know…"

"Could you find someone to take a message? A child, a boy?"

"Well, perhaps…" He seems to be considering this. "Who to?" he asks.

"To a priest, a man called Pierre Clergue, he's the village priest in Montaillou. You could send a messenger to tell him that I'm here and I want to see him. I promise you that you will be well recompensed when I am released. They surely can't refuse me a priest?"

"I'll see what I can do, Madame. Pierre Clergue, you say?"

"Yes, Pierre Clergue, the priest from Montaillou."

The room is hot, stifling, and flies buzz around the bucket in the corner and around scraps of food on the table. Thoughts flood her mind as she rests on the pallet. She tries to slow them down and order them. There has never been so much time to think before, there have always been children, grandchildren, men, a house to run. Those years in Montaillou, her marriage, her children, how quickly it has all passed. Of her five daughters, one was lost to sickness some years ago. And her sons, they left a long time ago. She hasn't seen them or their families in years – they are near Carcassonne, living on their estate. Her grandsons, her daughters' babies who live near her in Dalou, baby boys with soft downy heads that she loves to kiss gently, they make up in part for her lost sons. Will she ever see any of them again?

From time to time she rises and bangs on the door with her fists and cries out but no-one ever responds. As the square of sky turns from dusk to deep midnight blue, it is clear that she must spend another night in this foul place. She can't settle and the night seems eternal as she dozes off and then wakes up again and again, until eventually the square of sky pales into dawn. Her mind is full of dreams again, dreams of Montaillou. She is being chased and her legs won't move fast enough to take her away from her pursuer, and she wakes up shivering in a freezing cold sweat of terror in spite of the heat.

This is the aftermath of what happened all those years ago, the final clearing-up. Many others from Montaillou have been arrested and questioned. Béatrice had thought she had escaped this, that she was of no consequence. But the loose ends are being tidied up. The methodical and thorough Bishop Fournier does not tolerate loose ends.

Footsteps approach, but it's the young attendant bringing in the bread, cheese and water.

"I expect Bishop Fournier will see me today?" she says.

He shrugs his shoulders and stares at her.

She eats and drinks everything, then remembers that she didn't ask for her bag and more water. Whoever comes in next she will ask again to see both a priest and her family. Surely they must know what has happened. As a noblewoman, this treatment is intolerable. And there was a certain look that Bishop Fournier gave her, it made her think for a moment, that he is a man like any other man… would he be susceptible to seduction? She looks around at the disgusting, filthy room, at her dirty clothes, at the terrible state of herself, her naked head – no-one could possibly desire her like this. In any case, she must be mad, she's well past her prime. How ridiculous that she could even consider such a thing. To even think that Jacques Fournier might be interested in her as a woman. He might have been interested for a moment, but he won't be interested now. There is no point in thinking these ridiculous thoughts. This place is driving her out of her mind.

She paces around and tries to get clear in her mind what she might safely tell Bishop Fournier. The stories and beliefs of the heretics were the subject of conversations all over Montaillou when she lived there, and she listened and was interested. It was impossible to avoid it at that time in that village. It must be about twenty-five years ago that the Authier brothers from Ax gave up their lives as notaries, left their families and started the revival of the heresy. Bishop Fournier wants to know what happened in Montaillou and about the people who lived there then. Many of them are dead now and some fled to Aragon and Lombardy years ago. This is a last attempt to root out and destroy any remaining heretics. When she talks, she must be careful that she does not incriminate any of her friends who are still alive. Dead ones – well what difference will it make? What can he do now to them?

Bishop Fournier must know how much the Roman Church is hated by peasants and noblemen alike. Its greed, the extortionate taxes it demands, its debauched clergy, these are the matters which cause people to question and doubt. To talk, to mock, and to make jokes, often crude ones. People think, they question and they blaspheme, and show interest in heresy. This is how people have made themselves into targets for the Inquisition. Béatrice herself has asked questions about the Roman Church and the priests, and her own church attendance has been irregular and non-existent at times. But to the Bishop she will be a devout Roman who does not do these bad things. Surely he will send for her today? The young attendant brings more soup at lunchtime, with bread and water.

"I require water for washing and I would like my bag returned to me," she tells him. "I will see that you are paid for your services when I am released."

His eyes have a gleam of interest in them at the mention of money, but he shakes his head at her.

"I can bring more water, that's all."

"I'm sure that I will be going home as soon as Bishop Fournier has seen me again," she says.

But all that happens that afternoon is that Monsieur Belmas brings more water. She is relieved when she sees it is him.

"Do you have any news for me?"

"News?" he looks puzzled.

She wants to scream. "About the priest? Or my family? I asked you to find someone to take a message to them to tell them I'm here."

"I asked one of the guards whose son delivers messages, Madame. He said it is too far to send his son to Montaillou."

She stands up, moves around and sighs. "Isn't there anyone else? You must know someone yourself?"

"Perhaps…"

She interrupts him. "Have you worked here long, Monsieur Belmas?"

"About a year, Madame," he says.

"What did you do before you came here?" She paces the room.

"I was a shepherd, Madame, but I injured my foot and I'm unable to walk long distances. I came to Pamiers to live with my daughter and to seek employment."

She stops, she is nearly touching him, and she looks straight into his eyes.

"Monsieur Belmas, Jean, you can see how desperate my situation is. You must try and help me, I beg you to do what you can for me."

"Yes, Madame."

"Thank you, Monsieur Belmas."

"Madame." He bows his head.

"Oh, before you go, I also require water for washing and the bucket needs emptying. And, there's a dead rat in the corner. I would like you to remove it."

"I will do all that, Madame," he says.

"Thank you," she says as graciously as she can.

Can she believe him, can he be trusted? He is probably just agreeing with her, telling her anything to stop her pestering him. There is more soup, bread and water brought by the young guard later. As the light fades, she sees she must spend another night in this room. The marks and stains on the wooden beams of the loft are becoming familiar now, the idiosyncrasies of the underside of the roof tiles, the grey festoons of cobwebs in the corners. Dead flies hang in the webs which have been forgotten and abandoned by the spiders that made them. Things are forgotten and die in this foul place.

She seems to have slept for a while and the square of light high up in the wall shows that the dark blue of the night is being replaced by a light creamy blue. Another day is dawning and she is fast losing hope that she will be seen by Bishop Fournier today or any day. Will she die here alone without anyone she loves? She lies still, waiting, waiting for the Bishop to send for her, for Pierre Clergue to visit her, to be allowed home, to see her family. And for Barthélemy. Where is he now and why have they arrested him?

Chapter 6
Châtelaine

After the wedding, the weather changed. Freezing cold winds battered the walls of the château and when the wind dropped a dense mist enveloped it more often than not. The sky became a thick, grey blanket and snow fell. Walking around the steep tracks of the village became treacherous. Montaillou was a desolate place in the winter. The villagers stayed inside their homes, keeping warm near their firesides, carding and weaving the wool from their sheep, and making clothes. The shepherds had taken the sheep south at the end of September to overwinter in warmer pastures. They would be back at Easter with the lambs born at Christmas. During these winter months everyone ate from their stores of turnips, cabbages and preserved meat, with rabbits and chickens, trout from the rivers, the occasional wild boar or fat wood pigeon.

I fell in with the rhythm and routine of life at the château, which was not so different from my life in Caussou. I came to know the people who lived and worked there. Both Raymond, the steward, and the village bailiff, Bernard Clergue, were now familiar presences. They worked closely with Bérenger and would often dine with us at the end of the day. I needed to learn the business of the château and the estate because, as Military Agent to the Count of Foix, Bérenger was required to travel, sometimes for weeks at a time, and I was left nominally in charge of the estate. It was the end of November when Bérenger went to Foix, and I was left alone for the first time. The first evening I saw Raymond as he came into the château after working outside all day.

"Raymond," I said. "I shall need your help, Bérenger has told me I'm to rely on you for decisions about the estate whilst he's away. You'll have to guide me."

He nodded. "I can do that, Madame."

"So, you'll continue to dine with me in the evenings whilst my husband is away?"

"Yes Madame, if I report to you each evening as usual, you'll soon learn."

I was glad when Raymond arrived for dinner. I had never eaten alone in my life and I did not want to be by myself.

"I want to know about the villagers and their families as well the estate," I said to Raymond as soon as we sat down together.

"Who do you want to know about?" he said laughing.

"Well, for instance, who lives in the large house just below the château?" I said.

"Ah yes," he said. "That belongs to the Clergues, the richest family in Montaillou."

"Bernard Clergue's family?"

"Yes, and now their other son, Pierre, is our new village priest," he said. "You must have seen them in church?"

"Oh the priest… I have to confess that I haven't been to church much since my wedding," I said looking at him for his reaction to this. His green eyes widened.

"Madame, why ever not? You'll be in trouble."

"The weather has been too bad."

The truth was I did not care much for going to church. Ever since my father had to wear his yellow crosses, the experience I had loved as a small child I now disliked. The arguments between my parents about it tarnished the whole thing for me. So now I was no longer obliged to go to please my mother, I avoided it whenever possible. Bérenger only went occasionally when he was here – the needs of the estate took priority – and when he was away I did not feel like going, especially by myself. I was not used to doing anything alone.

When I next walked down into the village, I looked with interest at the Clergues' large house. Built into the hillside on several levels, the back opened onto pastureland. They had stables for their animals and storage barns beneath the house, and a wooden loft space built on top of the stone walls of the property. Their house reflected their status as a wealthy and powerful family. I looked forward to getting to know them.

I soon learnt from Raymond about the other villagers and where they lived. I wandered about the village and soon developed a friendship with three young women, Alazaïs Azema, Fabrisse Rives and Jacquemette Maury. They all had young families and lived en route from the château to the square. I met them often as they went to fetch water from the font canal near the château, or as they visited each other in their homes.

It was not long after Bérenger went to Foix in November that I suspected I was going to have something in common with my three new friends and in fact with most of the women of Montaillou. I missed my monthly bleeding. I could usually predict exactly on which day it would occur and this time nothing happened. I guessed immediately that I was carrying a child and soon other signs began to appear. My breasts swelled and tingled. My stomach developed a small curve and I alternately felt sick or ravenously hungry, often craving a particular food. I longed to walk over to

Caussou to tell my mother but I knew I must tell Bérenger first. My purpose in life was here, it was the reason for my marriage. My new life was starting to take shape.

Just before Christmas, a village boy came from Caussou, with a message to tell me that my family were intending to come over for mass on Christmas Eve at Sainte Marie de Carnesses. They would stay two nights at the château. This would be the first time I had seen them since the wedding and I was filled with excitement about telling my parents about the forthcoming child. Bérenger was delayed in Foix by the freezing, snowy weather which made travelling impossible, so I had to wait longer to reveal my secret. Finally he managed to return home the week before Christmas when the tracks were clear and the snow had stopped falling.

"My little lady," he said when I told him. "I knew you would fulfil your duties well. We will have a son, I know."

My parents and younger sisters made the journey from Caussou on foot in the snow and arrived on Christmas Eve. Philippe and Bernard had stayed behind to look after the animals and keep the farm going. We all walked down together to the church for midnight mass. I noticed that my father was not wearing his tunic with the yellow crosses sewn onto it. I guessed that he felt safe enough in Montaillou to attend church without them. That, the presence of my family, the child I was carrying, the stillness of the evening, the clear starry sky and the moonlight shining on the silent world of snowy Montaillou, lifted my heart. We walked past the village square and the houses on either side of the track, down to the flat pastures where the little church lay, looking so comfortably settled there as if it had grown up out of the earth itself and was a natural part of the countryside. The track was trodden hard and glassy by the feet that had gone before. We picked our way down carefully, our leather-booted feet slipping at times on the compacted snow. The white peaks all around and the pure, clean air tinged with the scent of wood smoke from the many fires made it a perfect winter's night. As we entered the church, the familiar musty smell of incense, candles, unwashed bodies and dusty ancient relics was in great contrast to the freshness outside. We settled into our seats and I looked around. I noticed an old couple, Monsieur and Madame Maurs, sitting together. They were always there when I attended church and I had noticed that he was the only person wearing the yellow crosses at that time in Montaillou. They kept themselves to themselves. I casually watched the villagers as they filed up the aisle to receive the sacrament at the altar from the priest, until I was startled to see another figure wearing a tunic with yellow crosses on it in the queue of people. The figure was familiar, surely… this could not be. But when he turned round after receiving the sacrament, I felt a shock, like a sudden whoosh-hit from an arrow piercing my flesh. It was Raymond Roussel. I let out a little cry, put my hand to my mouth and stood up. Bérenger, seated next to me said, "Béatrice, what's the matter?"

"I'm sick," I said. It was a good excuse. I had been sick recently on a few occasions so there was some truth in it, and I did at that moment feel some nausea.

"I'll go outside," I said.

"I'll come with you," said Bérenger. We pushed past everyone and, watched by the congregation, we walked down the aisle, opened the heavy church doors and went outside. I leaned against the wall and covered my mouth with my hand.

"I'm sorry," I said to Bérenger. I breathed slowly in and out, and after a minute or two I regained some composure. "I feel a little better out here in the fresh air."

"It's cold out here," he said.

"I think… can we go home?"

"Yes, that's probably the best thing," he said.

He took my arm and we climbed back up the track to the château. He escorted me to my room and I lay down on my bed. He brought me some water and left me to sleep after kissing me goodnight. I drank the water and closed my eyes. But my mind would not rest. I kept seeing the image of Raymond wearing the yellow crosses. Raymond of all people – it was hard to believe. I wondered why I had never seen him wearing them before. I'd heard he had a home in Prades, the next village, so it was likely that he usually attended church there. I'd never seen him wearing them around the château so, like my father, he must only wear them for church-going. He would know that no-one would be concerned about that in Montaillou, as long as he wore them in church.

I wondered what had happened to Raymond that he had to wear the yellow crosses. I knew very little about him even though I had grown used to his presence in my life. In the short space of time since I was married, I had spent more time with him than my husband. I had grown to rely on him. He knew the estate and the village well. We had talked together about the villagers, but I did not know much about him. Certainly he had not breathed a word about the heresy. Bérenger must know who bore the punishment, but it was an unspoken agreement between us that we never talked about it. I was determined that the curse of the yellow crosses would not contaminate our marriage as it had my parents'. I was curious to find out more about Raymond. I decided I would ask Sybille about him when an opportunity arose. And I could easily arrange that.

We spent Christmas Day with my family and they stayed another night at the château. They left the following morning and Bérenger went out on the estate. I asked Sybille to de-louse my hair. We were in my room where a fire was blazing and giving out much-needed heat because, as always, a freezing draught was coming in through the wooden shutters. Even the heavy tapestry in front of them flounced outwards as if it were a thin gauzy curtain. I put a cloth round my shoulders and sat in front of the fire, my long hair falling down over the cloth. Sybille stood behind me with a small comb which she started to pull through my hair.

"This is a very good little comb for this job, Madame." Sybille separated my hair into sections and pulled the comb through each section in turn. She wiped it on the cloth, examined the cloth and poked around on my head with her fingers pulling out any lice and eggs that had resisted the comb. She rinsed the comb in a basin of water and repeated the task all over my head.

"I think my mother bought it from a pedlar at the market at Ax," I said. We sat in silence for a few minutes as Sybille concentrated on her task.

"It's been a good Christmas, my first one in Montaillou," I said.

"Your family seemed to enjoy it," said Sybille.

"Especially your mother."

"My mother loves Sainte Marie and she's happy to see me settled here, and about the baby, of course."

"It is a special church with the footprints, people from a distance come to see it." Sybille combed through a strand of hair.

"Raymond was in church on Christmas Eve," I said.

"Oh, was he?" said Sybille. "Keep your head still, please, Madame. Your hair is so thick I'm having trouble finding these little devils... there, got one." She showed me a dead louse on the end of her finger.

"They're hard to see, I know, I used to do my sister's," I said. Sybille continued working through my hair.

"I don't go to church every week, but I've never seen Raymond there before, I suppose he doesn't usually go to church here," I said.

"He goes in Prades – he has a small house there."

"Oh, I see. Is he married?"

"His wife died a few years back, I heard. He has a son and daughter living in Prades. He goes over there on a Saturday night and comes back on Sunday night, I think."

"When I saw him on Christmas Eve he was wearing a tunic with yellow crosses sewn onto it," I said as casually as I could.

"Oh, was he? He probably only wears them in church."

"Do you know why he wears them? I mean... what happened?"

"Mersende, the cook, told me that there used to be a lot of heretics round here. But someone betrayed them and the Inquisition came and took Raymond and some others for questioning, you know, to Carcassonne. They kept them there in the prison, the Wall, for a while. When he came out, he had to wear the crosses. Na Roche, that very old lady in the village, she had to wear them along with her son, but then they were let off." Sybille paused for a moment. "Just turn your head to face the fire, Madame, there are a lot behind this ear."

"They seem to like that spot."

"They do."

"So are there any heretics round here now?"

"Well, who knows," said Sybille combing vigorously behind my ear. "I'm new here too."

"Ouch," I said putting my hand up to stop Sybille's hand for a moment.

"Sorry Madame, keep still a minute, there's another." Sybille parted my hair with her fingers. "Got it."

I bent my head over the other way. "Will you have a look on this side now?"

One evening around the fifth month of my pregnancy, Bérenger was away in Foix and I was dining with Raymond. We were eating trout with vegetables. We both ate steadily. Raymond had been working outside most of the day supervising the repair of some walls and fencing on our land. I had been ravenously hungry that day, craving fish and bread the whole time. He finished eating before me and looked idly around.

"I notice that you are busy preparing for your coming event." He nodded to my sewing which lay on a bench near the fire. It was the first time my condition had been mentioned between us, although I was not surprised that he knew – I could no longer conceal it for one thing and we had begun to tell people now we sure. I finished eating and smiled back at him.

"Yes, I am. My mother and sisters are busy too. My child will not want for much." I sat back. "You have children, don't you, Raymond?"

"Yes," he said. "My two eldest sons are married and live near Carcassonne. The other two, a son and a daughter, live in Prades. I usually go over and see them on a Saturday evening and then come back here on Sunday."

"Ah yes," I said. "I remember thinking when I saw you in church here at Christmas that I haven't seen you before in Sainte Marie."

"I stayed over, and you, I think were taken ill, Madame. Your husband took you outside."

"I was sick and…" I paused, then decided to ask him. "I was…"

"What?" he said.

"Oh nothing, perhaps I shouldn't say…"

"What's the matter, Madame?"

"Well, to tell you the truth I was shocked when I saw you wearing the yellow crosses," I said. "It's usually only Monsieur Maurs who wears them in Montaillou."

"I don't need to wear them here," he said. "Your husband doesn't object, but I have to be seen by the priest… and everyone else in church."

"Yes, I know." My voice came out shaky. I was surprised by how unsettled I felt. I cleared my throat. "Your father?"

"Yes." I nodded but said nothing more, feeling that perhaps I hadn't been very wise in mentioning this. Then Raymond cleared his throat.

"And you, Madame?" He said. "What about you?"

"What about me?"

"What do you believe?"

I studied his face. He looked serious but relaxed. I had no reason to mistrust him, in fact just the opposite – he had been a reliable steward for Bérenger for many years now.

"To tell you the truth, sometimes I do wonder about things." I put a piece of bread in my mouth.

"What do you mean?" he said.

"Well," I chewed and thought for a moment. "I remember an occasion when I was a child, we were staying with my cousin who lived in a place called

104

Celles. I heard a man say something that struck me as funny at first, but then it made perfect sense to me." I could see that Raymond looked interested, his green eyes fixed on me, so I told him the story about the idea of eating Christ's body at communion and the Pech de Bugarach.

"I've heard that said too." He smiled.

"And since then I've heard others say that if you take that idea to its logical conclusion, his body goes down into your body and then, well, it comes out at the other end." We laughed together at this. "Why would Christ want his body to be digested by people and then have it go through their stomachs only to have it excreted out by them? I thought it was a good point. I'd had similar questions myself, but I never dared say it to anyone."

"I've heard that said too, in much cruder terms than you put it, Madame. But the Church in Rome does not like people to question their teachings."

"I know," I said. "But people do talk, I've heard the villagers complain about the amount of money and goods the Church takes for taxes. The Church must be rich, but that's not how Jesus lived."

"The priests don't set a good example either." He looked directly at me. "You can understand how the Good Christians came about, can't you?"

"You mean the heretics?"

"They are only heretics in the eyes of the Roman Church – they are called the Good Men or Good Christians by those who believe in what they preach," he said.

"Yes, of course." I remembered what my mother had said about being cautious and not speaking of the heretics. I'd probably said too much.

"There are still believers in the Good Men around here. They're waiting for the new holy men, called Perfects to take them forward."

"Perfects?" My curiosity took over.

"Yes, their holy men are called Perfects because they lead such good lives. They don't go with women and they eat only fish and vegetables." Raymond was so serious and intense, I felt a stirring of fear and something else… excitement. He continued. "We will see Perfects soon, here in Montaillou."

"In Montaillou?"

"Yes, there are many believers here who are ready and waiting for the forthcoming revival." He looked at me. "It will happen, Madame."

"I think we shouldn't speak of such things."

"There is little to fear here," he said. "The wealthiest families in Montaillou are Cathar."

I was staring at him in a mixture of shock, fear and curiosity when we were interrupted by Sybille knocking on the door.

It began gently enough, a twinge of pain, a watery stain of blood on my undergarments. Then slowly, over a few hours, it built up. The pain came in waves, the muscles of my womb contracting, warming up to push out the baby. An iron band gripped my body each time there was a contraction. My mother came to help and Guillemette Benet from the village came too. She had several children of her own and had helped many others in childbirth. There were two more attendants: Sybille and one of the older women who worked in the château as a general maid. She was Guillemette Benet's regular helper.

I lay on my bed with layers of cloths beneath me. It was a hot, sultry August night and I was sweating with heat and pain. A wooden crib stood at the foot of the bed containing small garments and wraps, ready and waiting for my child.

Intense pain, like no pain I'd ever experienced before, gripped my front, my back and all round my body, increasing with each contraction. It engulfed me entirely. Warm fluid gushed from me, flooding the bed linen I lay on.

"That's your waters broken," said Guillemette.

I gasped and cried out as another wave of pain took me over. My mother wiped my forehead with a cool cloth and offered me a herbal infusion.

"Take some of this, Béatrice, it will ease the pain and increase the strength of the contractions. It will be over all the quicker."

I sipped and lay back as there was a moment's reprieve. Then another strong contraction and another. I groaned, and grabbed and squeezed my mother's hand.

"I want to push, I want to open my bowels," I said.

"Lie back, Béatrice, let me see, relax your legs," said Guillemette. "There's nothing to be frightened of, it's the baby coming, your baby's coming," she said. "It's the baby's head you can feel. That's quick."

My mother squeezed my hand. "It'll soon be over now."

"Stand at each side," said Guillemette to Sybille and the other attendant, "Then she can push her legs against your shoulders."

"I can't, it's too big." I screamed with pain and exhaustion.

"You can do it, Béatrice, when you want to push, push into your bottom, not your throat. Come on now, you're doing well, don't be frightened. Go with it. That's it, push, push, that's it, now rest."

107

The pain built up again, front, back, everywhere.

"That's a good girl, you're doing well, push now, push that baby out, it's got to come out," said Guillemette.

With a kind of groaning roar and feeling as if I would rip from back to front, I pushed out my baby's head.

"That's it, the worst is over, the rest will just slide out," said my mother. And with another push the rest of my baby slithered out into the world.

"It's a boy, a beautiful baby boy," said my mother.

Guillemette tied off and cut the thick bluish cord. The baby cried and I cried too as I heard him. It was the most beautiful sound in the world to me, my newborn baby's cry. He was where he landed, on the bed between my legs, looking like a little skinned rabbit covered in blood and slime, his face crumpled and red, his dark hair wet and shiny and stuck to his head. My mother wrapped him in a cloth and wiped his face and head as another wave of pain made me push out the large reddish-brown afterbirth. He cried strongly. They cleaned me, put fresh cloths under me, a robe around my shoulders and propped me up in the bed so that I could hold my son. I looked down at this tiny scrap of life with his little wrinkled face and his hair still wet on his little head. His gummy mouth puckered and stretched, his unfocused eyes blinked. I marvelled at his hands, his perfect fingers with their tiny gleaming nails. An overwhelming rush of love for this helpless child flooded my whole being. My son. Everyone was around me, telling me I'd done well and that I had a beautiful baby.

The birth of our son, named Bérenger after his father, was the start of a new era in the château. We had our second son, Philippe, eighteen months later and we employed a nursemaid, Rixende, to help care for them. The cries and laughter of babies and their nursemaid rang out and filled the once empty rooms at the top of the château, which had been cleaned and aired to accommodate them. The milky, faecal smells of infanthood mingled with the château's aroma of dust and wood smoke. My life now centred on the children. My conversations with Rixende and Bérenger were all about them, their nursing needs and habits, their eating, their sleeping, their teething and their ailments. The only break from children and their needs was when Bérenger was away, as I continued to dine with Raymond, so he could advise me about the estate.

"It's the only time I talk about anything other than my children, who I love dearly, but it's good to talk of other things for a while," I said.

"Motherhood suits you," he said his eyes wandering over my figure.

"I like being a mother," I said looking down to hide the blush I felt rising up my neck and face. "But I can talk about other things with you, Raymond."

"Such as?" he was laughing.

"Well, you know, the estate and the work…"

He laughed. "Béatrice, I think you like to know all the latest gossip about the villagers." He had been calling me Béatrice when we were alone together for some time now and I hadn't objected.

"Perhaps I do – there's nothing wrong in that," I laughed. "I have to know what's going on so I don't say the wrong thing when I'm with the villagers."

"Yes, that's important," he said. "For example, there are certain people you must never mention the

109

Good Men to because they are against them, but then again there are others who would expect and welcome some talk of the Good Men with you. So best to know who thinks what, I agree."

"We shouldn't speak of such things."

"Everyone will be speaking of them soon enough," he said. "The Good Men are coming." He looked intently at me. "You know, Béatrice, they are the only ones who can save our souls."

"What does that mean?"

"It means just what I said. The Good Men alone can save our souls."

I stared back at him as I thought about this. "That can't be true, surely?" I said. "Because if it is true, how is it that God made so many people that haven't been saved?"

"Because that's God's will."

I knew I should not encourage this dangerous talk, but I was fascinated about the beliefs and practices of the heresy. It did not occur to me then to speak to Bérenger of it, in part because of my determination to keep the subject out of my marriage but also, I had to admit, I did not want to stop the discussions with Raymond. Speaking together secretly about the heresy like this, with the air of dalliance there was between us and the intensity of Raymond's belief, gave these dinner-table discussions an exciting frisson.

As time passed, a change came over these discussions with Raymond. It was a gradual process, from Raymond inciting my curiosity by telling me about the Cathar beliefs bit by bit and my questioning what he told me, to the evening when he suggested that I should meet a Cathar Perfect. That this involved a long journey to Lombardy seemed to be no barrier in Raymond's view, nor did the fact that I was married and usually either pregnant or nursing an infant. Once he had mentioned this, he urged me regularly to go to Lombardy with him, where the Perfects were, telling me over and over again the same thing.

"When you hear the Good Men preach, you will be theirs for ever."

"I cannot go away with you, Raymond," I told him repeatedly. "I cannot leave my husband and children."

He quoted from the Bible, telling me it was better to leave a husband and sons in this life in order to be saved eternally in the next life. He persevered in this suggestion, leaving the subject for a while then bringing it up again. Although I tried to dissuade him I knew in my heart that I enjoyed the game we were playing, there was pleasure in his persistence and my continued refusal. We were in deep water together but I thought I was staying afloat and I must admit that I did not want to get out of that water. I did make one or two half-hearted attempts. On one occasion, I implied that the time might come in the future when I would consider his proposal. I thought this would stop him from pestering me with this idea of leaving.

"If we go now, whilst I am young, people will say we have gone to satisfy our lust and not for religious reasons," I said.

"This isn't something that can wait, Béatrice," he said. "It's too important, the revival is imminent – besides you wouldn't be the first noblewoman to do this," he said. "Stéphanie de Château-Verdun left her husband and baby to go to Lombardy."

I had heard rumours about Stéphanie de Château-Verdun, but the subject was not mentioned between us for a while, mainly because there was no opportunity until Bérenger went away again. I had just

111

come to realise that I was carrying my third child when Raymond spoke of it again.

"Raymond," I said. "I'm carrying another child. What would happen to my baby if I came away with you? From what you've told me, don't the Good Men regard a woman who is carrying a child as impure?"

"Well," he said. "That is true, but the holy spirit would enter your child if we promised to bring it up as a believer in the Good Men."

"I thought they didn't baptise infants because they felt that children should make their own minds up when they're old enough."

Raymond did not seem entirely sure of what he was talking about sometimes.

"I believe that is so," he said. "But you mustn't worry about these details, Béatrice. God will guide us."

"So, you think there are no obstacles to us going away together?"

"No, nothing that can't be overcome. If it's God's will, we will be guided by Him, we mustn't waste time on all these details and concerns of yours, Béatrice."

He stood up and moved towards me. He took hold of my hands. His face was close to mine as he spoke and I was conscious of the nearness of him, the male scent of him and his strong hands holding my hands. I pulled my hands away.

"I'm rather tired tonight, Raymond, I think I'll go to bed early."

He moved away from me. "Yes, yes, of course, you must take care of yourself, we'll talk again soon. You are looking well, though… it suits you, you know." His eyes roamed over my body, my breasts which were full with my condition and my slightly swollen belly.

112

"Goodnight, Raymond."

I climbed up the spiral stone stairs past my own room to check on the children, who were asleep in a room high up at the top of the château with Rixende. Everywhere was quiet, and the servants had gone to bed too. It was later than I had thought. I covered up little Philippe who had kicked off his blankets, and bent over and kissed each of the boys' soft chubby cheeks. I looked back at them both as I left the room. I could never leave them for a religion, for a man, for anything.

I went back down to my own room where I took off my clothes, folded them over a chair and squatted over the wooden bucket that was behind a screen in the corner to empty my bladder. I got into bed and after turning over once or twice, I fell asleep. Something, someone, woke me. I was warm and comfortable and I stretched a little. I felt strong arms around me and I relaxed into the naked, male body that was beside me. He ran his hand up my thigh and murmured in my ear.

"Oh Béatrice, I've waited so long for this."

For one moment I thought it was Bérenger, but I remembered he was away. I wriggled out of his arms and shouted out. "What's happening? Who is it?"

"Béatrice," he whispered. "Be quiet, it's me, Raymond."

"Be quiet? Who do you think you are? You peasant, get out of my bed." I screamed.

Raymond leapt out of bed, grabbed his clothes and disappeared before the servants, who, hearing my scream, came running to see what had happened. I felt so guilty knowing I had encouraged Raymond and then not knowing what to do about the whole thing, I told the servants I had been dreaming, that I'd had a nightmare. Early the next morning I sought Raymond out. He was outside in the château courtyard preparing

113

to go out onto the estate. He came over to me when he saw me and we went to one side away from the other workers.

"Oh Béatrice," he said. "Please forgive me, I should not have done that, but I thought you wanted it too. I hid under your bed until you fell asleep. I was mad for you."

"You can't stay here now," I said. "I see now, all your talk of the Good Men was a ruse to get into my bed and possess me. I ought to tell my husband, who would fling you into the dungeon beneath the château, except I fear that he would think something had already occurred between us. You will have to leave here and find employment elsewhere."

I knew I should have been firmer with Raymond from the start. I'd enjoyed his company and the attention he gave to me. I'd let it all carry on when I knew that all the talk about the heresy was a way of trying to get what he wanted, which was to climb into bed with me. I felt bad about the whole thing, but there was no other option. Raymond had to leave.

Chapter 7
The Third Interrogation

Béatrice wakes to the fresh, dawn light that is softly
shining into the dusty attic. The door is opening. She
turns her head. It's the young guard bringing in her
bread and water. No words are exchanged, she waits
until he has gone and then she sits up and drinks the
water. Soon after, she hears his footsteps again. She can
distinguish whose tread it is on the boards. Jean Belmas
is slow and his steps are uneven due to his lame leg.
This is the lighter, quicker step of the young one.
"Time to go," he says as he enters.
"Where to?" she asks, terrified of another visit to the
torture chambers.
"To see the Bishop."
She follows him through the Palace to the room where
she was last interrogated by Bishop Fournier. Thank
God he brought her here and not to the dungeons again.
Never would she have thought she would be glad to see
Bishop Fournier. A small glimmer of hope shines
within her. Now she has her chance. She can tell him
everything so that she will be released. She is ready. As
she enters the room, she notices a different scribe sitting
beside the Bishop. They both stand and she sees he is a
small, squat man, plainly attired in a black-and-white
monk's habit. His face looks smug and supercilious.
His black eyes, small and beady, are darting all over
her. The Bishop speaks.
"Brother Gaillard de Pomies from Carcassonne is
recording what is said here today."
Brother Gaillard smirks, bows his head to her briefly
then fixes her with a cold stare. She shivers and her
heart sinks. She knows of this man – he has a reputation
as a rigorous and ruthless Inquisitor. They must be

working together now, the two Inquisitions, Carcassonne and Pamiers. This makes them even more powerful. The Bishop looks stern.

"Be seated, Madame."

They settle themselves and the Bishop speaks again. His voice is cold, the tone low and menacing. "I must remind you that you are still under oath to speak the entire truth." He pauses. "That means I require you to tell all that you know and who you know connected to the heretical Cathar faith, starting with the time that you lived in Montaillou."

She looks up at the Christ figure on the cross. The Cathars did not consider that the cross should be revered because Jesus suffered on it. That makes sense to her. A lot of what they said makes sense. Is Jesus Cathar or Roman? Whichever one You are, Lord, give me strength. She looks back at the Bishop. She is weak and tired now, the glimmer of hope all but faded, but she takes a deep breath and starts to speak. She speaks about her time as Châtelaine. It pours out of her. She talks about Raymond Roussel, Raymond who she knows has since died so she is on safe ground, no-one is being betrayed. She tells how they spoke of the heresy when they dined alone together and how he asked her often to go away with him.

"He told me that the Lord said that man should leave father, mother, wife, husband, son and daughter to follow Him and He would give them the Kingdom of Heaven. He said that since the present life on earth is brief and the Heavenly Kingdom eternal, it was not necessary to care about the present life in order to inherit the Kingdom of Heaven. When I asked him how I could leave my husband and sons, he replied that the Lord had commanded it and that it was better to leave a husband and sons whose eyes were infected, than to

116

abandon Him who lives for all eternity and gives us the Kingdom of Heaven."

She pauses. How loquacious she is. But her words seem to have a life of their own. She had not intended to talk about Raymond. She has never told anyone about him before. She told Barthélemy, her priest husband, a little of what happened in Montaillou, but he had called her an old heretic, so she spoke no more of it. But now… she looks at the Bishop, who seems to be listening intently. Gaillard de Pomies is scribbling fast. The Bishop speaks.

"Madame, continue to speak until I say otherwise." He manages a tight smile. "For your own good, I suggest you comply."

She knows what he means. She is safe from nothing here. Her guts twist in terror. She opens her mouth.

"I asked Raymond why it was that God had created so many men if so few of them were to be saved. He replied that only the Good Men would be saved and no other. No religious men, no priests, no-one except the Good Men. He quoted from the Bible that just as it is impossible for a camel to pass through the eye of a needle, so it is impossible for those who have riches to be saved. Because of this, kings and princes, prelates and clerics and all who have riches will not be saved, only the Good Christians or Good Men. He told me that the Good Men remained in Lombardy because they dare not live here, where the dogs and wolves persecute them. By dogs and wolves, he meant the Dominicans, the preaching friars who persecute the Good Christians and drive them from this country. He said he had met several of the Good Christians and heard them speak. They were such wonderful speakers that once you had heard them, you would never leave them, and that if I heard them speak just once, I would be theirs for ever."

Oh God, what has she said? What she has just said applies to Brother Gaillard de Pomies, who she knows is a Dominican by his black-and-white robes. In her panicked state of mind she has been blabbering, the words tumbling out, falling over each other. She must take care that this tongue of hers does not lead her into danger. One wrong word and she could end up on the pyre, or the rack or some other unknown terror that could be waiting in the dungeon for her. The Bishop and Brother Gaillard are exchanging glances. She takes a deep breath.

"And did this Raymond tell you anything more about the Good Christians?" says the Bishop.

"Yes," she says. "He told me that in the beginning all the spirits sinned by the sin of pride. That they thought they knew more and were worth more than God. For this sin, they fell to earth from heaven and the Devil, who made earth, gave them bodies. The only way they could be redeemed and return to heaven was by receiving the blessing known as the *consolamentum* at the end of life from a Perfect. If this did not happen, the soul would migrate into another body, either man or beast. The souls could do this up to nine times – after nine times the soul is lost for ever. He told me that the child I was carrying would be saved by a spirit entering through any part of my body and then into the fruit of my womb. I asked him why, if this was so, babies did not speak when they were born. He said that was because God does not wish it. He encouraged me to leave my family by citing examples of other noblewomen who had gone to Lombardy."

She stops, her mind suddenly blank. She searches for words, something, anything. What can she say? Oh yes, Stéphanie de Château-Verdun.

"Raymond told me about her to convince me to leave with him but I didn't want to do that, but he continued to talk to me about the heresy and he continued to encourage me to leave with him for about two or three years more, after which he left our service."

Both men stare at her. Gaillard de Pomies has an expression on his face which looks as if he has just discovered a nest of cockroaches in his bed. She sits still, her hands in her lap with her eyes down.

Bishop Fournier, his eyes narrowed to slits, says, "Remember you are under oath here, Madame."

"Yes, my Lord Bishop."

"Have you believed and do you still believe that which he told you about the sins of the spirits in the sky and the reincarnation of spirits?"

"No, I did not then, nor have I since believed this," she says lifting her head to look at him directly.

"Have you revealed Raymond's propositions to anyone?"

"No, except on one occasion in confession at Limoux, to a friar."

"Has anyone else heard the heretical proposition that Raymond put to you?"

"No, I do not recall anyone else being there. A woman called Alazaïs Gonelle from Prades came to my house to talk to me once. She was a friend of Raymond's from Prades. He sent her to persuade me further. She told me it would be good to go to Lombardy with Raymond because the Good Christians would save our souls. She told me that she would accompany us, together with Algee de Martre from Camurac, who was the priest's aunt. But I told her that I could not leave my husband and family. It was after this that Raymond left our service."

119

"What did you understand by the Good Christians and the Good Men that Raymond Roussel and this woman talked about?"

"I understood them to be heretics…" She is about to say more when he puts his hand up and stops her.

"No further questions."

She looks at him. Why has he stopped now? She must continue, get it over and done with. She'll tell him everything, anything he wants to know.

"No, no, please let me tell you… I'll tell you whatever you want to know. Let me tell you because… I must go home now. I've done nothing, let me go, please." A sob escapes from her body.

He ignores her, makes the sign of the cross and says, "In nomine Patris et Filii et Spiritus Sancti, Amen."

"No, no." She clings onto the side of the table as the Bishop directs the guard by a gesture of his hand to take her away. She remains seated as the guard gets hold of her arm. She shakes him off.

"Get another guard," he says. He watches as another guard comes in and they grab her under her arms and pull at her. She resists and they pick her up under her arms and drag her across the room and out of the door. She screams and struggles but she is no match for their strength. Helpless and humiliated, she is pulled along by the guards, screaming, shouting and sobbing. They drag her up the stairs and throw her into the attic. She lands on the floor. She crawls over to the pallet where she curls up in a ball, her hands over her face until her sobs subside. There is so much more to tell him. A great deal more. If only he will let her.

Her marriage to Bérenger was arranged with the best of intentions, she sees that with hindsight, but marrying him did not protect her from the events which began to unfold in Montaillou. It was as if an

120

earthquake started rumbling there. At first it was quiet and only a few noticed it. A small tremor here and there. Then it gained momentum. More and more rumblings, everyone touched and shaken by it, impossible to ignore. It rose to a peak of disturbance and the earth opened up. Some were swallowed up by it, others escaped, and there was turmoil in Montaillou. She had been in the midst of momentous events which could not be avoided. Her marriage to Bérenger de Rocquefort which was in part to shield her from the curse of the yellow crosses had placed her at the epicentre of the earthquake.

She remembers, she dreams, not knowing at times whether she is asleep or awake. She has heard that a dying person sees all of their life flash past them and she wonders if she is dying. She does not want to die in this place, she must live to see her children and grandchildren grow older. Philippa, her youngest child, is a young woman now but not yet betrothed. She must see Philippa married. Then she will have done her duty as a mother; her life's work.

Chapter 8
Life and Death in Montaillou

In the autumn of the year that Raymond Roussel left our service, I gave birth to our third child, a daughter. We named her Béatrice. She became known as Baby Béa, or Béa. Now I had no moments of feeling lost, the needs of the children occupied me relentlessly. There was a baby almost every year. I bore another daughter, Esclarmonde, after Baby Béa. In five years of marriage I had born four children, and as the seventh year of my marriage approached, I knew that I was carrying my fifth child. I was weary at the beginning of this fifth pregnancy and sick. I was always sick when I carried a child but this one was worse than the others. I was fortunate that my children were alive and well. The births of my children had been straightforward and I had plenty of help, but it was exhausting. I could not help but think that the two boys and two girls we already had were enough for us. I had fulfilled my side of the bargain, done what was expected of me and I wanted a rest from babies, some time for myself. But I told myself I mustn't think like that. I had grown to love Bérenger – my mother had been right, age didn't seem to matter any more. There was no doubt he was a good man. I thought too of the innocent child within me, a product of our love for each other. This must be God's will. I must be strong.

At the start of this fifth pregnancy I decided to visit my parents, both to tell them the news and to give myself some time away from my small children. I wanted to walk over the Col de Marmare and imagine for a short time that I was the same carefree girl who had walked the mountain tracks a few years ago. I left the children in the care of their nursemaids. We had two by this time, with Gauzia joining Rixende after Baby Béa was born. Sybille stayed behind in the château as an extra pair of hands to help with the children and I set off alone to walk to Caussou. It was a rare treat to have this time to myself, and I enjoyed walking the mountain pathways in the fresh Feruary air, walking along at my own pace, relishing the pleasure of no little ones tugging at my skirts and needing attention. There was still snow on the top of the highest peaks but the meadows were full of wild flowers and the sky was the deepest blue.

It was a short visit to Caussou – I stayed only one night – but I noticed a change in my mother who looked thin and pale, and appeared to be picking listlessly at her food when we sat together at the table. I spoke to my father about it and he said that my mother had been ill for about a month. It had taken them a little while to realise that she wasn't recovering from a stomach upset and that her appetite had not returned. My mother made light of it, saying she would recover soon, she was sure, if she ate small delicacies of boiled fish, soup and jellies. I was not reassured and I insisted that my father send for a physician from Pamiers if there was no improvement in another week. Gentille, my sister, was due to be married in July and I wanted my mother to be well for that. I intended to go to Gentille's wedding too, even though my child was due to be born in August.

There was nothing more I could do, so I set out along the track towards the Col de Marmare and Montaillou. It was early spring, the sun was bright on the snow-topped mountains and it was peaceful, as the shepherds had not yet brought the sheep back from the south, where they had spent the winter. Fresh, lime-green grass gleamed at the side of the track studded with the soft lemons, blues, pinks and mauves of wild flowers. Butterflies were on the wing already, landing on the flowers and fluttering close to me, as if they'd lost their way for a minute. I smiled. The scent of the new grass, flowers and herbs coloured the air. The only sound was of insects humming. It had been a welcome break but worry about my mother clouded my mind. I had a feeling of foreboding about her. I vowed to make time to see her more often.

My mother's health did not improve. She was able to attend Gentille's wedding but she was thin, her skin hanging on her bones like a draped cloth, her face grey and lined. I decided to stay on in Caussou after the wedding to help nurse my mother. The children went back to Montaillou with Bérenger and the nursemaids. My mother faded away the week after the wedding and we had a small family funeral. My sadness at the loss of her was tinged with relief as during those days of helping to nurse her I saw how much she suffered.

It was only a week later that I bore my third daughter, who I named Condors. I took comfort from the fact that my mother knew she had a grandchild, my second daughter Esclarmonde, named after her. I was glad that my mother had known her namesake before she died. My new baby, Condors brought some much needed joy and distraction into our grieving household. We stayed in my father's house for six weeks after the birth. Before I left for Montaillou, my father spoke to me.

"When Ava is betrothed, which will be very soon – your mother and I made the arrangements before she died. I… well, I have something to say, Béatrice… I can only tell you, your brothers mustn't know…" He looked at me. "I have decided to devote the rest of my life to supporting the Good Men. I believe it to be the true religion. I believe that they are the only ones who can save our souls. I don't know how much time I have left but now that your mother is no longer here, your brothers run the estate and you girls are all married, I... I must be true to my beliefs. There is a great revival of the faith on its way and I shall be ready to support it in any way that I can."

"Oh Papa, please don't take any risks. I don't want to lose you... now," I said, feeling tears starting in my eyes. My father put his arms around me.

"I have thought a lot about this these last few months. I knew that your mother did not have long for this earth and I have thought about what I must do with the time I have left. The Authier brothers will return from Lombardy soon and they will start their ministry in this area. They will need support, somewhere to stay, food and clothing. Believers are preparing for their return. There will be a network of safe houses for them to stay in as they travel and they will preach in believers' homes. They don't need all the pomp and ceremony of the Roman Church." He looked at me again. "I must do this, Béatrice."

He sounded so passionate, it was clear he had made up his mind. I said, "Be very careful, that's all I ask."

I set off then to Montaillou, in the company of a mule and muleteer who carried my belongings. I carried baby Condors in a sling made from a large piece of cloth. As I walked, with the heavy warmth of Condors against my body, I thought that I couldn't and shouldn't do anything to dissuade my father from his chosen path; he must do what he felt was right. I was not entirely surprised by his declaration – there had always been a sense of his true feelings about the heresy. His mother, my grandmother had been a heretic too, it was in the blood. But I was now the mother of five children and

Bérenger's wife. There was little time for anything else. The revival of the heresy was gathering momentum, there was an inevitability to it and I was watching.

The following year, 1298, in February, on an ordinary morning, when I was busy upstairs in the château with the children, I heard a commotion in the hallway below. Urgent shouts for help were ringing out. I rushed down the stone stairs and saw Bérenger lying on a rug. Four of the estate workers were beside him.

"What's happened?" I asked.

"He collapsed after moving a sack of grain," said one of the men. "We carried him in."

I knelt beside Bérenger. His skin was grey and he was gasping for air. His forehead was clammy with beads of sweat. I picked up his hand – it was freezing cold.

"Bérenger," I said. "I'm here." He opened his eyes.

"Fetch a blanket and a cushion, they're in that first room off the stairs, and bring some water," I commanded the men.

Bérenger was struggling to speak. I put my head close to his lips.

"What is it? Have you got pain?"

"Here." He put his right hand on his heart and gestured down his left arm. "I don't want to leave you…" His voice faded as he whispered, "I love you."

"Hush don't try to talk, a little rest that's what you need, you've been working too hard…"

My desperate words tailed off as I saw his breathing had ceased. I waited, I shook him, I patted his face, gently then harder.

"Oh no, Bérenger, please, no!"

I shook him again as if I could shake some life into him. I lifted his heavy head but let it back down as it rolled horribly around in my arms. I knelt beside him and put my head on his chest. I could feel the life leaving him, the warmth leaving his body, his skin cold, mottled and pale, his face waxy. Sybille was kneeling beside me and I rested my head on her shoulder. I stayed with him for a long time but eventually someone covered him with a sheet and I moved away. Sybille guided me into a room off the stairs where we could sit away from Bérenger's body.

"How can this happen? Bérenger is too young and my children, what will I tell them? What will we do?" I appealed to Sybille. "I don't know what to do."

"It's a terrible shock, so sudden," said Sybille. "Your father and brothers will come and help you. And I'm here." Sybille and I cried together then.

Bérenger was buried in the graveyard next to the church of Sainte Marie de Carnesses. His mother did not make the journey to Montaillou again. She died shortly afterwards. Bérenger's brother came to stay at the château along with my father. The two men discussed the arrangements for me and the children as we sat round the table in the hall.

"Béatrice will, of course, have her dowry returned to her as is usual in this situation," said Jacques to my father. "As you know, the château belongs to the Count of Foix and must be vacated as soon as possible. A new Châtelain will be appointed in the near future. There is enough money for Béatrice and the children along with Sybille, the two nursemaids and a housemaid to stay in a house just below the château, which belongs to the Count also. After a year or so the two boys will come to live with my family on the estate which is their inheritance at Carcassonne."

"No, I don't want to lose my boys as well," I said. "How can you talk about that now?"

I could hardly take in what they were saying – how could they talk about me and my children as if we were animals being moved around the pastures? No-one asked me what I wanted and, apart from wanting to keep my family together, I had little idea of how I might go on. Sybille put her arm around me.

"You mustn't worry about that now," she said. "We must concentrate on getting you and the children settled in your new home."

Sybille and I, Rixende and Gauzia, and the housemaid, Brune, packed everything up in chests and bundles of blankets and, helped by some of the men who worked at the château, we moved the household into a nearby house, which until recently had been occupied by an estate worker. I didn't know what to say to the children. How could I explain to them why they would never see their father again and why they were going to live in another house? The words would not form in my mouth. Where could I say he was? In heaven? Is this what God does, takes the father from small children and a husband from his wife? I was so very tired, nothing interested me any more. Sybille and Rixende were cajoled into caring for my children and moving our belongings. Somehow, a month after Bérenger's death, we were living in our new home; one of the houses on the track leading down from the château to the village.

My children were growing up fast. Bérenger was now eight, and baby Condors was seven months old. I was so sad to think she would not have memories of her father. The children surprised me by their ability to continue as they always had. Their needs and demands were so immediate, and the nursemaids and I were constantly busy with them. I was thankful for them – they gave me a purpose and a structure that helped me through each day, moment by moment. It was all I could do, the next chore. I thought of Bérenger and my mother every day whilst mechanically carrying out my work. I would notice something I wanted to tell Bérenger about the children, then I would remember that he was no longer there. I woke up in the night certain that I had heard his voice, and another time I saw him disappearing round the bend in the track that led to the village. I wondered then if he really had died, even though I knew he had. I found myself crying whilst feeding Condors. Would this ever end? These painful feelings of loss and loneliness… would I ever be happy again? So many questions and God didn't seem to help me at all. The children asked for their father, especially the two boys, who had loved to play fight with him. I didn't want to tell them that he was never coming back so I told them he was in heaven with Jesus. I found no comfort in this idea for myself, but it was the only way I could think of to help my children. At first I thought about him all the time, then one day a few months later I suddenly realised that I hadn't thought of him for a couple of days. He said he loved me as he lay dying. It was the only time he had ever said it. I held these words in my heart forever. This was the only comfort I had.

The new house was pleasantly situated with the back of it giving onto a sloping, sunny meadow. As the weather warmed up I often sat out there with the children. I liked to play with them there but I also loved to sit and look at the green pastures beyond the village, which sloped away from the meadow, and the mountains still covered in powdery snow on their tops. The scenery was a constant in this world of change in which I now lived. Nothing seemed steady in this life except the mountains which withstood the elements. Dramatic storms with lightning and thunder that could easily kill people and animals left the great rocks untouched. I felt awed and vulnerable in their presence and so frightened of the fragility of human life. I saw God as a cruel God who played with people and I regularly questioned my belief in Him. After Bérenger's funeral, I told the village priest, Pierre Clergue, that I didn't want him to visit me as he offered to do, and he had reluctantly agreed to leave me alone for a while. I didn't attend church either – I couldn't face the well-wishers and I was too hurt and angry with God, and many questions were in my mind about His existence. Religion provided no comfort for me as it did for others at times of loss. Nothing could explain why Bérenger had to die so soon after my mother.

It was just a few short weeks after Bérenger's death that I was sitting on a bench in the meadow behind the house, playing a game with Baby Béa and Esclarmonde. Baby Condors was seated on a blanket at the far side of the meadow with Rixende and Gauzia. The two boys were playing with sticks they had picked up, using them as swords. I was giving Béa and Esclarmonde tasks to do. They were searching for differently coloured and shaped flowers and leaves amongst the grass in the meadow. They were dashing backwards and forwards to me with their finds when Sybille appeared at the back door of the house.

"The priest, Father Clergue, is here to see you, Madame," said Sybille.

130

"Oh, I don't really want to see him," I said. "But, I suppose I can't turn him away… show him out here, please Sybille." I stood to greet him.

Pierre Clergue emerged from the back of the house, a neat figure in his black priest's robes. Pierre was in his late twenties. His dark hair was well groomed and his dark brown eyes were shining. His aquiline nose and firm chin gave his face a good-looking strength. His warm smile revealed a full set of even teeth.

"Madame," he gave a little bow. "I know you asked me not to visit and I don't want to intrude, but I would be failing in my duties if I didn't visit to see how you are from time to time."

"Well," I said not knowing quite what to say to him. "I am living here now with my children and their nursemaids... and… I'm managing to get by."

Then I started to cry. I was surprised at myself, it came on me unexpectedly and I couldn't seem to stop. Pierre murmured something. I wasn't sure what he said but he sounded warm and kind.

"I'm so sorry," I said, between sobs. "I don't know why I'm crying… well, I do of course… I mean… it's not easy at times." I glanced at the children in the meadow. "I'm so sorry," I said again.

Then a fresh wave of tears caught me. He moved towards me and put his arms gently around me and I fell naturally into sobbing on his shoulder, like a baby with its mother. His arms felt strong around me. With only Sybille's arms around me of late, I was acutely aware of his masculine strength.

"I think you'll feel better afterwards," he said. "For crying, I mean… why don't we go indoors away from the children."

I nodded and he followed as I led him back into the house. I took him into the main living room. I started sobbing again as soon as we entered the room and he put his arms round me and patted me on my shoulder until I managed to control myself. I gestured to a bench for him to sit on and I sat opposite him.

"I'm sorry," I said. "I really don't know why I'm crying so much now. I try not to think about it all, you know… I just keep going as best I can, but I do miss him – Bérenger, my husband, it was so sudden… the way it happened, one minute he was there and then the next he was gone – I never expected that to happen. I apologise, I'm rattling on and on aren't I?"

"There is no need to apologise," he said. "I think you needed to cry… and I'm glad I came to see you, because I think you will feel better after this."

"I think I've been bottling it up, for my children's sake, you know, I have to keep going for them," I said.

"Children do have a way of keeping you going," he said. "But you must think of yourself as well."

"Well yes, I know," I said, "But there is always so much to do with so many little children. You can't just sit around feeling sorry for yourself."

"Of course," he said. He smiled at me. "But you can leave your children for a short time with their nursemaids. Come to the church anytime, I'm usually there. We can talk again, about anything – it might help."

"Thank you," I said.

He stood up to go. After he had gone, I sat outside again with the children. I felt somehow lighter. He had been so kind and was not put out in any way by my crying. He was right, I had tried to put my own feelings to one side, wanting to make life seem as normal as possible for the children.

The following week, I was on my way down to the village to visit my friend Jacquemette Maury when my eye fell on the church, sitting in the meadow. I thought that maybe I would call in and see Pierre Clergue on my way back from visiting Jacquemette. I carried on towards the village square where the Maurys' house was situated. The Maurys were farmers and weavers, not very well off, but Jacquemette was a warm and generous woman, and I had become closer to her, and to Alazaïs Azema and Fabrisse Rives, since Bérenger had died. I was a regular visitor to the Maurys' little house on the edge of the square, often in the company of Fabrisse and Alazaïs.

On this occasion, I had just settled myself next to Jacquemette's fire when another visitor arrived at the house. It was a woman I knew vaguely named Vuissance Clergue, who lived on the far side of the square and who was a distant relative of Pierre Clergue's. Vuissance acknowledged me briefly as she entered the house but she seemed anxious to speak to Jacquemette.

"Jacquemette, I couldn't rest... I had to come and ask – how... how was it with Agnès?" she said ignoring me. "Did it go *well*?"

"It went *well*," said Jacquemette.

"It was done... done *well*?" Vuissance looked intently at Jacquemette.

"Yes, very *well*."

"You weren't short of anything then?"

"No, not at all, as I said, everything went *well*."

"Thanks be to God," said Vuissance. "That's all I wanted to know, Jacquemette. I'm so relieved. I'll go now but I'll come back later, I'll need fire for my oven."

Vuissance nodded to both of us and left. I turned to Jacquemette with a question on my face.

"Would you like a drink?" said Jacquemette turning away. Her plump, pretty face looked as if she was about to cry.

"Jacquemette?" I said. "What is it? What was all that about?"

Jacquemette sighed and a tear fell down her face. "I… I can't say."

"Well, it's obvious something has upset you," I said. "Why can't you say?"

Jacquemette sighed. "Agnès died last night."

"Agnès, you mean your sister-in-law? Why didn't you say…?"

"It slipped my mind," said Jacquemette.

"What?"

"I just forgot… are you sure you wouldn't like a drink?"

"And what did you mean… it went *well*? What went *well*?"

"Nothing, no special meaning," said Jacquemette.

"Agnès dying…" I said, an idea coming into my mind. "And 'did it go *well*?' Why…"

"It's nothing, really," said Jacquemette.

"Really, Jacquemette?"

"I can't say," Jacquemette said. Her face was very flushed.

"Is this…? I hardly dare say it, but is this concerning the Good Men? It is, isn't it?"

"Béatrice! What do you know?" Jacquemette was clearly taken aback.

"Not a great deal, but I think you must know about my father... his yellow crosses," I said. "Everyone seems to know that and Raymond Roussel, the old steward at the château used to talk to me... at... at times about the Good Men and 'the understanding of good', *l'entendensa del Be*'."

"Yes, yes, of course, Raymond wore the crosses like your father," said Jacquemette. "I'd forgotten all that. There is so much going on here at the moment."

"Oh?"

"I don't know if I should say any more, it's so dangerous. A word spoken in the wrong place and the Inquisition... well, you know... you don't want them knocking at your door."

"Yes, I do know. What was all that about Agnès?"

"I'm so frightened of speaking about it – you must promise not breathe a word to anyone," said Jacquemette. I nodded. "Poor Agnès died last night, in her house just beyond the square. She'd been ill for a while with a terrible growth on her chest. We knew she was near to death last week. Her husband, Bertrand, said that she should receive the *consolamentum* before she died. It's what she wanted; she was a believer in the Good Men. So he sent for Guillaume Authier, the Perfect, who he'd heard was staying in Ax... so, he came and gave Agnès the *consolamentum*."

"Guillaume Authier was here, in Montaillou?" I said.

"Yes, he came to Agnès's house."

"Were you there?" Excitement and curiosity coursed through my body. I was being woken up after my weeks of feeling half dead with grief.

"Yes, I was."

135

"What happened?"

"Oh, it's hard to explain how wonderful it was," said Jacquemette. Her face changed as she spoke, relaxing into what I thought, with a shock, looked like peace, serenity. Jacquemette was quiet for a moment then she said, "I've never seen anything like it. Guillaume Authier asked Agnès some questions about her faith. She was very weak but she managed to answer him. Then he read from a book of Gospels, Saint John's Gospel, he said it was. He placed the book on her head and prayed, then he laid his hands on her hands and on her body, it was so beautiful."

"So it's true, it's here… the revival and the Perfects."

"Then, he told us she must take no food or drink to ensure the soul's purity, ready to be received into heaven, she must go through the *endura*."

"The *endura*?"

"The final stage of life," said Jacquemette. "When she took no food or drink."

"Guillaume Authier was so calm and kind. He seemed…" Jacquemette searched for a word. "Holy, I felt the holiness in him, Béatrice. He spoke like an angel."

"I remember seeing him dance at my wedding. He was a very good dancer and he had a lovely wife and family."

"Well, he gave it all up to become a Perfect, a holy man. His brother Pierre did the same. I believe they really are good, they don't lie, and they don't harm any living thing, not even animals for food. They say they are the only ones who can save our souls," said Jacquemette. "And I can believe it."

"Raymond Roussel told me about the Authier brothers going to Lombardy to become

136

Perfects. He said the same thing, that only the Good Men can save our souls. But what a risk you took… being there at the *consolamentum*," I said.

"Yes, I know," said Jacquemette. "But this village is safe because our priest, Pierre Clergue, and his family, the Benets, the Belots, the Forts and the Rives are all believers. They all support the Perfects," she paused, "You could help too, Béatrice, by giving some food for them."

"Our priest? And his family are Cathars?" I was incredulous. "But how can that be?"

"I thought everyone knew that," said Jacquemette. "It's not just them, there are a lot of people who are believers here, in Montaillou. They feel safe here because Pierre Clergue can protect us. The Roman Church and the Inquisition don't know what's going on," said Jacquemette.

"Raymond hinted that Pierre Clergue turned a blind eye to it all, but I didn't know he was involved in it. How can he be both a priest and a Cathar believer?"

"The Clergues have always been Cathars. Most people think he only became a priest to keep the Roman Church off our backs."

"But surely there are some here who are not believers in the Good Men? Surely they'll find out what's going on and report to the Inquisition?" I said.

"Yes, we must still be careful, but Pierre Clergue will deny any accusations at the synod in Foix, and to the Inquisition in Carcassonne. If anyone steps out of line they will be dealt with by Bernard Clergue, in his role as Bailiff. He can throw them into the dungeon of the château or confiscate their land. That's enough to stop most people from talking, people are frightened. You know, Béatrice, many people in

Montaillou, and in Prades and Ax, give money to the Clergues so that they will protect them. People are in awe of them and appreciate what they do. You know Pierre doesn't take as much as he should for Church taxes off the people either, he looks after us all."

The realisation of the extent of the Clergue family's power hit me in my guts as I sat listening to Jacquemette. With Bernard the village Bailiff, Pierre the village priest, and all of them Cathars as well, they had everything within their control.

Jacquemette continued, "Many of the shepherds including my son Pedro, and Arnaud Vital, the shoemaker, act as *passeurs.* They guide the Perfects as they move over the mountains in the night when it's dark to perform *consolamentums* and to preach in people's homes."

"This is a lot to take in," I said. I thought about my friends in the village and one in particular who both Jacquemette and I were close to.

"You said the Rives are Cathars, but what about Fabrisse Rives? She is a strong Roman, Jacquemette, how will her family keep it from her?"

"I don't know Béatrice, there's going to be trouble. The rest of the Rives family have told Jacques, her husband to bring her into line, I heard. But she's so strong-willed, I don't think she'll be persuaded."

"You can't change how people feel in their hearts," I said as I rose to leave. "That is one thing I do know."

"We need to support the Perfects in their work by providing food. I've given what I can, but you could give something too," said Jacquemette.

"I'll send a bag of wheat for them."

I walked home trying to digest what Jacquemette told me. I forgot that I had planned to visit

Pierre in the church. I had such a lot to think about now. Pierre was certainly a fascinating man. It was as if a whole new landscape had opened up before me. It was the first time in a long while that I found myself curious, interested and thinking about something other than my children and the losses I had suffered. I felt alive again.

I fell asleep thinking about Pierre Clergue and his involvement with the Good Men, and I woke up with him on my mind. Could I dare to ask him about it all? I felt compelled to go down and see him although I had no idea how to broach the subject with him. I left the children with their nursemaids and set off down the track to the church, passing the Clergues' large house on the way. I found Pierre sitting in the doorway of the church enjoying the sun. His legs were swinging over the side of the chair he was perched on. He jumped up when he saw me.

"Béatrice," he said. "How are you?"

"I'm feeling a little better at the moment," I said. "I found talking to you so helpful that I thought I'd come and see you again."

"Let's go inside the church," he said.

He made his way towards the front of the church near the altar and sat down on a bench at the side. He patted the seat next to him and I sat down.

"So, you are feeling a little better?" He smiled his warm smile at me.

"Yes," I said. "And I want to ask you something."

"Oh, what is it?"

"Well," I said, half wishing I hadn't started this conversation and wondering how I could ask him what I wanted to know. "I'm not sure how to put it… but I've been hearing some rumours."

He nodded. "There are always rumours in villages, Béatrice. There is nothing to worry about in Montaillou, now I'm the priest here. I will always look after the people."

"I wonder… is it possible that people can have different beliefs?"

"Life can be complicated," he said. "You know that, I think."

"Yes, but…"

He put his finger on my lips. "Don't worry Béatrice, I will look after you, if you come and see me here, or I can sometimes visit you in your home, I will teach you more about what is going on here, so you will be reassured." His finger traced a delicate line my lips. I felt a tingle of arousal. I licked my lips then stood up.

"I must get back to… my children."

He stood up with me and put his arms around me. "Béatrice, don't forget, I will look after you," he said and kissed me gently on my lips. For a moment I enjoyed the strength of his arms around me again, but he was a priest. This could not be, a kiss like this felt wrong.

"No, no, I must go." I pushed him away and ran from the church.

I ran home. I was confused about what had just happened. I had enjoyed being with him again, he was a man so different from any other man I knew, so much more interesting than any other man in Montaillou, but he seemed to challenge every idea that I had of a priest. His kiss and his touch had aroused feelings in me that had been lying dormant. But he had gone too far. I could not allow this to continue. I resolved to avoid him in future.

He arrived at my house the following day. It was early afternoon and the boys were outside with the nursemaids and the little girls were asleep.

"Oh, Pierre," I said.

"Can I come in?" he said.

"I'm not sure I should let you in," I said.

"I want to talk to you," he said. "Don't keep me standing outside." I took him into the living room.

"How are you?" he asked.

"I'm quite well," I said.

"Good, that's good," he said.

We looked at each other, his dark eyes were clear and shining, his expression serious.

"Béatrice…"

"I…"

We both spoke at once and laughed.

"Béatrice," he said. "I think I upset you yesterday, but I just want to be a friend to you, we could be friends, you know."

"Is that what you want, to be friends?"

"Yes, of course," he said.

"You kissed me."

"I couldn't help it, you are so beautiful," he said. "In fact I would like to do it again."

I moved away from him. "You should not, I think."

"Perhaps."

"You're a priest."

"Well, Béatrice, I can tell you that there are people who think differently about these things."

"I have heard that women who give themselves to priests will never see the face of God."

"Béatrice, I think there are some things you don't understand," he said. "As a priest, I know the

141

truth about the Church. Much of what goes on is done to please the people."

"Is that so?" I said. "So can you tell me what's going on in Montaillou? I've been hearing about… certain events."

"Ah yes," he said. "You mustn't worry about it."

"You don't know what I mean."

"I'll explain," he said. He looked at me steadily. "My mother looks after Na Roche, you know her, the very old lady in the village. She was in prison for a while, she was imprisoned for her beliefs, she supported the Good Men. My mother gives her food and clothing."

"Well…" I was lost for words, taken aback by his openness. "Your mother?"

"Yes, let's sit together and I'll explain it to you," he said. "My parents both look after the Good Men and their supporters. And I can look after the people here, the rituals of the Church are only what the people expect and want because that's all they know, but there are other ways of serving God and saving our souls. We cannot help but sin, but our sins will be forgiven at the end of our lives if we follow the right pathway. So Béatrice, we need not worry about what may occur between us."

Sybille knocked on the door at that moment and I had to go and attend to Condors who was crying for me, so Pierre left. But I couldn't stop thinking about him and what he had said whenever I had time to myself.

Not long after this conversation with Pierre, I visited my friend Alazaïs, who lived beside the track leading down towards the village square. As I arrived, Alazaïs's eldest son Jacques, who was about eighteen,

142

was leaving the house. He greeted me and turned to his mother.

"Everyone has gone down to Ax to the market now, Mother, so I'm going to take this bag of wheat across to Prades." He glanced at me as he spoke and Alazaïs also threw a look my way.

"Very good, Jacques, be careful," said Alazaïs and, with another glance at me, Jacques left.

"Is Jacques…? Is there something important happening?" I said.

"Don't be nosy," said Alazaïs touching her nose with her finger and laughing. "Tell me, how are the children?"

"Alazaïs, I know what's going on in Montaillou," I said. "You can tell me."

"No, no… Béatrice, I must be careful," said Alazaïs. "There are things we must not speak of."

"You can trust me, Alazaïs, I know the dangers – remember my father?" I said.

"Ah… your father?" said Alazaïs. I nodded and Alazaïs continued, "I have to be even more careful than most because my in-laws, the Azemas, are, well… against the…"

"The Perfects? The Good Men?"

Alazaïs nodded. "My father-in-law Pierre is set against them because of what happened last time. People were ruined by the Inquisition – they took people's land and burnt their houses. My in-laws had some of their land taken and it's been so hard since. They're very bitter so we daren't tell them how we feel. But you know you can't change what your heart tells you is right." Tears formed in her eyes. There was a small silence.

"Alazaïs, I promise you have nothing to fear from me. To be honest with you, I don't really know

143

what I believe sometimes, but then I've never heard the Good Men preach and everyone says that once you hear them you're theirs for ever."

"They need help, Béatrice, with money and clothes. If we all give something for them, they can devote their time to their mission."

"How would it be if I send some food and money to help them?" I said.

Pierre had taken to visiting me regularly in the evenings when the children were in bed and I told him that I had been asked to give food to support the Good Men. I guarded my friends' names and stories with care and he didn't ask.

"This village is full of believers," said Pierre, "and there'll be even more soon."

It was evening and we were sitting together on a bench next to the fire, watching the orange flames and the occasional burst of sparks from the logs. He put his arm around me and he kissed me gently on my cheek. Both his arms were around me and he drew me to him and whispered in my ear.

"Béatrice, I want you so much."

I pulled away. "No, it's not possible," I said.

"It's not an uncommon thing for a priest to love a woman, or for a woman to love a priest."

"Yes, I know," I said. "But I'm concerned about it – what would the Church think?"

"Ah, Béatrice," he said. "The Church understands these things."

"Wouldn't you be in trouble?"

"No, you must know that many priests live with their housekeepers as man and wife."

"Well, yes, of course," I said. "But I think it should not be so… that this cannot be between us, in fact I would rather give myself to four other men than to one priest."

"Béatrice, the sin is the same whether it's committed with a husband or a priest. In fact, it is a greater sin with a husband because the woman does not think it is a sin. Much of what happens in church is secular pomp, and nuptials are part of this pomp, but really men and women can live freely in this world according to their pleasure... it is sufficient to be received into the sect of the Good Christians to be saved and absolved of the sins of this life."

"How can you say such a thing when, as a priest, you know that what is said in church is that marriage was the first sacrament, and that it was instituted by God between Adam and Eve?"

"If that is so, why did God not guard Adam and Eve from sin?"

"I don't know the answer to that," I said.

"The Church teaches many falsehoods and the scriptures have been embellished and elaborated on, Béatrice."

"If that is the case, then the Church has a lot to answer for, as they have told people untruths," I said.

Our discussions on these subjects carried on over a number of visits. I had many questions and he always had an answer. He always gave me a lot to think about. He told me that sex with him would not be as bad as I had thought, that it was our nature and we only needed to receive the *consolamentum* at the end of our lives and we would be saved. I enjoyed being with him; his knowledge fascinated me and his masculine presence in my world of women and children filled a gap in my life. I started to change my mind about him.

One evening, he said again how much he wanted me. I was ready.

"I'm ready to give myself to you," I replied. "But I am worried that I will have a child, and if that happened… my father is still alive you know… I would bring terrible shame on my family."

Pierre pulled from his pocket a little sachet containing something. It was on a long string, which he placed round my neck. He smiled at me.

"I have the answer," he said. "Whenever I make love to you I shall put this round your neck, it will hang down between your breasts, so." He guided it between my breasts on top of my clothing. "Then it goes down here," his hands gently moved over my body, still on top of my clothes and down between my legs. I allowed his demonstration to proceed. "Then you must let it go inside you and when I enter you the herb inside it will prevent a baby being conceived."

"What sort of herb is it? Is it the one that the cowherds hang over a cauldron of milk into which they have put some rennet, to stop the milk from curdling?" I whispered to him.

"Oh, I'm not telling you that – you may be tempted to use it with other men," he whispered back. "Come, Béatrice, let's away to your bed and we will try it out. After your father dies, I would like to give you a child."

Chapter 9
The Fourth Interrogation

In the attic room, the minutes and the hours, the days and the nights merge and pass. The changing light in the high opening and the fluctuations of temperature give her clues as to the time of day. But she sleeps whenever she can and eats very little. She is weak. She waits. She hears Jean Belmas walking along the corridor and she sits up ready to ask him for news of Pierre Clergue. It is evening and he brings soup. He looks serious.

"Pierre Clergue has been arrested."

"That cannot be," she says.

"It's true, Madame. One of the Bishop's men told me. I was talking to one of the guards, about finding a messenger to take a message to Pierre Clergue at Montaillou. He said that he'd been at the Priory, the one not far from here just outside Pamiers, Mas-Saint-Antonin, and the talk there was all about the priest from Montaillou, who'd been sent there. Pierre Clergue is under house arrest there."

"On what charges?" she asks.

"They said it was heresy."

Someone must have given evidence against Pierre. Who would dare? Would anyone risk giving evidence against a priest? Especially such a priest as Pierre Clergue. If so, who could it be? He has had many lovers, maybe one of them has talked. And he must have numerous enemies. He has always somehow managed to be both a Roman priest and a Cathar supporter. Everyone in Montaillou knew this. She'd heard that both his parents had died a year or two ago. His mother was buried under the altar in Sainte Marie de Carnesses. Their funerals were said to be grand affairs. It was also said that they both received the *consolamentum*, the Cathar death ritual. Peasants who paid rent and money for the Clergues' protection, which she had grown to understand meant preventing Bernard the Bailiff from confiscating their land and their property, and Pierre the priest from naming them as heretics to the Carcassonne Inquisition, came from miles around to pay their last respects. Except it was out of fear that they came, not respect. The extent of the Clergues' empire was revealed at their funerals and with that realisation came the question as to what would happen now they had gone. Someone must have talked. It seems that the moment is drawing nearer when she must talk about him too.

Pierre Clergue – for all of his deceit and lying – the thought of betraying him does not sit easily in her mind, with her sense of who she is. Béatrice does not betray her friends. But she must tell Jacques Fournier something about her relationship with Pierre, because if she doesn't then it is likely that someone else will, if they haven't already. What she says about Pierre Clergue will go a long way towards explaining how she was caught up in what went on in Montaillou. She must choose, her own skin or Pierre's, and she must, she has to save herself. Besides, it could already be too late for Pierre. Jacques Fournier must have some information about him. People are talking. The last twenty years of secrecy, betrayals and losses have been too much. Rome's persecution of the Cathars has done its job. What can she say about him? She knows what Fabrisse and Alazaïs would say about him. Pierre Clergue believes in Pierre Clergue, he'll say whatever he needs to say to save his own skin. She knows he has done bad things and has made enemies. Eventually the reckoning came and he had to make a choice, just as she must

148

now. He betrayed his friends, neighbours and fellow believers to save himself, but it wasn't enough to save him – somehow the truth must have come out, otherwise why would he have been arrested? It makes it easier to know he has already been arrested; she cannot do much more harm. Even so, the thought of betraying him to save herself disturbs her. How sad she has been to hear how Pierre has become, how he has degenerated. She cannot save him, but can he save her? She has her children and grandchildren to think of, not just herself. And she wants to see them grow up. It's a confusing picture and she fears she cannot think clearly any more. All she does know is that she wants to talk to him.

She takes a mouthful of the soup and forces a few more mouthfuls of the watery, tasteless liquid down before feeling sick. She must try to keep her strength up. She puts the remainder to one side and tries to sleep. But her mind is busy and she is restless, tossing and turning, dozing and dreaming throughout the long, hot night. In the morning, she awaits the arrival of the guard. It's Jean Belmas' footsteps that approach the loft. Will he have any more information? She is up and pacing the room by the time he opens the door.

"Well?" she says. "Have you any news?"

"Of Pierre Clergue, Madame?"

"Yes, yes, of course." She holds in a scream of frustration. "What is it?"

"He has been seen in Pamiers. He is under house arrest at Mas-Saint-Antonin, but it seems he is allowed out in the evenings and he walks around the town and the ramparts, which pass close by the Bishopric."

"Oh, Lord!" she says. "You must be able to get a message to him now if he's so close by. To tell him that I'm here?"

"I will try again, Madame. It might be possible."

"When I get out of here I will pay you well," she says. "It might even be possible for him to come here, to enter the Bishopric and visit me here. Don't you think?"

"Yes, Madame, I will see if it is possible to pass on the message, that you are here."

His slowness, his lack of fire and initiative infuriates her, but she contains it. Jean Belmas is her only ally.

"Yes, yes, of course," she says. "Thank you, Monsieur Belmas."

Shortly after this he appears again to escort her down to see the Bishop. The Bishop wastes no time. He looks as serious and cold as ever. His eyes seem to search her soul. Brother Gaillard throws her a look of contempt.

"Madame, I remind you that you speak under oath and that you would be wise to co-operate," he says. "Please continue from yesterday."

As she sits there in front of the Bishop and the scribe, it is as if she has ingested some poisonous substance that her body must now rid itself of. The terror of torture has infected her and she must spew the words out of her mouth like vomit. They pour out of her, even more than at her last interrogation.

Shame suffuses her mind and body as she speaks, but it does not stop the outpouring. Rather the opposite. She feels she must get rid of all this. Too much has been kept inside her. Now she has permission, she lets it go – it must all come out. There have been too many secrets held in for too long.

"It was during Lent in the year after my first husband died that I went down to the church of Sainte Marie de Carnesses to make my confession. The priest there was Pierre Clergue, the son of Mengarde and Pons Clergue, who lived in Montaillou, and the brother of Bernard Clergue, the Bailiff. We were alone and he embraced me and kissed me, saying that he had been watching me, that I was the most beautiful woman he had ever seen, and that he admired me more than any other woman he knew. I was so surprised by this that I left the church quickly."

She catches her breath and wonders, is that how it happened? She's not sure if she remembers correctly, maybe it doesn't matter how it happened. She glances at the Bishop who seems to be listening intently. His eyes under their puffy lids seem to be dancing. She continues.

"After this, Pierre Clergue came to visit me several times at my home. On each occasion he would ask me to give myself to him, telling me how much he wanted me. I told him to stop speaking so to me."

She notices the Bishop shift about in his chair as she speaks and she stops for a moment. She avoids looking at Brother Gaillard, who she sees from the corner of her eye has stopped writing. She can't separate out what is relevant and what is not, what is correct or not. It cannot be censored, she is so terrified that she cannot think. She must just talk.

He says, "Continue, Madame."

"I told him to stop saying these things. That this could not be, I told him to leave. But he was very persistent and although I continued to try and push him away, he always came back. I told him that I wouldn't give myself to him, that it was wrong for a woman to give herself to a priest. He told me that I knew nothing

151

about it, that he as a priest knew the truth of the matter and that he would tell me that truth. And this was how our conversations about the Good Men started."

She pauses to try to gather her thoughts. Bishop Fournier is looking intently at her and says, "We have other witnesses who know the truth. If you do not speak the whole truth then we will… help you to find the truth."

She shudders. She has already resolved to tell him what she knows and what she remembers. It's on her lips, ready to spill out.

"He quoted again from the Bible, saying that Christ had said to the apostles to leave their loved ones to follow Him in order to have the Kingdom of Heaven. Peter had asked Christ about those who were sick and unable to follow Him. The Lord had said that his friends would come and place their hands on the heads of the sick. They would be cured by this and then would be able to follow Him. These 'friends' of the Lord are the Good Christians, the Cathars, who are called heretics. It is the ritual of laying on of hands that they perform at the end of life for the dying that absolves them of sin. This is the *consolamentum*. And it is only the Good Christians who can save our souls in this way. He went on to tell me that God did not forbid marriage between brothers and sisters, either. It was only when problems arose because many brothers were fighting over one or two beautiful sisters that the Church decided to forbid it. But before the eyes of God, the sin is the same. He gave me his own family as an example, saying it made sense to him. They were four brothers and two sisters. He said he was a priest and did not wish to marry, which left his three brothers. If Guillaume and Bernard wed Esclarmonde and Guillemette, their sisters, then none of their wealth or property would go out of the family. Only one woman needs to be brought in for the remaining brother. This is not a sin in the eyes of God."

Béatrice stops and takes a breath. She looks at the Bishop, wondering for a moment at the impact her words are having upon him. She can feel the sadistic gaze of Brother Gaillard upon her. He is enjoying this.

Bishop Fournier says. "Please continue, Madame."

She does not hesitate. "With these arguments and many others, he influenced me to the point that during the octave of Saints Peter and Paul, I gave myself to him one night at my house. This happened again often, and he continued to visit me for about a year and a half, coming to stay at my house two or three times a week. I sometimes went to stay with him in his parents' house where he had a room upstairs which had an outside staircase. He stayed with me one time on Christmas Eve and went on to say mass the following morning. I asked him how he could want to commit such a grave sin on such a holy night. He replied that this sin was the same on the night of the Nativity as on any other night. Since he had often gone on to say mass in the morning after spending the preceding night with me, without being confessed, this occasion was no different. I had asked him this same question before and he always replied that the only true confession is the one made to God, who knows the sin before it is committed, and who alone can absolve it. Confession to a priest is only done to please the people. He told me that I must never confess the sin committed with him to another priest but to God alone, who knew it and who could absolve me, which no man could." She breathes in deeply.

153

"He told me that Saint Peter was not a Pope in his life but that as soon as he had died, his bones were thrown into a pit where they remained for several years. When they were discovered they were washed and placed on the throne on which the Roman Pontiffs sat. And so, he told me, that the bones of Saint Peter did not have the power to absolve when they were enthroned and made apostolic, neither did any of the Popes who sat on that throne. It was only the Good Christians who suffered persecutions and death like the Saints Lawrence, Stephen and Bartholomew who could absolve, not the Bishops nor the priests subject to the Roman Church, who were heretics and persecutors of the Good Christians. God gave this ability to absolve only to the Good Christians, whom he had known and knew would suffer persecution. I asked him then if confession made to a priest was worth nothing, why he himself heard confessions, gave absolution and imposed penances. He said it was necessary to do this, as otherwise the Church would lose their revenues and no-one would give them anything if they did not do as the Church prescribed. But it would be those who submitted themselves to the Good Christians who would be absolved by the laying on of hands. The sins did not even need to be confessed; the *consolamentum* at the end of life was all that was necessary." She pauses for a moment, wondering if she has already spoken of this. She cannot think clearly, she only knows she must speak to avoid torture. If someone else has spoken – she remembers the assistant priest who knew about the bed in the church – she has to cover herself.

"He told me all this and more besides, as we sat at times near a window which looked out over the pathway and I de-loused his head. Sometimes we talked beside the fire and sometimes in bed. We were careful not to be overheard as we talked of these things, although my servant Sybille may have overheard on occasions."

Bishop Fournier sips some water and waits. She starts again. It continues to pour out of her.

"Pierre Clergue told me that God had created only spirits. But that the bodies which one sees, and the earth and the sky and all that is found herein, with the sole exception of our spirits, these were created by the Devil, who rules the world. It was God who made the spirits and the Devil who made the bodies. God breathed life into the bodies that the Devil had made and they could walk and talk. He also told me that God had made all the spirits of heaven and that these spirits sinned by the sin of pride, wishing to be equal to God. Because of this they fell from the sky and onto the earth where they dwell and penetrate into the bodies of men or beasts that they meet. The spirits that dwell in beasts have knowledge and reason just as those in human bodies, except that they cannot talk. That is why it is a sin to kill a beast or a man. These spirits enter into a human body to do penance for their sin of pride. This must be done before the world is finished. If they enter the body of a Good Christian then they will return to the sky from which they fell. If they have not entered a Good Christian then, when they leave that body, they can enter into another body. This can be done successively up to nine times but after this if they have not entered into the body of a Good Christian they are totally lost. Judas and the other Jews who betrayed Christ were lost immediately and forever. It is only those whose spirits enter the bodies of Good Christians, who believe in them and enter into their sect, they will be saved."

Fear drives her, has she made herself clear? Does she remember it correctly? She knows for sure the next piece of information he told her is as he told her.

"He told me that the Good Christians do not believe that Christ took human flesh from the Holy Virgin. That He only hid Himself in the Blessed Mother, without taking anything from her. He also told me that the Lord, although He dined with His disciples, never ate or drank, although it seemed as if He did. He also told me that since the outrage of the crucifixion was performed on Christ on the cross, no-one should adore or venerate the cross. He said that the Church of God exists only where there is a Good Christian. He told me that when Good Christians are burned for their faith, they are the martyrs of Christ, and that God would not allow the fire to pain them greatly."

The Bishop asks her, "These heresies and errors that Father Clergue told you, did you believe them then and do you believe them now?"

"For a few months from Easter to August, I did not know what to believe. All this was told to me by a priest. The priest of our parish who I trusted, so there were times when I did believe what he said for this short time. But when I went to live in Crampagna with my second husband, and I heard the preaching of the Minorites there and I lived amongst faithful Christians, I abandoned these heresies. Eventually I confessed to a Franciscan at the convent at Limoux. I did not see a heretic that I knew to be a heretic either before that time or since. I very much regret having heard these remarks and even more regret having believed in them. I am ready to undergo the penance which my Lord Bishop would impose on me for this."

Bishop Fournier makes the sign of the cross and speaks the words.

"In Nomine Patris et Filii et Spiritus Sancti. Amen."

"Amen," she says and crosses herself.

She follows the guard back along the familiar route through the Palace. There is no protest – she is exhausted. She is surprised at herself, how she spoke so freely of such things to these men of the Church. And there is more still to come.

Back in the loft, Béatrice collapses into her customary place and stares up at the opening. The sky is a hazy blue. If only she could be out there under that sky, to touch the earth, smell the air, the flowers and the grass. In Montaillou, there are places where the mountain peaks are so close at eye-level that you feel you could put out a hand to touch them. That's freedom. If only she could see Pierre and explain to him. If only… but it's too late, what she has just told Jacques Fournier seals the fate of Pierre. He is damned in the eyes of the Roman Church. But is he damned in the eyes of the Good Men? Cathar hell or Roman hell, she doesn't know which. If she doesn't tell what she knows, she will be the damned one. So she must talk.

Chapter 10
Changes

The two years after Bérenger died passed so quickly and I was dreading the time when my sons had to leave as it came ever closer. They would soon go to Carcassonne to live on the estate with their Uncle and his wife. These terms were arranged when Bérenger died and were legally binding. There was nothing I could do to change this. It was what my marriage to Bérenger had been for. To provide heirs for the family. And I had obliged perfectly. My brothers were the boys' guardians and would ensure their welfare. I could visit them whenever I wished. But I knew that would not be often. The reality was that they would grow up from now on without their mother and their sisters. It was not something I wished to face.

It was a cold, wet winter's day when my brothers rode into Montaillou to collect my sons. The mist which hung over the mountains and the château imbued the place with a dark dismalness, so different from the sunny beauty of a summer's day there, that it was difficult to imagine it was the same place. From the back of my house I had a view of the track leading through the outlying meadows below the village. I watched for them all day. Finally they arrived in the late afternoon.

I had not seen my brothers for at least a year, which was when I last went over to Caussou. My father had visited me once during that time, but Philippe and Bernard were always busy on the estate and did not come with him. These two were now big, strong men in their late twenties who had a reputation for thuggery. There had been rumours circulating about them a few weeks previously that they had killed a man, and that

158

one of the peasants on their estate had been blamed for it. They were not to be trifled with. I, although repudiating the rumours that had come to my ears publicly, privately thought that I could believe them. I heard the sounds of the horses, their hooves clattering on the stony track and their snorting, as they approached my home. I went to the door to greet them. They drew their horses to a halt when they saw me in the doorway to my house, and dismounted. Both of them had dark beards and thick dark brown hair, which was in wild disarray from their travels. Their clothes – wool tunics, cloaks and leather boots – were covered in mud and wet through. They looked like two of the shaggy, wild bears that roamed the remoter regions of the mountains. The animal smell of the horses and the men's wet wool clothing was strong. The horses shifted and squelched their hooves in the mud near my door and snorted gentle wickers of greeting to me as I approached them.

"Béatrice, you look well," said Bernard.

"Thank you, I am," I said. "But you look very wet and cold."

"We'll go straight up to the château, stable the horses and change our clothes before we come into your house."

I smiled at them as best I could. "Did you have a good journey?"

"Apart from the weather, yes, there were no problems."

"You'll eat with us later, then?"

They nodded and walked off with their animals towards the château. I shut the door leaning back against it, aware of my mixed feelings. I was partly pleased to see them – they were my brothers after all – but the purpose of their visit was not something I

159

wanted to think about. I walked into the main living room of the house where a fireplace with a bread oven always had a fire burning in it. The smell of baking bread filled the room and six large loaves sat on the table top. My two boys, Bérenger and Philippe, were sitting at the table eating some of the bread and the little girls were clambering up on the bench near the table asking for some. This was my family, soon to be broken up.

"You can all have just one piece each, otherwise there'll be none left for your uncles who have just arrived," I said.

"When are we going to Carcassonne?" said Bérenger.

"Tomorrow, I expect," I said. "You'll meet your uncles when they come to eat with us and they'll tell you what the arrangements are then."

"Yes! Yes!" the two boys shouted, excited about their journey.

Later my brothers walked down from the château to my house. I opened the door and embraced each of them.

"You look much better now," I said. They had changed out of their wet clothes and their wild hair had been tamed and tidied.

"That's a good smell," said Bernard.

"It's a large side of wild boar that's been roasting for the last few hours, for our meal tonight. The new Châtelain gave it to me," I said. "I know how much you like wild boar and you must be hungry after your journey."

The children were waiting to meet their uncles before they went to bed. It had been so long since they last saw them that the girls did not remember them at all. The children went quiet and still, and stared wide-eye at their uncles.

"They've all grown a lot – look at Bérenger and Philippe, such big boys now." Philippe ruffled Bérenger's hair with his hand. "What an adventure riding with us to Carcassonne."

Bernard rode an imaginary horse round the room holding the reins in one hand and using the other hand to hit the horse with an imaginary crop.

"I don't want Bérenger and Philippe to go. I want them to stay here," said Baby Béa.

"Hush, Béa," I said. "They will like it very much, and we can go and visit them whenever we want to." My voice was bright and cheerful.

"We'll be off early in the morning so you'd better all get a good night's sleep. You want to see them before they go, don't you?" said Philippe. Baby Béa nodded. Sybille gathered them all together.

"Come along girls, it's time for bed now. Say goodnight to everyone. I'll come back for the boys when you girls are all tucked up in your beds." The little girls all said good night and followed Sybille out.

"So, young Sires, it's off to Carcassonne tomorrow to learn to ride, to learn to read and write, and to learn about the estate you will inherit one day," said Philippe, my eldest brother.

I put my arms around them. "We shall miss you, but I know you will like it there. There's so much to learn about. It's exciting isn't it?" They both nodded.

I had to be strong for my beautiful boys with their dark eyes so like their father's, and their thick chestnut hair like my own, but to be separated from them... it was unthinkable, something I couldn't believe was happening – to me, they were just little boys in need of a mother's love and care. I wanted so much to keep them with me but I could not give them the upbringing they deserved as their father's sons. I had to let them go and claim their inheritance. There was no reason to believe that they would not be treated well and loved as Bérenger's offspring, but my heart was breaking.

After all the children had gone to bed, I sat down with my brothers to eat together. The roasted wild boar, served with vegetables, was succulent with crackly, crispy skin. It tasted delicious. An aromatic dessert of stewed apples and quince was perfectly balanced between sweet and sharp. A wobbly custard accompanied it. My brothers ate heartily. I had little appetite and picked at my food as they discussed the arrangements for the morning.

"We can only take a change of clothing for the boys, we can't carry much. It's just in case we need to dry our clothes out when we stop for the night. Whatever they need will be found for them when we arrive at Carcassonne. We'll take one each on our horses. We should make the journey in two days and then they'll be safe in their new home."

"I don't suppose…" I said.

"What?" said Philippe sharply.

"Is there any chance… could we postpone this for another year at least? They're still so young."

"You know they can't, Béatrice," said Philippe. "I'm surprised you even mention it. It's been agreed, they must go tomorrow. It's best for them… in any case they need to get away from here with all these women. There's nothing more to say."

I could only nod dumbly. There was no point in pursuing this, I could do nothing, say nothing that had any influence. When we finished eating, there was a silence. It was Philippe who broke it.

"Béatrice, there are some further changes needed here and… matters… err… to be discussed," he seemed to have difficulty choosing his words. This was not like him. Usually he was blunt and to the point; it was a de Planisolles family trait.

"Oh? What do you mean?"

"Well, first of all, you know… you are required to move from this house." Philippe played with his wooden spoon. "It was funded by the Count of Foix and the de Rocquefort family until such time as the boys could go to Carcassonne. Now that time has come, you must move to a smaller house. The de Rocqueforts will help with that, but the Count of Foix has no further responsibility for you. I think you knew that this would be necessary." I nodded again.

"Where shall I go?" It was all being decided for me again. I hated feeling so helpless.

"There's a little house in Prades near the church which should suit you. You will also have to manage without the maids, apart from Sybille that is. There will only be the three little girls to take care of and a small house. You and Sybille can manage that between you."

"Prades? Why can't we stay in Montaillou?

"There are no suitable houses in Montaillou." Bernard looked at me. "It is for the best, Béatrice, to get you out of Montaillou."

My heart was sinking. This was too much, to move and live in a little house in Prades, as well as losing my sons. I had hoped I could stay where I was in Montaillou. But I saw there was no other way, I had no money of my own, I had nothing to bargain with.

"There are some other changes required of you too, Béatrice." Philippe was saying.

"Oh?" I said dully.

"I think you know what I mean," Philippe looked at Bernard. "I'll come straight to the point, Béatrice. You are the subject of many rumours."

I remained silent, my head bent down, dreading what was coming.

"There are… some things that everyone is talking about," said Bernard. "First of all there's all this nonsense about a revival of the Good Men. People are getting caught up with the excitement of it all and they seem to have forgotten just how dangerous it can be. Either that, or they close their eyes to the dangers. And, you know these peasants just can't keep their mouths shut – that's all they do all day long, gossip about the Good Men – and – well, it's rumoured that you're supporting them."

"I… just, I didn't give much."

"Béatrice!" said Bernard. "People are thrown into prison, into the Wall at Carcassonne for less. You know the dangers better than anyone. You mustn't give anyone any cause to gossip about you. The Inquisition are watching and it won't be long before they find out what's going on here. It seems to be common knowledge that the priests, the so-called Perfects, have a base in Montaillou. Our family has had enough to deal with concerning the heretics, we don't need any more," Bernard sighed. "You know that, Béatrice."

"How is Papa?" I asked.

"He's well. We don't see as much of him around the estate. He's often away from home these days," said Philippe. There was a pause, a feeling of dread was creeping over me. I had an idea what was coming next. "There's something else, Béatrice." He looked at his brother. "There is another rumour going around. I just hope it's not true… it's about you and the priest."

164

A red-hot flush burned up my neck and spread onto my face.

"It's true, isn't it?" said Philippe, looking at me. "I can see by looking at you that it's true. Béatrice, it's got to stop. How do you think you can make a good second marriage if you are behaving like a common whore? It's not in your best interests… for your reputation to be the subject of such bawdy rumours."

"Another marriage?"

"Yes, we must find another husband for you. How else are you going to live? You need someone to take care of you and your children, someone to take you away from this… this miserable little village, this hot-bed of heresy and whoring. The money we have charge of, that Bérenger left for you and the children, isn't going to last for long. We need to find a wealthy husband for you," said Bernard. He leaned over towards me. "You should be thankful that you have retained your figure and your beauty in spite of all these children. You are a beauty, Béatrice. You've not lost any teeth yet and your hair's not grey. You'll be more marriageable now with only the three girls in tow and you're still young enough to have more children. We should be able to find a rich nobleman for you. Just think, if you have a child out of wedlock with this priest – no-one will want you then, certainly not anyone with money. You'll be condemned to live like a poor peasant, glad of any passing pedlar who wants a quick poke."

"I won't have a child out of wedlock," I said. "You shouldn't speak to me like this." I was close to crying or screaming or both.

"You can't be sure of that. If you're fucking that priest, you could have a child, Beatrice, and it would ruin you," said Bernard.

165

"I think going to live in Prades will solve these problems." I was trying to remain calm in spite of the intense frustration I was feeling. My life was not my own but I knew too that there was some truth in what they said. Life could not carry on like this.

"I hope so, Béatrice," said Philippe. "Because if you don't put a stop to it, we will."

This was no idle threat. It did not seem fair that they could get away with whatever they wished to do, I was sure that they both could and more than likely did have any village woman they wanted, and even father a child or two out of wedlock and no-one would consider that any barrier to a future good marriage.

I slept badly that night and woke early sobbing. I dreamt of my mother, of leaving her like I did when I married, but in the dream I knew I'd never see her again. I was searching for her and realising she'd gone for ever. I rose early from my bed with a leaden heart. This was the day my sons were leaving and I must say good-bye to them. I prepared breakfast with Sybille, cutting up bread and cold meat and setting out preserves. Sybille had already been to the font canal for water. My sons were sleeping when I went to wake them. They were curled up together, Philippe with an arm around Bérenger. Their chestnut heads together. I knelt at their bedside and stroked the soft skin of Bérenger's face. He was no longer a baby, but he was still too young to leave me. I kissed his cheek and leant over to kiss Philippe. Tears were waiting but I blinked them away knowing I must be as cheerful as possible to help them leave. Both of them stirred at my touch and opened their eyes. I smiled at them.

"It's time to rise, boys," I said. "You must be ready for your uncles when they come down from the château to collect you. Here are your clothes," I pointed

166

to the piles of garments at the end of the bed. "Put them on and come downstairs for some breakfast. You've a long journey to make today."

Breakfast was like it always was, the children chattering, annoying each other, spilling water, preserves spread anywhere but on the bread. I sat quietly and left Sybille to sort out the arguments, mop up the spills and wash sticky hands and faces afterwards. I toyed with a piece of bread, unable to eat anything. I sat amongst the debris of the meal and watched Sybille as she performed the necessary tasks. These boys, who I had borne, nursed and nurtured were to leave me and their sisters. It went against all my instincts as a mother. No-one could love them as I could. But I had to let them go. It was the law and it would cause terrible trouble if I started to make a fuss about it.

My brothers were at the door and the children were milling around them.

"Are you ready, Bérenger and Philippe?" said Bernard. "Say good-bye to your mother and sisters, then."

The boys came over to me. Philippe's head hung down and he started to cry. He clung to my legs. The sight of his little face crumpled up and the tears flowing was unbearable and I started to cry too. I tried to stop and looked at Bérenger whose lip was trembling as he tried to hold back tears. I knelt down and gathered both of them into my arms and hugged and hugged them.

"That's enough of that now," said Bernard in a gentle tone of voice I'd never heard him use before. "Come along now, boys, off we go, one on each horse, that's it."

Both boys were up on a horse in front of each of my brothers. Their small bundles of belongings were fastened onto the horses and they were off, the horse hooves sliding and slithering down the steep track through the village. The boys turned to wave and kept waving as they progressed onto the flatter area of the pastures. I waved back at them until they disappeared from my sight.

"I'm going to rest, Sybille, I slept very badly last night," I said. I went upstairs and lay on my bed where I wept until I fell asleep. The next day I kept busy – after all, there was a lot to do. But the faces of my little boys kept intruding as I went about the daily tasks of looking after my little girls and preparing for the move to Prades. I prayed that their Aunt and Uncle would be kind to them even though I did not think that God would listen to me. Maybe God was punishing me for my lack of faith. My brothers might be right, the move could help me recover from losing my sons and help to resolve the… the other matters.

But the move to the smaller house in Prades did not make any difference at all. I made a half-hearted attempt to talk to Pierre about not continuing with the relationship when I moved to Prades, but he quickly brushed aside anything I said about it being too far away. It was after all just a half-hour stroll away from Montaillou. The truth was that I was not ready to give up the relationship and Pierre showed no signs of wanting to either. Pierre gave me a lot of attention, more than my busy husband had ever had time for. He stayed in my house for three or four nights each week, and I would also stay with him in his room in the loft at his parent's house. This loft had an outside staircase so we could come and go as we pleased without disturbing

168

the rest of the household. It all continued in Prades just as it had in Montaillou. When we weren't in bed together, we talked, mainly about religion. It was wrong, I knew, but it was hard to envisage life without Pierre. It would be much duller.

The talk with my brothers prompted me to ask Pierre about the Inquisition in Carcassonne. After our love-making, I was de-lousing Pierre's hair one day beside the open window when I asked him if it was true that the Inquisition could fling people into the Wall without reason.

"Well, it's true they're a law unto themselves in many ways," he said. "But they are kept busy up there negotiating with the King of France, and a Franciscan friar called Bernard Délicieux. He's whipped up a lot of support on behalf of the people who have had enough of the Inquisitors' power to throw people into the Wall without good reason. The King of France thinks they have too much power as well, so he's involved in trying to curb them. They're not at all worried about us up here in Montaillou."

"Are you sure of that?" I said.

He laughed heartily at this. "Of course I'm sure. It's me that they ask about heresy in Montaillou. He said. "And I tell them only what's necessary." He laughed again. "Do you see?"

"Yes," I said. "I do."

The house was quiet and empty without my sons. I missed their noisy, boisterous behaviour. I missed their love and affection. The three girls too missed their lovable, annoying big brothers who would tease them cruelly at times but who would protect and love them as well. We were all bereft. I hoped they were being treated kindly and I longed to see them. It felt strange in our new small household. There was just enough space for us all. My three little girls no longer babies and Sybille and I, with occasional help from a woman in the village, could manage easily by ourselves. The little house in Prades was a stroll away from the church of Saint Pierre and adjoined the priest's house. There were only two rooms upstairs and two rooms on the ground floor with some outhouses at the back. The girls all slept with Sybille in the largest room and I had the smaller one. The only problem was that the walls were thin and I was fearful that my love-making with Pierre could be overheard by the priest next door when we were in my bedroom. This was always the source of a lot of muffled laughter between us but it was a real concern too. One evening I opened my door to find Pierre's assistant priest Jean, who had a message for me.

"Father Pierre sends a message to you Madame," he said. "He asks that you meet him in the church and that I escort you there." He seemed slightly ill at ease.

"Has something occurred?" I asked. "Is Pierre well?"

"Yes, Madame," he said. "He's well."

"I'll just get my mantle and tell my maid that I'm going out," I said.

Jean took me from my house to the church door in the dark which wasn't very far. Whatever was Pierre up to?

"What is this?" I asked Jean.

"He's inside waiting for you," he said. "You'll see."

I pushed open the church door and walked in. The church was bright with candles and I could not immediately see Pierre. The familiar musty smell of ancient relics, dust and candles wafted into my nostrils as I stood there. He spoke to me from in front of the altar.

"Béatrice, come in and see what I have made ready for us." He pointed to a space in front of the altar. I walked up the aisle, looked where he was pointing and gasped.

I put my hands up to my face and said huskily, "Oh, Pierre, how could you? In the church of Saint Pierre?"

There, before the altar was a makeshift bed of rugs and blankets on the floor of the church. Pierre never failed to shock me with his lack of respect for the Church, even though I knew his views. He laughed when he saw the look on my face.

"Come, Béatrice, what harm will it do to Saint Pierre? And the priest can't hear us here."

I was unable to answer him for once and I allowed myself to be led to the makeshift bed. I sat down upon it, encouraged by Pierre. He kissed me and we lay down on the bed together. Pierre's desire seemed heightened by the excitement of our wickedness and I soon responded to him. We stayed together all night in the church. He escorted me back to my house early the following morning before anyone else was up and about in the village. I blushed when I thought about this incident afterwards, firstly with the excitement of it but then I blushed again with fear and shame, when I thought of my brothers and what they might do if they ever found out about the night of sin in the church at Prades.

I opened my door to Alazaïs one morning. Alazaïs, normally placid and easy-going, looked red-faced and animated. Her dark eyes shone and she could hardly wait to get inside, almost pushing past me in her haste.

171

"Can I come in?" she said. I followed her into the living room of my little house. This was the biggest room in the house with a fireplace and a bread oven, the usual wooden benches by the fire, and a table for us five inhabitants. It was simple but serviceable. Sybille had taken the children down to the field just outside the village where the donkeys were kept. They had taken some stale bread to feed them.

Alazaïs and I sat down facing each other. Alazaïs seemed excited, full of something.

"Whatever is it?" I said.

Alazaïs lowered her voice. "Is Sybille here?"

"No, there's no-one else here."

"I don't know where to start," said Alazaïs. "But last night I heard Guillaume Authier and Prades Tavernier preach! I wish you could hear them. It was the most moving thing I've ever heard. Béatrice, you must come and hear them. You would feel the same I know, if you heard them."

"This is what everyone says," I said. "Where was this?"

"It was in the Belots' house," said Alazaïs. "I'll tell you… Yesterday I was in and out of my house all day. I went down to the field, where Jean was working on our strip of land. I took some food and water for him at midday. He wanted to work there all day before the weather gets too hot. Then I went to the river to wash some clothes, and then I went to the font canal to collect water twice." Alazaïs paused for breath and looked at me; I just gave her a questioning look. "Well, each time I passed along the track between the Clergues' house and the Belots', I saw Mengarde Clergue going from her house, backwards and forwards to the Belots' house. She was carrying pots of food, loaves of bread, and some pieces of woollen fabric that

172

looked to be of a very fine quality, over to the Belots'. She just nodded to me as I passed and we exchanged the time of day. But I thought it seemed very strange. I know that Mengarde does help some of the poor in the village, but the Belots aren't poor – they don't need any gifts of food or cloth. Then later I saw some more people going to the Belots' house. This was early evening, just as the light was going. I hid and watched." She stopped again. "Can I have a drink, Béatrice, my mouth is dry."

"Yes, of course." I fetched a goblet of water and sat down again. "So who did you see?"

"Well, I saw Na Roche and her son," she said.

"Well, that's not unusual, she's often there or at the Clergues'," I said.

"Yes, but that's not all, two of the Maury brothers and their father, and Sybille and Guillaume Fort, and Raymonde Guilhou."

"Raymonde Guilhou. She's one of the Clergues' servants isn't she? What was she doing there?"

"Well, that's what I wondered. So I thought that if they were all going there, then I could too. If they asked me what I wanted, I would just say that I wanted fire as mine had gone out," said Alazaïs. "Anyway, Mengarde Clergue opened the door to me, she never asked me why I was there, just invited me in. She seemed very warm and friendly. I thought afterwards that she must have thought that one of the Belots had asked me to go. Anyway it took me a few moments to adjust to the light in the room as it was quite dark. There were no candles, just the firelight. All the people were sitting or standing around the room. In the middle in front of the fire were two men sitting on a bench." Alazaïs paused and looked at me. "It was Guillaume Authier and Prades Tavernier."

173

"Oh! Are you sure it was them?"

"Yes, of course I am. Guillaume Authier started to speak. He told us about the *consolamentum* and how we could save our souls through that deathbed ritual," she paused again. "I can't remember everything he said... oh yes, I know, he said that God made our souls but the Devil made our bodies and the world we live in."

"Everyone says they are wonderful speakers."

"They are," said Alazaïs. "Prades told the story of the souls falling from heaven and how the Devil made tunics or human bodies for them. He told it so well."

"What is it? What makes them so compelling?" I said.

"They tell such stories and they promise us salvation," said Alazaïs. "Guillaume said that the Roman Church is a bawd and a whore, she takes our money and our animals for taxes and the Church officials spend it on themselves. And they are ruthless if anyone dares to disagree. He told us that we must all be very careful who we spoke to about the evening. And then, Mengarde Clergue motioned to me and Raymonde to kneel before Guillaume and Prades, and pay our respects by saying three times, 'Bless me Good Christians and pray to God for me.' Each time we said it, Guillaume Authier said, 'May God bless you and bring you to a good end.' Then he kissed my forehead and I swear to you, Béatrice, I felt something when he touched me. I was nearly crying, I was so moved."

"Why three times?"

"It's the greeting ritual, showing your respect for them. It's called the *melioramentum*. It's the custom to do it when you meet a Perfect, or when taking leave of them," said Alazaïs. "Everyone performed it as they left. Then Gauzia Belot told me and Raymonde to ask the Perfects if they would give us the *consolamentum* when we are dying and they said they would. Then Guillaume brought some pieces of bread out of his bag and gave Raymonde and me a piece each. It was blessed bread. Bertrand Maury came forward and asked for a piece and said he would give them something in return. We all said we would give what we could. Raymonde and I were completely overcome by the whole experience. When we walked home together, she told me that she'd been de-lousing Mengarde Clergue this afternoon and that Mengarde had told her all about the Good Men and invited her to meet them at the Belots'. And, she said that Pierre Clergue was present and heard the whole conversation and never batted an eyelid the whole time."

"He protects us from the Inquisition, I think," I said.

"I hope so," said Alazaïs. We looked at each other in silence. The sound of high children's voices chattering outside prevented the possibility of any further discussion.

As springtime came and brought warmer weather, the villagers moved away from their firesides. They dug over their strips of land in preparation for the new season's crops and leaned on their implements, lingering a little longer in the sun, talking to their neighbours. The days lengthened and cockerels crowed loudly at dawn, and chickens began to lay and became broody. The melting snow from the mountains swelled the rivers and streams with pure, clear water. The green tips of foliage and flowers pushed through the earth and early butterflies were on the wing, and I had a journey to make.

My sister Gentille, who lived in Limoux, had
given birth to her second child at the end of January and
had sent a message to me, asking me to visit as soon as
I could, when the better weather made travelling easier.
She wanted me to be her child's godmother and the
baptism was to be at Easter. It was a long journey to
Limoux, especially with small children, and although it
would take us at least four days, I was keen to go. The
atmosphere of subterfuge and secrets building up in the
villages was becoming more intense. It felt suffocating.
The stories of Perfects moving like phantoms in the
night, and resting in people's lofts and barns by day,
seemed evermore the only thing that was talked about,
and they were getting bolder. Prades Tavernier had
been seen walking down the main track in Montaillou. I
was finding it increasingly difficult to continue to avoid
meeting the Good Men, either by chance or on purpose.
I had a sense of being inexorably drawn into something
I wanted to avoid. Or maybe I didn't. I was both
appalled and fascinated by the events in Montaillou.

Then there was Pierre. I loved being with him,
he was so interesting and full of life. His company took
my mind off my sadness about my boys. His irreverent
attitude to the Church and his audacious delight in
brazenly defying Rome excited me but also unnerved
me. Nothing had changed in this relationship since I'd
moved to Prades, and I was certain that my brothers
would soon find this out. They would not tolerate my
disobedience for long. There were financial and status
aspects I was acutely aware of as well. I was a
noblewoman living like a poor peasant at that moment.
I had three children to bring up, three daughters who
themselves must make good marriages. I could not find
the best husbands for them living as I was. Something
would have to change. As my brothers had so clearly

told me, I had only my face and my body at my disposal. I must use my advantages as best I could. I could do better than a village priest, especially this dangerous village priest.

It was the Monday after the first Sunday in Lent when Sybille and I set off with the children on the journey to Limoux. We had two donkeys with us to carry our belongings and for the children to ride on when they were tired. I told Pierre we would be away for a few weeks and would not be back until after Easter. He said he was heartbroken, but I would not agree to stay. It was time for a change.

The journey was long, tedious and strenuous. After a day of walking, the sky turned from a pale spring blue to an unremitting dull grey. The rain fell heavily in straight rods and penetrated our clothes and bags quickly. A dense mist of rain enveloped the mountain peaks that surrounded us. The trees along the track dripped steadily and the pathway became a muddy landslide. The donkeys kept their heads down, their long, furry faces looking miserable. As we reached the place where we were to stay the first night, we decided to delay our journey. We waited for the skies to clear, not wanting to risk the children getting wet and becoming ill. The children were bored and irritable cooped up inside the small tavern where we stayed. Sybille and I invented games and pastimes to keep them occupied but we were all relieved when eventually, on the third day, we awoke to a clear sky and a fresh wind. We started again on our journey. It took three more days of walking, and encouraging the girls to move, and of taking turns to ride a donkey. One of the donkeys was slow and could turn bad-tempered at times. He would stop still when he felt he'd had enough. He kicked out at Baby Béa and bruised her leg on one occasion. We were all exhausted when we arrived at Limoux.

Gentille was married to a wealthy and influential man, Paga de Post, who was distantly related to the Count of Foix. She had chosen the other godparents for her new child for their importance and connections; I was the family representative. Gentille's home was a large mansion on the outskirts of Limoux. It felt like a haven to me. There was more space, there were more servants and there was a lot more comfort than in my little peasant's cottage. I noticed how safe and happy I felt there amongst my family, all there for the baptism. Sybille and the children enjoyed the comforts that were provided too. It was in great contrast to the wet, uncomfortable journey we had just made and the miserable little house in Prades.

The evening before the ceremony, Gentille asked me to go to church with her to make our confessions. I felt obliged to go but it created a conflict within me. Pierre had told me that I must not confess the sin I committed with him to another priest. It would be only on my deathbed when I would be cleansed of my sins by receiving the *consolamentum.* When I was with Pierre, I often questioned what he said, but on the whole I believed what he told me. He was a priest, after all. But here in Limoux with Gentille, who was a good Roman, well, I found myself wavering. So I compromised by going to confession, but not mentioning Pierre Clergue.

There was a celebratory meal after the baptism. My brother Philippe was seated on one side of me and one of the other godparents was on the other. Philippe introduced us. "Othon, my sister, Madame de Rocquefort, from Montaillou. Béatrice, the Knight Othon de Lagleize, from Dalou."

178

"Enchanted, Madame," murmured Othon. "You are the widow of Bérenger de Rocquefort, of Montaillou, I believe?"

"Yes, I am," I said.

"I knew him a little. We met at the Count of Foix's Palace a few times," he said. "It was a sad loss, he was a good man."

"Yes, he was." I looked at Othon de Lagleize. I saw a young nobleman perhaps a year or two older than myself. He wore an elegant tunic cut from fine fabric. His dark hair and beard were neatly trimmed and framed a strong-looking, high cheek-boned face. He had a full mouth and his eyes were a light grey, shining in the candlelight. I looked away and we both started to eat the food that had been served us. I was enjoying having such high-quality food prepared for me and I ate with enthusiasm. There were excellent dried sausages and meats with bread to start the meal. This was followed by pheasant, pigeon, venison, cabbages and turnips, all beautifully cooked and presented. The new season's cheeses were followed by preserved fruits prepared with sweet wine. The wines for each course came from the vineyards owned by Gentille's husband. They were of exceptional quality.

"Madame," said Othon. "I hope you won't think me impolite, but I notice you have a very good appetite for a woman."

I felt myself blush. I wiped my mouth and looked at him. His grey eyes were laughing.

"I'm not very lady-like, perhaps, for a woman, Sire." I laughed too, remembering I'd been accused of this before by Bérenger. I blushed again. I raised an eyebrow at him, and I knew that my eyes were sparkling with fun.

"It's good to see a lady eating well," he said. "I don't find picking and poking at food an attractive quality. Besides a lady needs some flesh on her bones."

His eyes travelled up and down my body and back to my face. The expression on his face was of appreciation. I returned his gaze for a moment and then lowered my eyes, saying, "Well then, I'd better carry on eating."

"Have a sip of wine first," he said, taking a mouthful of his wine. He savoured it in his mouth, swallowed and licked his lips. I lifted my goblet to him and took a sip, then with the very tip of my tongue I licked my lips. We both laughed. The warmth of arousal slowly sizzled in me. I was enjoying myself. I noticed Philippe's eyes on me and this time they held a look of approval. Gentille remarked later, "You seemed to be getting on well with Othon de Lagleize."

"Yes, I like him," I said.

"Good," Gentille smiled. "I think it's good thing for you to get away from Montaillou. It's a dreadful place. You didn't talk too much about the children to him, did you?"

Géraud Othon de Lagleize was a prosperous nobleman from the lowlands, where he owned houses in Crampagna, Dalou and Varilhes. Everyone called him Othon. He was good-looking, wealthy, and, above all, he was Roman. During my two-month long stay in Limoux, he visited me regularly and at the end of my visit we announced our betrothal. We were to be married in August of that year, 1301. This was a solution to my problems that suited both me and my family. Othon would whisk me away from the dangerous stew of heresy that was boiling up just below the surface in Montaillou. Babies would be born legitimately and I would be safe from marauding priests and other chancers. But this was no calculated move on my part. I had fallen in love with Othon, but, on Gentille's advice, had kept him at arm's length.

"Keep him waiting, Béatrice, it'll be worth it. Otherwise he may grow tired of you, or think you are ready to sleep with anyone who asks you. You need him to marry you."

I felt my face reddening at this comment and recognised the truth of it.

I started the journey back knowing that during the next few weeks, I must tell Pierre and all my friends of my betrothal, pack up the house in Prades and leave behind my life there.

"You've broken my heart," Pierre said when I told him.

"You'll survive perfectly well without me," I said. I had my regrets about leaving him. His neat figure in his priest's robes, his warm brown eyes, the intimacy we had enjoyed together, our lively talks about the Good Men and religion, and his intrigues with the Church authorities were so much part of my life then. But both of us had always known that it would have to end, that I must remarry and find a better life for myself and my children. There was gossip about me in Montaillou and probably elsewhere. It had certainly travelled to Caussou and my family knew far too much. I caught the drift of it on the wind. There was always someone ready to call me a whore, and a Roman priest's whore at that. It could only be time before the gossip reached Carcassonne, no matter what Pierre said about it. I must be seen to be leading a life that was proper for my station, a Roman life.

Alazaïs, Jacquemette and Fabrisse visited me several times before I left. Alazaïs and Jacquemette said they were concerned for my soul. We sat at the back of the little house in Prades in the shade of a fig tree. It was July, and very hot.

"Are you sure that you're doing the right thing?" said Alazaïs.

"I have no doubts, Alazaïs, really," I said. "I must have a husband to provide for me and my children. What else can I do? There's no-one here for me to marry, there are no noble families in Montaillou. The new Châtelain is an old married man, so he's no use to me. I'm running out of money. I can't go and live back with my father, my children wouldn't be safe there. I don't think I want them involved with what he's up to. If I don't get married soon, I'll lose my teeth and my figure, and no-one will want me. And Pierre, well, he's a priest, for God's sake!" They all laughed at this and Jacquemette said, "That's apt, Béatrice."

"Bernard Belot is coming over to visit you," said Alazaïs. "I saw him in the square the other day and he told me he is concerned for your spiritual welfare. He said you were going amongst the dogs and the wolves in the lowlands."

"I suppose he means the Roman Catholics, but it's of no use you all trying to keep me here, I can't carry on like this." They recognised the truth of what I was saying.

Fabrisse visited just before I left. "It's becoming very difficult for me in Montaillou," she told me. "Did Alazaïs tell you anything about Bernadette Benet?"

"I know she died last week," I said.

"She came back to her parent's home to be looked after as she was very ill. She was in a bed in their living room. I went to see her. She looked terrible. So pale and thin, I would hardly have recognised her. She was my friend in the village before she left to

182

marry a few years ago. Alazaïs, Gaura Fort, Raymonde Guilhou and myself, we were all friends as children and we offered to help nurse Bernadette. We took it in turns to stay with her and nurse her so that there was someone with her night and day. Her poor mother had been looking after her and she was exhausted. On Sunday evening I went over to relieve Raymonde and Gaura. Alazaïs arrived just after me and we could see that Bernadette had deteriorated. She was drifting in and out of consciousness. She could only take drops of water, most of it dribbled down her chin. But she opened her eyes and responded to us and gave a little smile as if she was pleased we were there." Fabrisse sighed. "Anyway, Guillemette Benet, her mother, and Gaura Fort went into a huddle in the corner. Bernadette's father, Michel joined them and they talked for quite a while. Gaura then left, saying she would come back later, and Michel left as well. Guillemette didn't rest but sat with us. She kept saying, 'I hope that they arrive before Bernadette sinks any further and cannot be roused.' We tried to comfort her as best we could. Eventually, just before dawn, Michel arrived with Bernard Belot. Michel came over to us, looked at Bernadette and spoke sharply to us. He said, 'You two must go now.' We were so surprised at this that we just sat there. He spoke fiercely then, saying, 'Go on, get out!' Alazaïs took hold of my hand and said to him, 'Don't worry, we will.' And we left."

"Why did he speak like that to you?" I said.

"That's exactly what I said to Alazaïs when we got outside, although I had a good idea of what was going on. Alazaïs said that she thought they'd gone to fetch a Perfect to give the *consolamentum* to Bernadette. I said, 'Well, why didn't they just say so?' Then as I said it I realised it was because of me. They

183

knew I wasn't a believer, so they didn't want me to know. But, I said to Alazaïs, they surely knew I wouldn't betray them. They couldn't be sure, she said, so they had to get us out of the way." She paused. "Anyway, everywhere was quiet, everyone was still asleep behind their closed doors and shutters, so Alazaïs and I crept back to the Benets' house. We put our heads round the corner of the barn and sure enough, there was Guillaume Authier wearing his Perfect's blue tunic, just disappearing into the house."

"I would have thought they'd have trusted you," I said.

"So would I," said Fabrisse. "But there's more. A couple of days later, after Bernadette had died, I was just on my way to the font canal, walking past the Belots' house, when suddenly Bernard Belot appeared from nowhere. He got hold of me and pulled me round the side of the house, slammed me against the wall and threatened me."

"Oh my God, he's a thug!"

"He said that I'd better watch my mouth, otherwise I might find my head separated from my body." A tear rolled down Fabrisse's face as she spoke.

"Oh, Fabrisse." I was shocked.

"And that's not all," said Fabrisse, blinking away more tears. "A couple of days later, Jacques became angry with me. He told me I must change my ways – meaning become a Cathar – or else he'd have no option but to get rid of me as his wife."

"What are you going to do?"

"I don't know yet. I'll just have to lie, or maybe I won't. I just don't know. You can't win here. If you're Cathar, then you risk the Inquisition at Carcassonne finding out and the consequences of that. If you're a Roman, you risk being killed by the Cathar believers in

184

Montaillou – they're as bad as each other. I'm just warning you that Bernard Belot said he's going to visit you to try and stop you from leaving. He said you're going amongst the dogs and the wolves in the lowlands and he's concerned for your soul."

"Alazaïs told me the same thing," I said. "At least I've got time to prepare for him."

True to his word, Bernard Belot visited me, out of his concern for my soul, he said. I managed to appease him with the gift of some money for the Good Men and I was not persuaded to stay in Prades. In August 1301, Sybille, myself and my three little girls left the villages behind for good.

Chapter 11
The Fifth Interrogation

Béatrice is silent when the young guard enters the loft with bread and water. She must conserve her strength for the interrogations, and for negotiations with Jean Belmas. There is nothing left for small talk. She sips the water and tries to prepare herself to look presentable. She has spent most of the previous night sobbing quietly and sleeping very little. She must look dreadful. Her clothes are dirty and her head, shorn of its hair, still feels naked and strange. She will have to tell more secrets today and betray more people. Speaking of Pierre, betraying him like this, more and more each time she is questioned, disturbs her profoundly. It is all growing more and more difficult.

Later that morning she goes with a guard down to the usual room. The Bishop and Gaillard de Pomies, the scribe, are waiting for her. The Bishop, cold, severe and pasty-faced, looks as if he never goes outside into the sunlight. Gaillard de Pomies is fat, smug and nasty, his red face looking as if he has drunk too much red wine. Both of them repulse her. The Bishop speaks.

"I remind you again, Madame, that you are speaking under oath here. That means that you are required to speak the whole truth. We have many witnesses who can corroborate your evidence. If you are found to be lying or omitting evidence, then you will be punished and questioned again."

She shakes with weakness and fear, and her mind is paralysed – unable to find the words – but she must speak.

"My Lord Bishop," she says, "I cannot recall what it was I said yesterday exactly…"

"You spoke of Pierre Clergue and your second marriage."

"Oh yes."

She remembers now. How could she possibly forget that? She'd been awake most of the night thinking about it.

"I recall now that when I told the people of Montaillou that I was leaving, they were concerned for me." Her voice is weak. "Bernard Belot came to see me twice. The first time was in Prades. He came to my house and tried to persuade me to stay in Prades. He was concerned for my soul, saying that where I was going there were no Good Christians."

She mustn't make the same mistake again, of calling the Dominicans dogs and wolves.

"Then after I was married, he visited me at Crampagna, at my husband's estate, Carol. I was desperate to get rid of him, I wanted to cut my ties to… to all that, so when he told me that a gift to the Good Christians would ensure that they prayed for my soul, and that he would leave me alone if I sent some money for them, I gave him twenty sous for them."

She tells of the rumours in Montaillou that the heretics stayed at the houses of the Belots and the Rives. Then she tells of the conversation about the *consolamentum* of Agnès Faure with Vuissance and Jacquemette. About the Maurys' support of the Good Christians and what they had told her about them. How the Maurys', not as well off as herself, gave to the heretics and how this inspired her to give some food and money to the Good Men. How Alazaïs Azema had told her that her son took food for the Good Men. At this point, she is unable to continue to speak as distress overtakes her and tears well up in her eyes. These are her friends, she is betraying them, this is not who she is,

187

someone who betrays her friends. She is overwhelmed by grief and shame and cannot contain her sobs of anguish. Why is he putting her through this? Why can't he let her go home? She thought it would all be over with by now. Jacques Fournier is silent for a few minutes. He looks at her intently.

"That's all for now," he says quietly to the guard, "take her back to her room."

He stands and makes the sign of the cross.

"In Nomine Patris, et Filii et Spiritus Sancti. Amen."

She finds herself automatically murmuring the response.

"Amen."

She is led away.

Chapter 12
Madame de Lagleize

The journey from Prades to Crampagna, where I was to marry Othon, was a long and arduous trek. Othon had arranged for two men with mules to escort us and carry our baggage. Sybille, myself and the three little girls were a slow-moving party. Our first stop was in Caussou, where we stayed with my father, who was to accompany us to Crampagna. I was shocked when I saw him. He seemed to have aged considerably. After we had eaten in the evening, Sybille went to put the children to bed and left us alone together.

"I have been thinking, Béatrice," he said. "It would be for the best if I don't come to your wedding."

"Oh, Papa, why ever not? I want you to be there," I said.

"If I come to Crampagna, which, lying as it does between Foix and Pamiers, I will have to wear the crosses. There will be people at your wedding who know my history, and if I don't wear them, there will always be someone ready to run to the Inquisition. And I don't want to be at your wedding wearing the cursed things. I don't know if de Lagleize knows of my conviction or not?"

I shrugged my shoulders. "I've not told him, we haven't spoken of it at all," I said.

"I think it would be a bad omen for your marriage if I went wearing the crosses. I would more than likely be the only one there wearing them."

He looked down, his face lined and sad looking. I went round to where he was sitting and, standing next to him, I cradled his head against my chest.

"I understand, Papa, I shall think of you on the day and Maman too, and my sons who can't be there either, I shall miss you all."

"I give you my blessing, Béatrice. Philippe and Bernard say that de Lagleize is a nobleman of some standing and that he will be a good husband to you. I wish you well."

We arrived at Othon's estate feeling very tired from our journey. The estate was named Carol after the river, which formed part of the boundary. It lay in a fertile valley and the land around the large manor house was mainly vineyards. Wheat and vegetables for the table were grown there too, and chickens and pigeons were kept for food. There was a mill on the land beside the river and there were plenty of servants to work on the farm. The whole place was well-maintained and tidy with an air of abundance and prosperity. We were to be married from there and after the grape harvest in September we would move to the château at Dalou. Baby Béa, Esclarmonde and Condors were so happy to be free again after the boredom of the journey. They ran around their new home laughing and screaming, and getting in the way of everyone as preparations for the wedding took place.

The manor house at Crampagna was light, airy and spacious. The noblemen and women who, as for my first wedding, came from the surrounding villages and towns to celebrate the marriage, were accommodated in the nearby village. The family were mainly in the manor house. The preparations brought back memories of my first marriage, but this time it was different. For one thing, it was I who had made the decision, although I had my suspicions that my meeting with Othon had been arranged by my brothers and sisters. But they could not have arranged how Othon and I would feel about each other. This was very different from the first time, when I had no choice in the matter at all and was so innocent. That it had turned out well was pure good fortune. This time I was sure that I had done the right thing. Not least because of leaving behind Prades and Montaillou, and all that was going on there. It had become too dangerous – the heresy was impossible to avoid, and Pierre Clergue and his family were at the heart of it, and being the priest's mistress was not a good thing for my reputation or my safety. It was as if suddenly now I could move freely; I could dance and sing. I hadn't realised how much of a burden I had been carrying. The way we had been living, with less and less money, and more and more danger from several sources – Pierre, the Church, my brothers, Bernard Belot, the Inquisition at Carcassonne – now I was well away from all of that.

The wedding ceremony was the same as I had gone through with Bérenger, but this time was joyous and relaxed in comparison. When we took our vows, there was no pretence or uncertainty for me. I spoke from my heart. Othon too seemed relaxed and happy. Everything was on a grander scale than it had been in Montaillou, but the church in Crampagna, although bigger and also prettily decorated with flowers and greenery, was not as charming as Sainte Marie de Carnesses. There were more guests at the wedding breakfast and they were served slices off a whole wild boar and also huge sides of venison. The meat was roasted outside on spits, and decorated tents with tables and benches inside to provide shade had been erected in a flat field beside the house. The de Lagleize family coat of arms was on display amongst waving pennants of their colours, yellow and blue and red. An army of

191

servants waited on our guests, who were local noble families all wearing the finest clothes. I had chosen the fabric for my wedding clothes before I left Gentille's house in Limoux, and my measurements had been taken. The kirtle, then tack-stitched into place, was waiting for me at Crampagna, when a last-minute fitting ensured that it could be finally sewn for me. It was similar to my first wedding dress, made of the customary bridal blue silk. I wore another gold coronet, this time from the de Lagleize family, and my hair was plaited and woven around my head. A finely embroidered and jewelled belt was the finishing touch.

The children were all dressed in white kirtles with pretty floral wreaths of white roses in their hair. I did not know many of the guests, I recognised only a few other than my own brothers and sisters, and their families. Othon's parents had died a few years ago and as Othon was an only child, he had no close relatives there. Othon was so attentive and smiling, and looked so handsome and noble in a brocade tunic of pale grey, which matched his eyes. Rather like my first wedding, the day passed in a dreamlike way, except it was a dream that I felt more in control of and more at ease with. I was comfortable and happy with my new role, the Lady of the Manor. It was what I had been born for, trained for by my mother, and the contrast with those last two years in Montaillou was stark.

After the marriage, I stayed on with Othon at Carol for a few weeks. I spent my time familiarising myself with the domestic arrangements, whilst most of the household was outside helping with the wine harvest. One afternoon, a visitor arrived unexpectedly. My heart sank when I heard the servant announce, "Madame, there is a Monsieur Belot here – he says has some legal papers for you concerning your first marriage, that were lodged with the priest."

I sighed with frustration. I really thought I had left all that behind in Montaillou. I knew that the reason given for this visit was not the real purpose at all. I knew too that I must make it very clear to him that he was not welcome at Carol.

"Show him in," I said. As soon as Bernard appeared, I dismissed the servant.

"What is it, Bernard? What do you want?"

"Madame, Pierre Clergue and all your friends in Montaillou have sent me with a message for you. We are all concerned for you living down here where there are no Good Men." His big, red peasant's face and his working tunic looked alien to me. He should not be at Carol.

"I thank you for your concern, Bernard," I said, "But you must understand that I no longer wish to have news of the... events in Montaillou."

I knew I sounded cold and haughty, but warmth and pleasantness could be misconstrued. He looked wounded.

"But Madame..." he said.

"You must leave me alone," I said. "Now that I am living here, I have to leave all that behind me. My husband would be very angry if he knew why you had come."

"I can see that you have forgotten all the good words of your friends," he said. He was reproachful now and I was concerned that our conversation might be overheard by one of the servants or, worse still, that my husband might find out about the real reason for Bernard's visit, or that, through his presence at Carol, one of the many other things I wanted to keep from

193

Othon might come to light. I was desperate to get rid of him. I spoke in a fierce whisper to Bernard.

"You must leave me alone."

"If you give me some money for the Good Men, they will pray for your soul," he said. "And I will not trouble you again."

I stood up and reached for my bag that was nearby. I fumbled in it and took out some money.

"Take these twenty sous, and never, ever come here again."

Thank God he left me then.

Not long after Bernard's visit, there was another visitor to Crampagna. Almost everyone was outside helping with the wine harvest and there were only a few servants remaining in the kitchen. I was sitting on a bench at the front of the farmhouse, enjoying the September sunshine. The fields of vines were spread out before me and beyond them lay the rocky-peaked, blue-green mountains. The grape-harvesters were working in the fields furthest from the house, as they had already harvested the grapes that grew close by. I noticed a figure walking up the track which ran between the vineyards. I stood up to better see who it was and recognised Sybille, my old maidservant. Sybille, who, after some heart-searching and indecision, had decided to return to Montaillou after my wedding. She was now living with Pathau Clergue, Pierre Clergue's cousin, as his mistress in Ax. I was pleased to see her and I ran towards her and embraced her.

"Sybille, how good to see you. What brings you here? Are you alone?"

"Yes, well no, I am alone at the moment, but I am accompanying Pierre Clergue and Pathau, who have someone to see in Carcassonne. We're on our way there."

"Who are they going to see in Carcassonne?" I said.

"I don't know," said Sybille. "Sometimes it's better not to ask, and usually it's better not to know as well."

"Yes, you're probably right," I said, remembering that the Clergue family were involved in some nefarious activities. "Is everything going well for you?"

"Yes, we stopped last night at Saint Jean de Verges, at a hostelry there, and we'll be there another night. Pierre wants to see you, Madame, he's sent you this." Sybille produced a parcel.

"Come inside, Sybille." I began to feel nervous.

We went inside to a small wood-panelled reception room. The room was furnished simply with sheepskins on the floor and benches in front of a small fireplace. It wasn't used often and felt impersonal.

"We won't be disturbed in here, everyone is out harvesting the grapes." I knew that this was something I must hear well away from any stray servants. "Come in and sit down, Sybille." I ushered Sybille in. "You're fortunate to have found me here. We're moving to the château at Dalou as soon as the wine harvest is over. That will be any day in the next week or so," I said. We sat and looked at each other. I thought Sybille looked strained.

"How are you, Sybille?" I said.

"I'm well, Madame, and you?"

"Very well, I'm busy preparing to take my clothes and belongings to Dalou, which will be our main residence. Some of my clothes are already there and we'll soon be gone from here."

"And the children, Madame, how are they?"

"They're very happy. They're with their new nursemaid, Mathende, and my new maid, Alisette, at the moment. They've gone to help with the harvest. They like it here, but they miss you, Sybille, they often ask about you. You must see them."

"I will, Madame, but first I must give you this and a message from Pierre." She handed over the parcel.

"What is it?"

"Open it, Madame." Sybille smiled.

I lifted the gift from its delicate packaging of thin paper to reveal a silk blouse which had red and yellow trimming at the neck.

"Oh, that's beautiful," I said.

"It's from Aragon," said Sybille.

"The colours are lovely," I said. "But what is Pierre doing sending me presents?"

"There's a message to go with the present." Sybille looked embarrassed.

"What is it?" I said. "Tell me, Sybille, I know him, nothing will shock me."

"He wants to see you tomorrow. He will come here disguised as a messenger from Limoux, as if from your sister. He wants you to find a private place, somewhere like the cellar, he said, where you two could be together, you know..." Sybille tailed off.

"Yes, I do know Pierre," I said shaking my head. "But he can't expect… I'm married to Othon now, I have to leave all that behind."

"He said I could keep watch in the doorway so no-one would discover you and if anyone came I'd say that you were showing this friend of Gentille's the wine-cellar."

"Oh no, Sybille, I can't agree to that." I laughed at the audacity of it.

"He told me to tell you that we'll turn up in the late morning when everyone is outside working, and then you can be alone for a while."

"No, Sybille, I cannot agree to this, will you tell him that this is not possible, that he must leave me alone."

"I'll tell him, Madame," said Sybille. "But you know what he's like, he's a law unto himself."

"Sybille, you must impress upon him that I cannot see him."

Nevertheless they arrived the next day, as I thought they might. I was outside the house watching for them. I had hardly slept for worrying that Othon would find out who Pierre really was, and that my past relationship with him could somehow be revealed along with my support for the Good Men. I had no idea how I could persuade Pierre to leave. I really didn't know whether to laugh or cry when I saw them walking towards the house.

"Pierre, what on earth are you doing, coming here?"

"Béatrice, my dearest, how I've missed you. Let's go somewhere where no-one can see us," he said.

"Come round here, then," I said, not able to think straight with him there in front of me. I took him around the side of the house, hoping no-one would see him. Sybille hovered behind us.

"Pierre," I said. "You should not have come here, you could put me in a difficult position with my husband if he finds out."

"I want to see the wine casks," he said. "Take me into the cellar."

"If you must, but you must not linger," I said thinking that perhaps he would go if I allowed him to see the cellar, at least we would be out of sight down there.

We went down the stone cellar steps. It was quite dark but we picked our way past one or two of the barrels, then Pierre stopped. Sybille remained in the doorway. He put his arms around me.

"I've missed you, Béatrice." He gently pushed me against a barrel and began to lift up my skirts.

"No Pierre, I cannot do what you want, I am married to Othon now." I pushed his hand away.

"Oh Béatrice, would you refuse me?" he said.

"Yes Pierre, you know I must."

"I just wanted to see you one last time," he said. "I miss you."

"I know, and I miss you, but it cannot be."

"I know," he said and gave me a kiss and a hug.

"Come, we must move out of here before anyone finds us, it would look very bad," I said. As we emerged from the cellar I told him, "You must go now, you must leave me alone. I have another life now."

"I'll always love you, Béatrice."

With that, Pierre and Sybille wandered off down the track. He turned and waved and blew me a kiss. I was certain no-one had witnessed any of this, but I was left feeling that I had done something wrong and I felt very guilty about it. I decided on balance that it was better not to speak of it to Othon. I couldn't think clearly about this at all. I wanted so much to leave my past behind me and I was so frightened of getting into deep water if I tried to explain who had visited and why. I knew I would have to tell lies, which I would probably later forget and get into a mess with it all. No, it was best left alone.

A few days after Pierre's visit, Othon and I were dining together in the evening.

"The grape harvest is all in now," he said. "And I can leave the labourers to continue with the next stage of the wine-making. Albert, my steward will supervise them. I wish to go to Dalou in the next day or two. Are you ready to leave here?"

"Oh yes," I said. "I'm looking forward to going there. I shall be ready whenever you wish to go." I ate a piece of meat from off the bread trencher that lay on the table before me.

"Good," he looked at me. "You're not missing your old life and your friends in Montaillou?"

"No, not at all." I smiled at him. "I'm very happy to be here."

"You haven't seen any of your old friends then?" he appeared to be concentrating on the food in front of him.

"No… err, I haven't." I concentrated on my meal. Oh God, what's happened? Did someone see Pierre yesterday, after all? My face was red hot.

"How odd then," he frowned at me. "That Albert said he saw your old maid servant – Sybille, wasn't it? She was with another man entering the wine cellar a few days ago."

He stopped eating and looked at me. His light grey eyes, which had seemed warm a moment before now looked cold, and his good-looking features, set in hard lines, looked as if they were carved out of stone. I sat paralysed under his gaze trying to think what to say.

"Oh, how silly of me, I completely forgot, Sybille came with her husband. They were on their way to Foix to... err... to see some relatives. I told them about the wine-harvesting, that everyone was working, and they were interested in the wine and so, err… I took them to see where it was kept."

I stopped. I was breathless and the words tumbled out fast. My face was on fire. He continued to stare at me. A pulse in my neck throbbed heavily. I was sure he could see it.

"I see," he said. "Relatives in Foix? Why would they come up here on their way to Foix? It would be out of their way."

"No, no," I said, "Did I say Foix? I meant to say Pamiers."

We sat in silence. My appetite had gone and I picked at my food, chicken and vegetables, whilst Othon ate steadily. When he had finished he said,

"I think an early night is in order."

"Yes, of course," I said.

"I require you to come with me, Madame," he said, standing up.

"I'm a little tired myself," I said. He walked round the table to me and took hold of my arm. He held it in a tight grip and put his face close to my ear.

"I require you in my room, Madame," he said.

"Yes, yes, I'll come with you, but please let go of my arm, you're hurting me," I said.

We walked up to his room. He pushed me in ahead of him and locked the door. He grabbed my arm and took me over to the bed where he pushed me down onto my back. I tried to get up but he knelt across me, a leg on each side of my body. He pinned down my arms with his hands. He put his face close to mine.

"Never lie to me, Madame, because I will find out if you do."

He was pulling my kirtle up and loosening his own clothes. I didn't resist, as it would have been pointless, but I didn't respond either. Then he was inside me, thrusting hard. He quickly climaxed with a grunt and moved off me. I lay still, determined not to cry. He lay beside me on the bed and turned to look at me.

"Go now, Madame. I don't want you near me tonight."

We both got up and straightened our clothes. I kept my eyes down. He stood in front of me.

"Madame," he said.

I looked up at him. He slapped me hard across my face. My head spun round. I cried out and staggered back under the impact. My face was stinging and intensely painful. I put my hand up to touch it and there were drops of blood on my fingertips. He moved to the door and unlocked it.

"So that you don't forget," he said. "I'm giving you a warning," His eyes glittered at me.

I ran to my own room and bathed my face with water. It wasn't bleeding much – one of his rings must have scraped the skin and my lip had burst – but it hurt a great deal. I lay on my bed. Silent tears rolled from my eyes onto the pillow. They were tears of frustration, at myself and my past, and the fact that it was affecting the present. The next day my face was bruised and my lip was badly swollen. It took three weeks for the bruises to fade. As I thought about it, I realised how foolish I had been. I should at least have told Othon about the visit and then he wouldn't have been suspicious.

The escapade in the cellar receded into the background as I settled into my life in the lowlands. It was spent between the three houses that Othon owned. The manor houses were all spacious and light. Even the château in Dalou, where we spent most of our time, did not have the same dark and forbidding appearance as the one in Montaillou. It was in the centre of the village and was at the heart of life there. Those mad, heady days of love-making and religion with Pierre Clergue soon began to seem like a lifetime away to me. Othon expected me to conform to his lifestyle and I had to ask permission to do anything out of the ordinary, which irked me. But it was the way of things and I learned the limits of my freedom and his power over me. The incident when he hit me was never repeated. But it took time for the cool detachment which it had caused between us, to melt again. I was wary of him and he, I suppose, was uncertain whether he could trust me. Maybe he suspected that I had something to hide. I had acted so foolishly and caused the very problems I was trying to avoid. I vowed to myself that I would be honest with him from now on and I was committed to making our lives run smoothly. We gradually became warmer towards each other.

Othon had a large estate to run. He employed a lot of people and he was occupied most of the time with estate work. He enjoyed hunting wild boar, and fishing with his fellow noblemen. There were times when he went to Carcassonne for a few days to meet with other noblemen, to follow the politics there, he told me, but he never took me with him, although together we visited other noble families nearer to our home. In all, I felt my life was good, as long as I conformed to what was expected of me as Othon's wife and the lady of a large estate.

There was plenty to keep me busy. There were three houses to run and Othon passed much of the running of these homes on to me. My experience of running the château in Montaillou, and my own childhood, stood me in good stead, and I enjoyed organising, planning and managing the smooth running of the households. My responsibilities were many. I

instructed the maids on how to look after the animals –
the pigs necessary for their meat, salted and smoked in
the winter, the geese, ducks and chickens – these were
all my responsibility. I tended and supervised the
growing of vegetables and herbs in the kitchen garden,
the broad beans, the cabbages and the turnips as well as
the orchard fruits. I ensured that the maids knew how to
store and care for sheets, coverlets and furs to keep
fleas, moths and lice to a minimum. I oversaw the
preparation and storage of food supplies, and was
involved in the daily selection and preparation of
ingredients for the table. I dealt with tailors,
shoemakers and washerwomen, with reapers, mowers,
threshers and grape-harvesters, with wine-pressers,
coopers, farriers and candle-makers. And I enjoyed it
all.

I attended church on Sundays with Othon, and
the heresy and the events in Montaillou were never
mentioned between us. I was nervous of what might be
revealed that would anger Othon, if the subject of life in
Montaillou was opened up. It was too, as if by not
speaking of the heresy, that the yellow curse of my
father's punishment could be erased. The following
year, in August, I knew that I was carrying a child. This
was what Othon wanted. My position and my life with
him would be consolidated.

At the end of September that year I received a
message from my brothers in Caussou, to say that my
father was seriously ill. I wanted to go and see him and
I was greatly relieved when Othon agreed to allow me
to visit. I made the journey with my maid Alisette, and
a muleteer and his mule accompanied us. Othon gave
me a warning as I set out.

"Be careful who you mix with up there, I've heard of all kinds of things going on. And take no risks with my son and heir." He patted my stomach.

"I shall be very careful I assure you, Sire. I shall be with my father. I must make his last days on earth as comfortable as I can. He will be my whole concern whilst I'm there," I promised him. "As well as our child, of course." To myself I vowed that I would not go near Montaillou or become involved in any heretical doings.

I arrived in Caussou to find my father very ill. He was bed-ridden, hardly able to walk, and had great trouble breathing. His lungs seemed to be full of fluid and he sat up half the night coughing up copious amounts of frothy phlegm. He was in great discomfort and very weak. It was obvious that he could not survive long as he was. My brothers' wives had been looking after my father, along with two women from the village. One who had been helping came to apply hot vessels on his back to try and relieve the symptoms. She told me and my brothers that it seemed to be the same malady that her own father had suffered from, and the application of the vessels on his back had relieved him a little. It seemed to draw the fluid out temporarily and made breathing easier. But any relief gained from this procedure was short-lived, and my father's condition deteriorated rapidly in front of my eyes. His legs and feet were badly swollen and his whole body was a sodden, bloated mass. He seemed to be drowning in fluid. I had no doubt about it, he was dying. I sat quietly with him, holding his hand as he struggled to breathe. In spite of our differences and his sometimes rough treatment of me as a child, I loved him. I knew he had loved my mother too and that they had been on the whole happy together. As I sat with him he struggled to speak to me.

"Béatrice, I want you to help me. I must receive the *consolamentum* before… You are the only one I can ask to do this."

He spoke in a breathless whisper. His old eyes were rheumy but the fierceness of his passion shone through and I could not deny him his last wish. In fact I had been expecting this.

"I will arrange it, Papa." I told him. "I will ask them to come in the night when the rest of the household is asleep."

He nodded and closed his eyes. I had to do this for him even though it was what I had dreaded – that I would be drawn into the heresy again. I sent a message to Alazaïs in Montaillou with a child from the village asking her to come and see me. I hoped that she would know how to arrange it. I could not venture into the feverish atmosphere of heresy that prevailed in Montaillou and risk being assailed by Pierre Clergue, or any of the other fervent Cathars there. But timing was of the essence as my father had not long to live, and he must receive the last blessing whilst he was still able to respond to the questions. I hoped it would be arranged in time and his last wishes could be granted.

Alazaïs walked over to Caussou the next day. I told my brothers and their wives that I needed a break from sitting with our father and that I was going for a walk with Alazaïs. We walked through the familiar meadows towards the river bank. It was the end of September and the fields were scrubby and bare, the earth dry and the grass bleached. The mountains were a dull green with a few spots of russet from early fading leaves on their slopes. We sat on the dry river bank and watched the water eddying and flowing, the sparkle of sunlight on the quiet ripples. After a few polite exchanges about our children, I spoke about my father.

"My father is very ill," I said. "And he wants to receive the *consolamentum*." Alazaïs nodded. "He has only a short time to live, just a few days I should think." Tears rolled down my face as I spoke. "I could only think of asking you to arrange it. I dare not venture into Montaillou myself or send for anyone else to arrange it. Can you do this?"

"I'm not sure, but Bernard Belot always knows where the Good Men are. I can ask him," said Alazaïs.

"Tell him it's urgent and that they can only come at night. I am the only one who sits with my father at night-time. My brothers and the rest of the household will be in their beds."

"They're used to that," said Alazaïs. "They only ever travel at night, the shepherds guide them from death-bed to death-bed. That's all… "

I wiped my eyes with the back of my hand and put my hand up to stop Alazaïs. "Please," I interrupted. "Don't speak of it any more to me, the less I know the better, and you must ensure that any message must be sent to me, only me, not my brothers or the servants. Find someone you can trust to deliver it, to tell me when they are coming."

Alazaïs nodded again. "I'll be very careful."

"I can't be involved in it. I will leave the door unlocked and I will wait for them. I will show them where to go to find my father, but I must keep away from the ritual and from the Perfects, as far as possible," I said.

It was quickly arranged as the Perfects were in Prades, not far away, and they came the following night in the company of Bernard Belot, and one of the shepherds who had guided them from Prades over the rocky pathways in the dark. I spoke briefly to the shepherd when they arrived, being careful not to look at the Perfects who were with him. I had no idea which Perfects they were. I melted away into the darkness and left them to perform the ritual without me. It all passed without incident and they left quietly. No-one in the house ever knew what had taken place that night. The following day, my father grabbed my hand with his shaky, damp fingers and whispered to me, "Thank you, Béatrice."

"Papa," I said and kissed him.

It was two days later, that my father died. Fabrisse came to see me the day after the funeral. We embraced when we met at the front door of the house. Fabrisse stepped back to look at me.

"You look tired," she said.

"I am." I passed both my hands over my face. "I kept watch over my father at night and tried to sleep during the daytime, but there was noise from the servants and my brothers. Now the funeral is over I think it's catching up with me. Oh, and I'm carrying a child again," I said with a faint smile. I had almost forgotten this fact.

"Oh, Alazaïs never mentioned that," said Fabrisse.

"I forgot to tell her, I was just so caught up with arrangements for my father that it went to the back of my mind," I said.

"You must be worn out. Can you rest here for a few days before starting back?"

"I'll stay for another day or two but I must return to Dalou as soon as possible." I realised that we were still standing in the entrance to the house. "Come in, Fabrisse, come and sit down. I want to know how you are."

Fabrisse sighed. "A lot of things have happened since you left."

"We'll go to my old room," I said. "We won't be disturbed there. I'll go to find some water and some grapes for us. You go on ahead."

We sat together on the bed, as the room was sparsely furnished and not used much since me and my sisters had left. Its empty atmosphere seemed to mirror how I now felt. I wanted to leave there as soon as I could.

"I'll try and tell you everything in the order in which it happened," said Fabrisse. She nibbled on a grape and spat out the stones into her hand. "One thing led to another, you know," she said. "Do you remember the shepherd boy, Guillaume Guilabert?"

"Yes, I do," I said. "Didn't the family live on the far edge of the square?"

"Yes, that's them, a little way out of the village. They weren't very well off." Fabrisse continued. "It was heart-breaking, Guillaume was their only son, only about seventeen years old. He'd been working with the other shepherds near Montaillou all last summer, but he wasn't well. He had a bad cough and he was very thin and weak. Eventually he was forced to stay at home. He didn't get any better. In fact he got worse. Then he started spitting blood and he was so ill that they had him in a bed in their living room so that his mother could nurse him. He brought up a large amount of blood one day and they knew that he didn't have long to live. His mother was worn out with looking after him, so Alazaïs and I went to help her. Two of the shepherds came to see him and they spoke to him about the heresy and about the *consolamentum*. He said that he knew he was dying and that he wanted to receive the *consolamentum,* so that his soul would be saved. His

208

mother and father were distraught. They didn't know what to do. They were so frightened by the idea of the Perfects coming to their house. The shepherds said that they would send Bernard Belot to talk to them and that he would be able to arrange it all for them." Fabrisse paused and sipped her water.

"Fabrisse, I don't want to know too much about the Good Men. I'm frightened of being implicated in some way and of my husband finding out. He would be so angry," I said.

"I'm only telling you this because of what has happened to me. Everyone knows I'm Roman so talking to me won't cause any problems, will it?" said Fabrisse. I shook my head caught between wanting to listen to my friend and my fears about the heresy.

"The Guilaberts were very frightened too. They'd seen what happened before – you know, what the Inquisition was capable of. They are not well off, so they were worried that they might risk losing what little they had if they were in any way involved with the Good Men. But Guillaume badly wanted it. He had heard the other shepherds talking. Most of the shepherds are Cathars and he strongly believed that it was the only way to save his soul. Anyway, Bernard Belot came and told them not to worry, that he would arrange it all and that they must agree to it for their son. It was his dying wish. Then I decided I would go and leave them to it as I didn't want Bernard Belot threatening me again. But Alazaïs told me what happened."

"They wouldn't dare to disagree with Bernard Belot," I said.

"Hm," said Fabrisse. "It's all supposed to be secret but everyone knows it's going on. Some people are very keen believers, others are very much against it.

Mainly those who were punished the last time the Inquisition found them out. Some of those who lost land and property or who were imprisoned want nothing to do with the revival. Some people sway in the wind depending who they are with." She sighed again. "It means people don't know who to trust. The Clergue family seem to be at the heart of it. Pierre is our priest but he's also a Cathar and he uses it all for his own ends." She looked at me.

"What do you mean?" The pulse in my neck throbbed.

"I think the best way to explain it is to tell you what's happened to me. I spoke to Pierre about a few things. But I wish that I hadn't."

I listened with a knot of anxiety twisting in my stomach. Fabrisse continued, "I know for sure that he has bedded so many women by threatening to denounce them as Cathars, or if they're Roman, he still threatens to say they are Cathars. After the *consolamentum* of the shepherd boy, when the boy's own father was too frightened to be present at his son's death, I thought I'd put it to the test. I wondered what Pierre Clergue would say if I told him there had been a *consolamentum* in the village. I was on my way down to the fields one morning. I was going to prepare the land for sowing. I noticed Pierre sitting in his favourite place in the church doorway, taking the sun and I just thought, let's see what he has to say for himself. So I went up to him and told him about the *consolamentum* of Guillaume Guilabert. He immediately jumped up and told me to shut my mouth, that I didn't know what I was talking about, and that there were no Cathars here in Montaillou, because if there were he would know about it and he would report them."

"Oh God. What did you say to that?" I put my hands up to my face.

"I told him what I thought of him," said Fabrisse. "Which was a mistake – I should have realised that he would make me pay for that. I told him he was a two-faced bastard, that he knew full well what was happening and that it was all leading to trouble. I also told him that he shouldn't be bedding so many married women in Montaillou." She looked as if she was going to cry. I put my arm round her shoulder.

"Anyway," Fabrisse sniffed, "he told me that I should mind my own business and then he said that if I thought there was trouble, he'd show me what trouble was really like. I walked away then and went on my way down to La Cot, and I worked there all day, getting the land ready for the crops. When I went home later, Jacques was waiting for me. He told me I must change my ways, there was no more time left, I was causing trouble for all his family and if I didn't change he would throw me out. I told him what I'd told him before – that I had to follow my heart. I could only be true to my own beliefs and why couldn't he just accept that we had different ideas about the way to salvation. So he beat me, and told me to go."

"Oh, Fabrisse, where did you go?"

"I went to stay with Alazaïs, and I took Grazide with me. We stayed there for a few weeks whilst Alazaïs's husband helped me set up a tavern in the village. They helped me get a small house ready for myself and Grazide, just out of the village, and I go to buy wine down in the lowlands and bring it back up here to sell. It's quite successful – everyone buys wine off me including the Clergues, who act as though nothing has happened. In fact I saw Guillaume Authier in their house one time when I went to collect my measuring jug that I had left behind there."

"So do you think that Pierre told Jacques to do that?"

"Oh, I'm sure of it." She looked at me and her face seemed to collapse. "There's more."

"What is it?" I looked at Fabrisse's troubled face.

"On one of these occasions when I went down to buy wine it seems that Pierre Clergue visited my house. Grazide was alone in the house, and well… to cut a long story short, he took her into the barn, where he de-flowered her." Fabrisse looked down as she spoke.

"Oh no." I sighed. "Did he force himself on her?"

"No, that's not Pierre's way is it?" said Fabrisse. "No, he persuaded her with sweet and clever words, and reassurances about how it was acceptable in God's eyes. A fourteen-year-old girl doesn't argue with a priest, does she?"

"Wasn't she betrothed to Paul Lizier?"

"Yes, and Pierre married them six months later, and he still continues to have her as his mistress. Paul knows and everyone knows; no-one can do anything about it."

We looked at each other in silence.

In 1303, my daughter with Othon, Ava was born. We named her Ava, after my second sister. Othon was disappointed that we had not had a son, but he was soon charmed by her and we both hoped that next time we would have a boy. Life became even busier with a new baby, and Othon and I fell into a comfortable routine, both occupied with our respective jobs but getting along together well. Sometimes after his visits to Carcassonne, he talked to me about events there. Politics and religion were the usual topics, usually intertwined and impossible to separate.

"There's a great deal of unrest in Carcassonne," he told me. "It seems to be whipped up by a friar by the name of Bernard Délicieux."

"Who is he?" I asked, vaguely thinking the name was familiar from somewhere, but always cautious when it came to religion.

"He's a friar from a Franciscan monastery in the Bourg, close to Carcassonne."

We were eating together at midday, with the children, so there were various interruptions to our conversation – which in a way helped, because as I became busy with a fallen napkin and a spilt drink, I remembered that Pierre Clergue had mentioned Bernard Délicieux to me. I feigned disinterest in the subject, even though I was fascinated, wondering if the unrest in Carcassonne was connected to the Cathar revival. Othon talked on.

"This Bernard Délicieux seems to be causing rebellion amongst the people of the Bourg, who hate the prison and hate the Dominicans, who they say have too much power."

"It was the Dominicans who founded the Inquisition, wasn't it?" I said.

I noticed that Condors wasn't eating. "Let me cut your meat into smaller pieces for you, then you can eat a bit more," I said, taking her trencher.

"Yes, and it's certainly true that the Dominicans have a great deal of power, throwing people into the Wall and keeping them there for a long time without a trial. And there are rumours of terrible goings-on there." He looked at the children, put his hand over his

213

mouth, patted his lips a couple of times with his fingertips and raised his eyebrows quickly to me.

"Um," I said, understanding that he thought he had said too much in front the children. "Oh well, perhaps this Bernard Délicieux is just saying what the people think." I gave Condors her trencher back.

"Yes, I think you're probably right about that." He looked at me thoughtfully. "They say he's trying to get the King and Queen of France on side. It will be interesting to see what happens."

"He must be a brave man to take on the Inquisition," I said. "Condors, are you going to eat that meat, or are you just going to play with it?"

"Brave or foolish," said Othon.

In October 1305, I gave birth to Philippa. My fifth daughter, she was healthy, strong and beautiful, but not a boy. I loved her just the same, of course, and Othon, although he was pleased with her, was disappointed again that our second child was not the longed-for son. But there was still time for more children, next time we would have a son, for sure.

A few weeks after Philippa was born, Sybille turned up alone one day at Dalou. I was in my room just putting Philippa down to sleep in her wooden cradle. Alisette came up to say that Sybille had arrived.

"Oh bring her up here, Alisette, and bring some refreshments. She'll need something after her journey," I said.

Sybille appeared with Alisette, who went off again to get the food.

"Oh Sybille," I said. "I'm so pleased to see you – how are you?"

Sybille looked at the cradle and smiled at me. She moved over to look at Philippa.

"A new baby," she said.

"Yes, this is Philippa, she's four weeks old."

We both peered into the cradle at Philippa who was already closing her eyes. Her chubby little face was contented with milk.

"Oh she's beautiful, Madame," said Sybille. "She reminds me of Baby Béa when she was just born."

"Do you think so?" I said. "I can see a look of Baby Béa too. She's a good baby, doesn't cry much, just sleeps and nurses." I turned to look at Sybille. "Anyway, what are you doing down here? Are you with Pathau?"

"No," Sybille shook her head. "I'm not with him any more. I've left him."

"Oh, Sybille," I said. "I'm sorry."

"I didn't trust him. I found him out in some lies and I didn't like… some other things that were going on." Sybille sighed. "He told me a lot about the Clergues and he did some things… anyway, he did a lot for Pons Clergue, Bernard and Pierre's father, as well as for Bernard and Pierre. In a way, I wish he hadn't told me because if they ever found out what I know, well it could be the worse for me."

"What do you mean?" I was alarmed by Sybille, both what she said and her demeanour, which was sad, defeated somehow. She had that strained look which I'd noticed last time I saw her. Alisette knocked and came in with the refreshments, and I waited whilst Sybille drank some water and ate some bread.

"There's so much going on, I don't know what to tell you. And I don't want you to know everything as it could be dangerous for you too, I think."

"I'm well away from it all down here," I said. "I don't think you need to worry about me."

"That's true, I suppose," said Sybille. "It all worries me a lot. Do you know that the Clergues have the Perfects, the Good Men, staying with them now sometimes? I saw Guillaume Authier there one day when I went in their house with Pathau."

"That's incredible, to take such a risk," I said.

"Yes, they think they've got everything covered, that they're above the law." Sybille nodded. "Some very bad things have happened in Montaillou. Do you remember the Maurs family?"

"Yes, I do – wasn't he the one who wore the yellow crosses?"

"Yes, that's right. Well, he died a few years ago, and Madame Maurs never went to church after that. She kept herself to herself, speaking to very few people. Her two sons lived with her. Everyone knows that her sons hate the heresy. They're so poor now because they had most of their land confiscated when they were convicted last time round. The sons blame the heresy. So you can understand that they might prefer to keep out of it this time."

"But that must be difficult, the way things are there."

"Yes, that's true, but if Pierre Clergue had left them alone, they would be still be plodding on as usual. But one day in the village square there was a confrontation between Pierre Clergue and Madame Maurs. Pathau told me what happened and there were a few others who witnessed it at the time and it seems to hold true. Alazaïs was there too and heard it all. For some reason, I don't know why, Pierre took it into his head to confront Madame Maurs about her church attendance, or lack of it. He's just so full of himself now and he's just getting more and more reckless. He thinks he can say and do whatever he wants."

Sybille paused, and I said nothing.

"Anyway the story is that he said to her, in a loud voice as if he wanted people to hear it, 'Why, Madame Maurs, I haven't seen you in church for a long time.' Everyone stopped talking, apparently, and turned to see what was going on. Madame Maurs said, 'No, and you're not likely to either.' 'Why is that?' says Pierre. 'Because I don't like the priest,' says Madame Maurs. 'He's not a proper priest. He's a debauched, double-dealing bastard who uses his position for his own ends.' She spoke in an intensely angry way and everyone was open-mouthed. Then she spat at him, and Pierre said, 'You will live to regret that!', then stormed off. Madame Maurs looked around at everyone, didn't say a word and then walked on, looking very dignified, by all accounts."

"My God," I said. "No wonder that caused trouble, Pierre would not like that one bit."

"No, he didn't." Sybille looked down. "The following week, her sons went down to Ax to the market to sell a few vegetables and eggs. They usually go each week and then they stay the night at the inn. On this occasion when they returned they found a terrible scene in front of them when they entered the house."

Sybille put her hand over her mouth. Her face expressed her distaste and distress.

"What had happened?" I said, feeling frightened.

"Their mother had had her tongue cut out." Sybille said. Her voice was shaky.

I put my hand up to my mouth. "Oh, my Lord! Who would do that?"

Sybille looked at me. "I don't know who actually did it, but I know who arranged it."

"Not Pierre... surely he wouldn't go along with that?"

"It was him and Bernard, they cooked it up between them. Pathau told me. Even Pathau, who's not averse to roughing someone up if they don't pay their protection money, even he was shocked to hear them planning it. 'Let the punishment fit the crime,' Bernard apparently said. 'That'll stop any more tongue-lashings.' Pathau said that they had both laughed at that."

"How is poor Madame Maurs?" I said.

"She's dead." Sybille drank some more water. "She lost a lot of blood and was very weakened and shocked by her ordeal. She lived for a couple of months but she wasn't eating, she was quite old, you know – anyway it just finished her off."

"It's unbelievable," I said. "I can't believe that Pierre would stoop so low."

"There's more," said Sybille. "Do you want to hear it?"

"I do and I don't," I gave a rueful smile. "I never thought Pierre had it in him to go along with something like that."

"It's almost like open warfare in Montaillou now," said Sybille. "The battle lines are drawn. The Clergues, the Belots, the Benets and the Rives on one side. The Maurs, the Azemas and the Liziers on the other. There have been at least two attempts on Pierre Clergue's life."

"There are probably many who would like Pierre out of the way. He seems to have lost all sense of right and wrong," I said. "And to do it in the name of religion makes it worse."

"He's in danger from all sides," said Sybille. "People are beginning to see through him, although

218

most are too afraid to do anything but toe the line. The Clergues have so much power between them."

"Sooner or later you would imagine that the Inquisition will find out that he and his family are harbouring Perfects in their house, at the same time as he's carrying out his duties as a Roman priest," I said. "If people are angry enough to try to kill him, then someone will start to talk soon enough."

"Yes, one side or another will betray him – or kill him – although Pathau says that the Carcassonne Inquisition are too busy with Bernard Délicieux, the mad friar… you must have heard about him?"

I nodded. "Or Pierre's contacts there are looking out for him," I said.

"I still think he's playing with fire," said Sybille.

"I'm sure you're right," I said. "If someone can be bought by one side, they can be bought by the other side as well. And I've heard dreadful stories of what conditions are like in the Wall, from Othon. He tells me what's going on up there when he's visited. It's the worst prison, they say. The cells are tiny and filthy, and people can be cruelly tortured until they confess in the dungeons. Most people would confess to anything if they're hurt badly enough."

"They say the Carcassonne Inquisition is ruthless." Sybille said. "They have so much power. They can arrest people and incarcerate them in the Wall without evidence, and keep them there for as long as they want. The people in Carcassonne are terrified, they hate the Dominicans and the Wall. I've heard they call them crows because of their black-and-white robes, and they make cawing noises when they pass. Bernard Délicieux is doing us a favour. He keeps them occupied in Carcassonne, so they don't look at Montaillou. Pierre

219

Clergue is supposed to be hand-in-glove with a man named de Polignac from the Carcassonne Inquisition as well, and that keeps them off the back of the heretics in Montaillou. But it can't last, this uneasy peace. They must know what's going on, it's common knowledge about the Perfects and Montaillou, although everyone says it's secret."

"Sybille, what are you going to do now?"

"I don't really know," said Sybille. "I need to find employment. I'll look for some around here, in Foix and Pamiers. I don't want to stay in Ax. I want to get away from it all."

"I'd love to have you back as my maid," I said.

"Oh no, I wasn't asking for that," said Sybille blushing.

"You've arrived at the right time," I said. "Alisette is with child. She told me only last week. She married last year – the head groom – they live above the stables. She'll have to stop working soon and I shall be needing a new maid. I'll ask Othon if we can find you some other employment until she leaves. In fact, I think you could help with the children, there are so many now and there will be more – Othon wants a male heir!"

"That would be perfect." Sybille's pretty face was flushed with pleasure.

Chapter 13
The Sixth Interrogation

She tries to eat, she must eat, but the bread is stale and hard and the cheese rancid. Her stomach is sick and she manages only a few mouthfuls of warm water. As the sky darkens and the night takes over, she lies still on the pallet, her eyes closed. Images, ghosts and memories stream by. She sleeps and dreams, waking in a sweat, certain that the black-hooded torturer is in the room with her, that she is in the dungeon of the château in Montaillou. She lies still, drenched in sweat and panic, unable to distinguish nightmare from reality. She dare not look at the corners of the room to see what lurks there. She fears sleeping again but is so very tired that she craves it. She is still awake when a creamy, blue dawn arrives and everything starts again. Her life is going on and on forever in this place.

She hears the guard. She moves shakily, trying to stand up ready to be taken down for the next interrogation. It takes all of her strength to follow the guard along the familiar route through the Palace. The Bishop is waiting with the recorder, Gaillard de Pomies. The two of them are sitting there looking pleased with themselves. They are growing plumper as she becomes thinner. She loathes them now. She wonders what they had for their dinners last night. Mutton, chicken and pigeon, no doubt, with fresh bread. Followed by cheese and fruit, plums and apples, cherries preserved in alcohol, all taken with wine to sip and savour. The sound of the Bishop's voice jerks her out of these thoughts. She stares at him.

"Madame, I remind you again that you are speaking under oath. If you are found to have lied or omitted information, you will be punished until you tell the whole truth."

She shudders at this threat. It clouds her mind as it did the previous day and she casts about wildly, trying to collect her thoughts – what can she say? She opens her mouth and what comes out is the story of the time, after her second marriage, that Pierre arranged to visit her and he wanted to have sex in the cellar. She stops and closes her eyes. Why on earth did I say that? He doesn't need to know all that. God help me, I don't know what I'm doing here. She's hot and weak, and her body aches, her back, her legs… she licks her lips, her mouth is dry

"Madame, are you able to continue?" he says.

"Yes," she opens her eyes, "but I would like some water."

She is brought water and a piece of bread. She sips at the water and nibbles a little at the bread. The bread is fresh. It seems like years since she has eaten soft, fresh bread. She takes a bite of it and savours it in her mouth. The water is cool and fresh – such a small thing, but it fortifies her. She must explain something, she must justify herself on one point at least.

"I remember when I was at Dalou and I was present at the last sacrament of a dying man. I quoted what someone had once said to me about the body of Christ – I meant it as an example of what some people say. I did not mean to say that I believed that."

At this point, Jacques Fournier puts up his hand and says, "Have you ever believed that the body of the Lord was not in the sacrament at the altar?"

"No," she says. Everything is so complicated.

"Have you ever said these words or their equivalent to anyone?"

"I do not recall, but if I do, I will confess it."

"Please repeat what you said, I did not hear you, and remember, Madame that you are speaking under oath."

She repeats her words. Her voice is hoarse and low.

"Have you spoken to any other people about the heretical teachings which Raymond Roussel and Pierre Clergue told you? And have you instructed any person that you have not already named?"

"No."

"Madame, please speak up"

"No," she clears her throat.

"Has anyone ever told you that the Devil was the maker of human bodies and the bodies of other creatures on the earth? And that the Devil was there in the beginning just as God was in the beginning, not made, or produced by any other spirits?"

"No," she says.

"Have you ever heard it said that there is a good God and an evil God?"

"No. They call God he who made the spirits, and the Devil they call the creator of the world, and the one who directs the world." Does that make any sense. Is he is trying to confuse her?

"Have you ever heard it said that the good God made ten worlds and the evil God made ten other worlds, and that those who are in the evil worlds fought against the good God, and that a part of the good worlds were conquered by the evil God?"

"No."

"Have you heard it said that the spirits are from the substance or parts of God?

"No, only what I said before," she says.

"Have you heard any of the people you have mentioned or any others, whoever they might be, say that there are two spirits in man, one which is of the Devil and the other which is of God?"

"No." A hot headache is throbbing behind her eyes.

"Have you heard them say that all the spirits created by God were of the same nature and condition?"

"The priest, Pierre Clergue, told me that all the spirits were created by God in heaven in the same condition, but that some of them rebelled against God, and that these were sent to hell and are demons. Some spirits did not rebel but followed the rebels and fell to earth, and these are the spirits which enter the bodies of men and beasts on earth."

"Have you heard it said that the Devil, out of pride and envy of God, made this world and all that is found in it, except the spirits?"

"No, only that the Devil has made all things that are visible on earth. Why he made them I was not told." Her head is throbbing.

"Did you hear them say that the scriptures of the Old Testament were not of God?"

"Not exactly, Pierre Clergue told me that the scriptures were elaborated upon and fabricated with the exception of the Gospels."

"Have you heard that the Son of God descended into the Virgin Mary and hid himself in her?"

"The priest said that it was the Holy Spirit who hid himself in the Virgin Mary."

"Do they call the Mother of God, Sainte Mary, because, according to the priest, the Holy Spirit did not take human flesh from her?"

"Yes." Is that was what he said?

"Did you hear anyone say that Christ was dead?"

224

"The priest said He was crucified but I don't remember him saying He was dead."

"Did he say that Jesus Christ was resurrected from the dead?"

"He said Christ was resurrected, but I don't remember if he said He was resurrected from the dead." She cannot think what else to say.

"Have you heard him say that Christ would judge the good and evil in the Last Judgement?" He is barking out these questions to her, each one is like a hammer blow to her head. Her headache deepens and swells with every question.

"Yes."

"That all the men resurrected with their bodies would come to the Judgement of Christ?"

"He said that we will all come to the Last Judgement of Christ, but that only those who were Good Christians and who had received the *consolamentum* at their death would be saved. Even those who were Good Christians would not be saved unless they had received the *consolamentum* at their death. No-one else would be saved." She must give the right answers. The headache bangs and thumps.

"Did the priest or others deny the baptism by water, the confirmation, the sacrament of the altar, ordination or extreme unction?"

"I never heard anyone speak of the sacraments or deny them except those of penitence and marriage."

"Is there anything more you can tell me about that priest?"

She looks at him. His face and that of the vile Brother Gaillard swim before her eyes. Brother Gaillard has stopped writing and is looking at her with what she thinks is hatred. There is no mercy here. What can she say? What can she tell them? She passes her hand over her forehead – she is sweating, burning hot.

She takes a deep breath and launches into the story of the time he made a bed for them in the church at Prades and the arrangements he made to meet her there. She glances at the Bishop as she talks about this and stumbles over the words. His face is stern and serious; he shows no reaction to this, the most outrageous of Pierre's many flauntings of the sacred Roman Church. Then she tells the intimate details of his contraceptive arrangements and the conversations they had about it, how he told her to keep the little sachet of herbs conveniently around her neck whenever he slept with her, ready for use, sometimes two or three times in the night. She tells how he said that after her father died he would like her to have a child of his. She lays her head on her hands on the table in front of her and sobs at this point. Why has she said these things? She hardly knows what she says now. It's unbearable. How shameful and humiliating to talk of this and how bad she feels about betraying Pierre. But she must save herself, she must tell the Bishop everything, or be tortured or burned alive. She is ashamed at her weakness, at the things she has told him. She doesn't take in what the Bishop says. Someone takes her by her arm and guides her back to the loft.

Chapter 14
1308

In December 1307, Othon came home one evening complaining that he felt unwell. His chest was sore and felt tight. He was hot in spite of the freezing weather outside.

"I'm going to bed straight away to rest," he told me, "I hope I've not contracted the malady that seems to be affecting some of the estate workers. I think an early night and a good night's sleep should help me to ward it off."

"Should I send for a physician?"

"No, there's no need for that, I'm quite sure a good night's rest will be enough to get rid of it," he reassured me.

But the following morning, Othon was worse. He suffered intense shivering fits and his breathing was laboured and rasping. He was burning hot. He agreed this time to let Father Martin, a monk from the abbey nearby, known for his skills in medicine, to be sent for. Father Martin arrived later that day and prescribed steam inhalations and a poultice of balsam, a preparation that he brought with him. This was to be applied to Othon's chest at regular intervals. There was a linctus for his cough and he was to be given plenty of fluids – water, soups and gruels – and he must be helped to sit up and cough to clear his chest. The monk took me to one side. His kindly face was serious.

"Madame, I'm sorry to have to tell you, but as you can see, your husband is very sick. There is a malady passing through the area," he hesitated. "He is showing the same symptoms others have had, his chest is very tight and he is having difficulty in breathing. He also has a high fever. I think you should know that this is very serious."

"What can I do?"

"Pray, Madame," he said. "Pray."

Othon had always been so strong and healthy, I was sure he could recover from this illness. But as the day and following night passed, his breathing became more laboured. I sat with him and applied the poultices regularly, and gave him drinks and the cough linctus. His breathing did improve slightly after the application of the poultices, but each time this proved to be only a temporary respite.

"People often are worse before they are better," said one of the maids who was helping to nurse Othon. "My father had such an illness for about five days and then he began to improve. You're looking after him so well he's bound to recover."

I fed him broth and drinks of water, whenever he would take them. I sponged his hot forehead with a cool cloth. I changed his sweat-sodden bed-linen and washed his burning body with cool water. I made him as comfortable as I could. He slept restlessly and then woke feeling temporarily better. Then he started shivering and coughing again. When he slept, I tried to snatch a few hours' rest myself, leaving instructions with the servants to wake me when he awoke. After four days and nights of this, I began to wonder if he would survive the illness. He thrashed about, muttering and mumbling and it was impossible to get him to eat or drink. He did not seem to see me and although he was weak and exhausted, he seemed to find strength from somewhere, and he fought me and the servants off whenever we tried to do anything for him. I feared he could hurt himself or one of us, so I sent for Father Martin again.

"Can you help him?" I said.

"I'll sedate him, but we'll have to restrain him," he said.

I sent for a servant who held Othon's arms down whilst Father Martin tried to get Othon to drink the sedative. Othon knocked the servant and the sedative flying.

"We need more hands to hold him down," said the monk. "Fortunately I have plenty of the sedative with me, I was expecting something like this."

It took four male servants to hold Othon down whilst the monk administered a draught of sedative. I watched helplessly as this procedure took place. I was distraught.

"Have you seen this before?" I asked the monk.

He nodded gravely. "He is very ill, Madame. Pray for his soul."

Gradually Othon became calmer and slept. I did as the monk said. I prayed. Later that evening, Othon seemed so settled that I hoped that he would awake refreshed. I left him to sleep myself for a night but after a few restless hours I went to check on him. His breathing was strident and I could not rouse him. I shook him gently but he was deeply asleep. His breathing rose up to a crescendo in a series of rattles and wheezes in his chest and then stopped for a long minute until it started again. Each time this happened, my own heart and breathing stopped along with his, until ten days after the first symptoms, his breathing ceased altogether. It was the New Year, 1308.

Othon's death shocked me deeply. Although his illness was serious, I had expected him to recover. He always seemed so strong and indestructible. That he was gone seemed so wrong. I didn't know what to do. What would I do? Our longed-for son would now never be born and I mourned for this. I woke up each morning expecting Othon to be by my side or downstairs eating breakfast. There was an empty place at the table and that was what touched me most, the empty chair where he no longer sat. It broke my heart, that empty chair. I took my meals in my room to avoid seeing it. Many thoughts and images passed through my mind about Othon and our marriage. The start had been threatened by my links to the past and my guilt about all that. I had also had to learn to accept certain limitations. I had promised to obey him and although inwardly I railed against this, I found him more amenable if I did not challenge him directly. He would be more open to accepting my ideas if I bided my time and kept my mouth shut. It had been hard for me, used to fighting my corner in my family in a more straightforward way, but it paid off. He was generous in many ways, and was loving and warm too. He appreciated my work with the household and we made each other laugh. We shared a love of our children and the hope of more to come. I had become deeply committed to him and I had imagined our life together to continue long into the future, and that our family would be increased. All this had been lost and I was sad, dull and tired. Life became a chore; the joy had gone. I could only continue to carry out the tasks and duties that fell to me as Othon's widow. That and the children kept me going.

I dreaded the funeral but in fact I found some comfort from my family and friends and the wider community of Othon's estate. But they of course all went away to continue with their lives. They all remarked how well I seemed to be coping. I told them I was managing, that I had Sybille, that I had the children and that I had a very full life, which I must get on with.

I inherited Othon's estate and I was determined to run it well for Ava and Philippa, who would eventually take it over. I wanted to make a good job of looking after the children's property for them and I set about re-organising all three households. I decided that I must make an inventory of everything and make sure that all was in order and under control. I had been too lax – I must keep a firmer eye on the housekeeping and the servants. The houses needed thorough cleaning. I hadn't noticed how dusty some of the corners were. I sorted and folded Othon's clothes. I organised his manuscripts and books. I saw his lawyers. I counted all the animals to be sure that none of the servants were helping themselves to the odd chicken or pig. It was of great importance, this counting of sheets and pillows, the correct storage of furs, the mending of garments and coverlets. Now that I was solely responsible, I must run the place efficiently so that the servants respected me as they had respected Othon.

Alazaïs and Fabrisse arrived at Dalou one afternoon a few weeks after Othon's death. They found me busy counting linen sheets. Sybille showed them up to the linen room where I had told her to bring them. As they mounted the stairs, I could hear them chattering to Sybille. I went to the top of the stairs. They stopped when they saw me.

"You don't know, do you?" I said.

"What do you mean?" said Fabrisse. They all stared at me.

"Othon… he died," I said.

"Oh Béatrice," said Alazaïs.

"Lord save his soul," said Fabrisse crossing herself.

They both reached the top of the stairs where I was standing.

"I'm so pleased to see you," I said, moving towards them both to embrace them. "There is so much to do at the moment, I'm ready to rest for a short time."

"What are you doing?" said Alazaïs.

"I'm counting linen." I gestured to them to follow me and we entered my room which was full of piles of linen.

"You seem... very busy," said Fabrisse.

"Othon died two, or was it three months ago?" I said. "I think it's nearly two months now. We buried him – let me see – well, not long after, of course. So I've a lot to do now."

"Oh Béatrice, I... I'm so sorry," Fabrisse struggled to find words. "How are you?"

"I'm keeping busy," I said.

"What a dreadful shock, we had no idea," said Alazaïs.

"Yes, it was a shock," I said. "But, you know, you have to carry on, don't you? I've got five daughters to bring up and an estate to run, I can't just sit around feeling sorry for myself."

"Oh Béatrice." Fabrisse walked over to me and put her arms around me. "Oh Béatrice."

I didn't know how to respond to this so I just stood rigidly in her embrace. When Fabrisse backed away slightly, I said, "I'll have a break for a little while – let's have some refreshments. I'll ask Sybille to bring something up."

We all sat in my room before the embers of a fire. It was March but still cold and Fabrisse and Alazaïs were glad of the warmth and the comfort after their journey.

"What happened? I mean was Othon ill?" said Alazaïs when we had eaten some of the soup and bread that Sybille had brought up for us.

"It was his chest. He had difficulty in breathing." I looked down. I didn't really want to talk about it.

"How did the funeral go?" asked Alazaïs, "Did all your family come?"

"Yes, it all went as it should have done. They all said I was brave. Gentille offered to stay but I said I could manage."

"And are you? Managing I mean?" said Fabrisse.

"Yes, I'm looking after the estate. I've got so much to do, everything must be in order for my daughters when they come of age and inherit the estate. I know how to run the estate and the households, you know. I have lawyers to see, and servants and labourers to attend to and supervise. Everything must be done properly."

I stopped. Alazaïs and Fabrisse were staring at me. There was a pause.

"Béatrice, you seem so… distracted," said Fabrisse.

"Do I?" I said. "I'm fine."

"Where are the children?" asked Alazaïs.

"They're with their nursemaid. The little ones don't understand, so I haven't said much about it to them yet," I said. "They came to the funeral, of course." There was a silence. Fabrisse and Alazaïs looked at each other. "But I've not asked you how you are, you must think me rude."

"I've come to see a healer in Pamiers about my bad foot," said Alazaïs.

"Oh, what's the matter with it?"

233

"I had an accident a few years back when I tripped and fell on a pathway near Montaillou. It was nothing really, I just stumbled and my ankle bent over, it was painful afterwards. But I just wrapped it up and eventually it went a bit better. But it's a funny shape now," she lifted up her foot and leg. A bundle of soiled rags was wrapped around her ankle. "It gives me a lot of pain and I can't walk far with it."

"She sat on the donkey most of the way, we've been travelling for two weeks and we'll hire a mule to take some wine casks back to sell when we return to Montaillou," said Fabrisse.

"Will you stay for a few days here?" I said.

"I think we should rest here," said Fabrisse looking at Alazaïs. "I'd like to see the children and see how they are."

I made arrangements for them to stay. I continued with my chores and was so busy with it all that I hardly sat with them. On the second day they insisted I sit down with them to eat in the evening. I told them I wasn't hungry but Fabrisse was firm.

"You're looking thin and pale," she said. "You're no use to anyone like that. Your children need you to be healthy for them."

We ate in silence. I picked at my food, I really wasn't hungry. Eventually I stood up to leave. Fabrisse stood too and moved round to face me. She put her hands on my shoulders. "Béatrice," she said.

We faced each other, Fabrisse gently put her arms around me. I laid my head on her shoulder. I felt a tear slide down my face, and then another, and another, until I was sobbing. Fabrisse held me whilst I continued to cry and waited patiently until I stopped.

"I haven't cried much since Othon died," I said as I calmed down and dried my face with a piece of

234

cloth. I gave them both a small smile as I sat down again and faced them. "Now," I said. "I feel suddenly so tired. How am I going to manage all that I have to do?" I stood up and started to wring my hands. "It's all down to me now, it's all so… daunting." Then I sat down and cried again.

"You have people to support you and help you and we're here now, we can stay for a while," said Fabrisse.

"I'm so tired," I said again.

"Crying is exhausting but you will feel better for it in the end," said Fabrisse.

"I think I will go and lie down, and try to sleep. I've not been sleeping very well since Othon died," I said. As I left I said over my shoulder, "Then later I want to hear about what's happening in Montaillou."

The following morning I lay in my bed, still tired but thinking about all that had happened. Eventually I got up and went to find the children, hugging them and talking to them about their father. It was true that Philippa was too young to fully understand what had happened to her Papa, but she could understand the idea of Papa being in heaven and not coming back. The three eldest girls were less close to Othon, but they loved the little ones and all five of had them had lost their fathers. The bonds of shared loss bound them together. In the evening when the children had gone to bed, I talked with Fabrisse and Alazaïs about Montaillou.

"It was just before we came away," said Fabrisse. "There had been another *consolamentum* in the village. It was old Na Roche. Yes, she finally died," she smiled at me. "No-one knows how old she was, but she must have been over eighty. She was like a little bird, so tiny and frail at the end, just skin and bone.

Prades Tavernier and Guillaume Authier came to perform the *consolamentum*, that's all they seem to do nowadays, move around from one death-bed to another. Anyway, this was an important *consolamentum* – Na Roche had been a strong Cathar all her life. She'd never wavered and she'd spent time in prison for her beliefs. So it was done one night, and the Perfects were staying at their usual places: Prades in the Rives's barn and Guillaume Authier in the Belots' loft space that they built for him. They'd been there for a few days after the *consolamentum*, resting. Mengarde Clergue was forever going over to the Belots' with presents for them. She took food and sheepskins, and some clothes-mending to do. Apparently the Perfects sewed fur linings into Pierre Clergue's clothes for him. She sent the very best of food over for them: honey, wine, trout and fresh bread. I've seen it for myself and you have too," she nodded to Alazaïs.

"Yes, I have, and Raymonde Guilhou told me – you know her, she works at the Clergue's house," explained Alazaïs.

Fabrisse continued, "Then after a few days, the Perfects were woken early one morning by Pierre Clergue. He told them they'd better move quickly and get out of Montaillou because there was a group of horsemen on their way from Prades, where they had raided some houses looking for Perfects." She paused for breath.

"Oh, my God," I said.

"Pierre said they'd had no warning from anyone, not from any of his contacts that is, one of the villagers just sent a shepherd over from Prades, with a message to him saying that a man called Pierre de Luzenac, from Comus, had turned traitor, and was riding toward Montaillou looking for the Perfects. They

236

think it was Guillaume Authier's nephew, Géraud de Rodes, who'd talked. He'd been arrested by the Inquisition just before this. The Inquisition is offering money for information and making bargains with people if they tell about the Good Men. Pierre de Luzenac was also trying to win favour with the Inquisition, realising it was all getting much closer to home." Fabrisse stopped for a moment.

"How dreadful it must be in Montaillou," I said. "Not knowing who to trust."

"It is, I can tell you. Anyway, the Perfects were dressed up as shepherds, wearing big brown cloaks like the shepherds wear, which covered up their blue-and-green Perfects' tunics. They had axes over their shoulders. Arnaud Vital, the shoemaker who often guides the Perfects, took them into the woods. The shepherds, all Cathars, were in the nearby field at the time and saw them as they left Montaillou. They were laughing at first, not realising how serious it was, and one of them said, 'Are those two woodcutters from Lavalenet? Because I don't think so!' They just about got away in time before the horsemen entered the village. They went immediately to the Belots' house and to the Rives's house, so they knew where to look," said Alazaïs. "Then they went to the Forts' house, arrested Guillaume Fort, took him to the château and put him in the dungeon, and then torched the Forts' house. His wife and their little daughter just got out in time."

"Oh and they arrested Guillemette Benet, Raymonde Capelle and Rixende Julia," said Fabrisse. "And along with some others from Prades, they were all flung into the dungeons too. They've been taken elsewhere since, to Carcassonne, I think."

237

"I sat with Rixende Julia when Na Roche was dying, and we laid her out together with Mengarde Clergue," said Alazaïs. "That was partly why I came away with Fabrisse now. I was so scared of staying in Montaillou."

"I'm not surprised," I said. "But one thing I'm puzzled about is why Pierre didn't know this was going to happen, I thought he was supposed to be hand-in-glove with the Carcassonne Inquisition?"

"Yes, it does make you wonder. He must be feeling pretty worried himself now," said Fabrisse.

In the autumn of 1308, I began to feel increasingly tired and unwell. I was at the manor house in Varilhes with the children, when I decided to rest in bed for a few days to try to recover my strength. Since Othon's death earlier in the year, I had struggled on and I was physically and emotionally exhausted. I had never fully regained my appetite and now just walking round my room and dressing myself in the morning tired me out. I wasn't sleeping well. I had felt better when Fabrisse and Alazaïs visited in the spring. The spring sunshine helped, but now, as the cycle turned to autumn, and the sky lost the dense blue of summer, the whole world seemed duller, and I was struggling with a feeling of intense and painful sadness that seemed to suck the life out of me. Even simple tasks seemed beyond me. I worried that I might be very ill and die too, leaving behind my children as orphans. This was an unbearable thought, although I found myself thinking at the same time that perhaps death would be better than this existence. This thought decided me then that I must look after myself, eat good food and rest. I asked for Father Martin, the Franciscan herbalist. He listened carefully to me as I tried to explain to him how I felt.

"I think your mind and your body has suffered too much and cannot carry on," he said. "It's the result of your husband's death, I think. You know," he said, "a loss like that has more impact on us than we sometimes realise. You lost your first husband too, I believe? It will take you time to recover, but you will, with rest and good food – even if you can only eat small amounts – fish, chicken, eggs, milk and honey, fresh fruit and vegetables. And I will give you some herbal remedies to help you rest and sleep."

"I hope so."

"Do you have good men and women to work on the estate?"

"Yes."

"Then you must leave them to get on with it. You need complete rest for a few months, if not longer. You could start to take a little gentle exercise after a month or so and gradually increase this. I'll leave some valerian to help you sleep and St John's wort will help you to feel better. I will speak to your eldest daughter – she's quite grown-up now?"

"She's fourteen," I said. "And there's Sybille, my maid – speak to her as well."

"I will come and visit you every two weeks or so. Between us, we should help you to get back to normal in time."

"You are very kind, Father. I will make a regular donation to the Priory."

"Thank you, Madame, I shall be back towards the end of next week and I will pray for you."

At the end of September, I had two visitors within days of each other. The first was Fabrisse again. Sybille showed her up to where I lay in my wood-framed bed, and Fabrisse sat down on a chair next to it. Her strong features were serious. Her dark eyes subdued.

"I heard you were ill, and I wanted to see you," she said. "How are you?"

"Not well at all," I said, "But very pleased to see you."

"What's the matter?" asked Fabrisse.

"Father Martin says exhaustion, so I'm following his advice and taking the remedies he's given me. I'm not improving much… well, perhaps I am just a little better for taking them. But it's very slow. Some days are better than others. But I don't want to talk about my miserable complaints, I don't have much energy for talking. I want to hear how you are and all the news from Montaillou."

I smiled, the first smile for a while, and my jaw felt tight, it had been stuck in a sad, unsmiling expression, mirroring my empty, internal state. Fabrisse's warm presence was good for me.

"It's bound to take time, you must rest and follow his advice," said Fabrisse.

"Talk to me Fabrisse, tell me what's happening… it will take my mind off myself."

"Are you sure? Some of it's… well, upsetting."

"Yes, I'm sure," I gestured to the bed. "Sit here next to me and tell me."

Fabrisse moved next to me. "It was Sunday, the Feast of the Nativity of the Virgin, when we usually have a feast in the square… you remember?"

"Yes, of course."

"Well, we didn't have a feast because at dawn there was another raid. This time though it was very different from the one earlier in the year. There were a lot of soldiers, and they surrounded the village and cut off all the escape routes. They were led by Jacques de Polignac from Carcassonne. We had no warning that they were coming, but it was obvious that Pierre

240

Clergue was in on it because he guided them round the village. They were knocking on the doors of 'suspected heretics', they said, and arresting anyone over the age of fourteen who was a suspect. Pierre was identifying people for them, helped by his brother. Those they arrested were thrown into the dungeon of the château."

She spoke calmly and fluently, but the words pierced my mind like so many little arrows. I shivered. I'd always hated those dungeons when I lived in the château. But Pierre Clergue telling Jacques de Polignac who to arrest – it didn't make any sense. I didn't want to think why he would do that but at the same time I really had to know.

"Why would Pierre do that?" I said, knowing what the answer would be.

"Why, to save his own skin, of course. He's a traitor, Béatrice. De Polignac even stayed overnight at the Clergues' house. In the very house that has sheltered the Perfects." Fabrisse shifted. "People were herded into the dungeon, Alazaïs included, then later they read out names from a list and some were let out and given dates when they must appear before the Inquisition at Carcassonne for questioning. Others were subjected to an open-air public trial in the courtyard of the château later that afternoon, and another group were taken with the soldiers the following day when they left."

"Who was rounded up?"

"Jacquemette Maury, Alazaïs – she's been given a date to go up to Carcassonne, the Maurs brothers, Raymonde Guilhou – there are too many to name. Most of them are still in Montaillou awaiting the dates when they go to Carcassonne."

"Oh no, not Alazaïs? How could he betray his friends and neighbours like that? It's as if he's changed sides."

"I think he's on whichever side suits him best."

"I must see him," I said.

"Are you sure that's wise?" said Fabrisse.

"I just need to… it's important – will you to take a message to him?"

It was only a few days after Fabrisse's visit that Pierre called to see me. He had received my message and was on his way to the synod at Pamiers. The story of the raid on Montaillou and his part in it had occupied my thoughts since Fabrisse had left. I had many questions for him. I was still resting in bed, attended by my daughter Béa, who was proving to be a capable nurse. I lay against my cushions and pillows. Pierre sat on the bed and gently took my hand. He stroked my arm as he asked me how I was.

"Not well, I fear," I said. "But I have been thinking of you a great deal since I had a visit from Fabrisse last week. I have some questions to ask you."

Pierre nodded and, looking at Béa, he said to her, "Will you leave us alone for a while, Béatrice, as your mother and I want to talk." Béa glanced at me and I nodded, and she left us.

"What is it, my dear?" His face showed real concern.

"I've been very worried since Fabrisse told me about the raid on Montaillou," I said.

"Ah, yes," he said, "you know about that."

"Yes, I do," I said. "And it's made me think, you know I've never confessed about my relationship with you and the conversations we had all those years ago, and now all those people arrested in Montaillou, I fear I will be sent for too." Tears welled up, I was weak and tired.

"You have no need of confession," he said. "Always remember what I told you before, Béatrice, all those years ago. It is God alone who can absolve sins, you have nothing to fear."

I closed my eyes for a moment. Battered and hurt as I was, I had to find some strength within me to question him more. "Pierre, I want to know, what has happened in Montaillou? I must speak plainly to you, I… I don't know how much time I have, I've been ill for weeks now and I'm hardly improving. Was it you who denounced the believers there? Tell me the truth, Pierre. I cannot believe that you betrayed my friend, Alazaïs, and the others – people who you once called friends."

"Things have become complicated in Montaillou," he replied. He was the same old Pierre, not fazed by my questions. "There have been many problems there. Some of the faithful turned against me – they don't know how much I have protected them, they have no idea how I have ducked and dived, twisted and turned, to protect the believers in Montaillou. I put myself and my family in danger for them. It came to a point where I had to make some choices. It was not easy, but it had to be done." He was becoming agitated as he spoke, but when he looked at me, he took a deep breath and calmed himself down.

"Sometimes there is no clear pathway that is right, and sometimes you have to do things that you don't want to do for the sake of the greater good. I have only taken revenge on the people who have done me wrong. Believe me, I only did what I had to do, Béatrice. I can assure you that I am still sympathetic to the Good Christians."

243

"But Alazaïs, Pierre? She has done you no harm – how could you?"

He stroked my hand. "Bystanders may be burnt if they stand too close to the fire… but you look tired, Béatrice, I don't want to weary you, my dear."

"I am tired," I said. I wanted to ask more of him but I knew he would find a way to worm his way out of it and I was so weary, it wouldn't be worth the effort. He would always have an answer for anyone who questioned him.

I was not strong enough to talk much more with him and he left shortly afterwards, kissing me gently on my cheek. I was deeply affected by what he had told me. What he said was true. I realised that there are times in life when difficult choices have to made. But I knew too that he had betrayed the people of Montaillou and that disturbed me. I thought it unlikely that he could or would implicate me in anything, but I resolved to make a confession to a priest as soon as I felt well enough to do so.

It seemed to be a turning point. Whether it was that God had pardoned me for my new resolve to make my confession, or whether it was that I had faced up to what I had done, I don't know, but over the next two months leading up to Christmas, I slowly regained some of my energy. I felt as if something deep inside me had changed, shifted and strengthened. I followed a routine of walking around the estate with one or other of the children, and as the weather grew colder I stayed close to the house with its log fires, its warm sheepskins and hot bowls of soup. I had still not seen a priest to make my confession. Something held me back. I wasn't ready. I would know when the time was right.

Two weeks before Christmas, as I was gaining strength, Béa came into my room one morning, saying that she had pains in her stomach, and felt sick and unwell. I put my hand on her forehead.

"You feel hot, Béa, I think you've got a fever, you should rest in bed for a while," I said. "Just take water, no food. It's a stomach upset, by the sounds of it – I'm sure it will pass soon enough."

Later that morning I went to see Béa, who was lying in bed in the room she shared with Esclarmonde and Condors.

"How are you?" I asked.

"I feel worse, I've been sick a few times."

I felt Béa's forehead. "You're very hot. Have you still got the pain?"

"It's a bit better. It went a lot worse just after I came to you, in one spot there." She pointed to her right side. "Then it spread all over there." Béa pointed to her abdomen.

"I'll sponge you down, that may help a bit," I said.

I went back with cool water and cloths and carefully applied the sponges to Béa's face and abdomen.

"You're very hot, Béa, I'm sure this will help," I said.

"It doesn't hurt quite so much in one place, it's all over," Béa said, as I sponged her abdomen.

"Rest now, Béa and I'll come back in a while." I dried her soft skin, placed the bedclothes over her and gave her a kiss.

"Béa isn't very well," I said to Esclarmonde and Condors. "She needs to rest so leave her alone today."

I looked round the door an hour later and saw Béa sleeping. At midday, I went in again. Her face was red and her chestnut hair was wet and ragged with sweat. I moved the bedding off her and covered her with a light linen sheet. She was still sleeping. It seemed best to let her continue to rest, that way the fever could reach its crisis point after which Béa would cool down. That's how it seemed to work for these ailments – all the children had suffered similar maladies at one time or another. An hour later, I went in to sit with Béa, who seemed now to be even hotter. There were beads of perspiration on her flushed face. I stripped the bed down and called for Sybille to bring cold water and together we sponged Béa's body to try and cool her down. We changed the sweat-soaked linen and covered Béa lightly with a cotton sheet. Béa was deeply asleep and didn't wake through any of this.

"We should send for Father Martin again," I said. "She's worse."

"I'll send someone to get him," said Sybille.

I sat next to Béa and held her hot hand. Her hand clenched mine, her fingernails buried into my palm, a tremor ran over her body and she convulsed in a rigid spasm. The bed banged against the floor and shook violently. I shouted for Sybille who came running. We watched in helpless fear as the frantic shaking continued. Béa's face was distorted into a grimace, her fists clenched tight, she was frothing at the mouth. I held my hands over her, her arms, her legs, her body, attempting to still her jerking movements. There was a choking, gurgling sound in Béa's throat and the shaking stopped. She lay still, her flushed face pale. I touched her and gently shook her. I put my head over her heart and listened. I felt for her heart beat. There was none. I touched Béa's face which was changing, growing paler still and waxy looking.

"Béa," I said. "Come back to me."

Death was on the face of my beloved daughter – one moment my beautiful girl was alive, the next moment her life was extinguished forever. I could not believe what had happened so quickly. I sat beside her body and stroked her hand which was limp and cold. I rested my arms on the bed and leaned forward with my head on my arms. I sobbed and sobbed until I could sob no more.

Béa had to be buried according to the rites of the Roman Catholic Church. There really was no other way although I wished with all my heart that there was an alternative, as I now felt sure that God had deserted me. There was no reason to take my beautiful, innocent daughter. I went to look at my daughter's body as it was prepared for the burial service. She was laid out on her bed, dressed in a white dress, a wreath of flowers around her pretty hair. I looked at her waxy face, beautiful, even in death. I touched the eyelids of the eyes which no longer saw, I ran my finger down the nose which no longer breathed, and over the lips, mauve and lifeless, and no longer able to speak. A collar of stiff fabric encased her fragile neck and the wreath around her head appeared to anchor her to the bed. I remembered Béa's affectionate care of me when I was ill myself, how she sat with me, how she helped me to wash and change my clothes, how she played with the little ones, how loving she was and how I loved her. I was unable to support myself then and collapsed into a heap on the ground and wept again for the loss of my lovely daughter. This was the moment when I was sure that there was no God.

I was still weak from my own illness, but against all odds I managed to find within myself a core of strength that had slowly developed over the last few months since Othon died. There was a great deal of support amongst friends and neighbours, and life continued in its remorselessly, trivial way. Esclarmonde, Condors, Ava and Philippa and me. They'd lost their fathers, and their eldest sister. I had lost my husbands and my daughter. My sons, their two brothers, whilst still living, were not close by and were as good as lost to me. We clung together, us five survivors and formed a close group.

I had never been an avid church-goer – I had gone out of duty with Othon – but since his death, my attendance had been sporadic. After Béa's death, I found myself thinking a lot about God, and why, if He existed, He would take so many people from me. Was this a punishment for listening to the Cathars, for allowing doubts to enter my mind? Was it punishment for my behaviour with Pierre Clergue? My faith, never strong and my attendance at church, never regular, now dropped off altogether. I just couldn't bring myself to go to church. I wondered about other losses, everyone suffers loss – is it God punishing us all? Or is it simply the way life is? Are we God's playthings? Does anyone really understand these things? Is there a God or is life just a series of random events? At times, I was sure there was no God, but then I wasn't. Would I suffer in hell for these thoughts, or are Pierre Clergue and the heretics right, that the only way to save your soul is through receiving the *consolamentum* ritual at the end of life? I found no answers to my questions, no explanations for my sorrows. The pain of the loss of Béa was unbearable and overwhelmed me at times, and I could only rest until it passed. Afterwards I was restless and unable to settle at anything. A few weeks after Béa's death, I decided to go and stay in Limoux with Gentille, who was always asking me to go and stay with her. I took my daughters with me. Maybe the change would help.

After I had been there for about a month, Gentille spoke to me one evening once we had eaten.

"You seem to be a little better now, Béatrice," she said. "I think you're eating more and you've put on a bit of weight."

"Yes, I think that's true. But you know, I don't think I shall ever get over losing Béa."

"No," said Gentille. "But…" she hesitated.

"What is it?"

"It may help if you come to church."

"My faith in God has been sorely tested," I said. "I no longer know what to believe or think. Sometimes I believe, then other times I don't. I often wonder how God could take both my husbands and my lovely daughter." Tears, always in waiting welled up.

"I know, dear, it is very hard to bear." Gentille put her arms round me. "We cannot understand all that God does, but praying and going to church may help you to see why these things have happened. God will show you."

"I am thinking of going to confession," I said, which was true, I had been considering this ever since Pierre's visit, even if just to do what looked to be the right thing. Perhaps the time had come. "I may go to church for that."

"I will go with you, if that will help," said Gentille.

Later that week, I went with Gentille to her local church where I made the confession I had been considering for a while. I did feel a certain lightening in my heart afterwards; perhaps that was something I could now leave behind.

When I was leaving to return home two weeks later, Gentille tried again to encourage me to attend church.

"Do think more about going to church, Béatrice?" she said. "Not just for yourself. Your daughters – they need to be set an example."

"I cannot go to church yet," I said. "Maybe in time."

I had confessed about Pierre. That was all I could do. Finally, the year 1308 was over.

Chapter 15
The Seventh Interrogation

Weak and sick, Béatrice slumps onto the pallet. Her stomach is bloated and uncomfortable, and her headache is blinding. Nausea lurking in her guts now creeps up on her. She moves towards the bucket in the corner. The urge to vomit overtakes her and she violently spews forth a stream of fluid. It misses the bucket and spreads on the floor. She kneels next to the bucket and heaves up more foul fluid. Again and again she retches until there is nothing left. Still retching, a small amount of bitter-tasting yellow bile comes up. She shudders as she spits this out and leans back against the wall. Her head spins. She closes her eyes but the sick dizziness does not ease. Her guts are in a vice-like grip, and she clutches at herself and groans. Another wave of pain hits her and she struggles to her feet, pulls at her clothes and squats unsteadily over the bucket. A rush of stinking, steaming fluid floods from her, another gripping pain and more fluid bursts out of her guts until she thinks there must be nothing left inside her. The pain subsides and she looks around for something to clean herself with. All she has are her own garments and the filthy sacking on the pallet. She crawls to the pallet and pulls off her kirtle. She rips at her undershift but she does not have the strength to tear a piece of fabric off. She uses the skirt of her discarded kirtle to roughly clean herself, throws it away from the pallet and collapses. She pulls the filthy piece of sacking over her body and drifts off into sleep.

She is disturbed by the sound of the door being unlocked. She opens her eyes but feels so weak that even to turn her head in the direction of the sound seems too much of an effort. The face of the young attendant swims into her field of vision. His hand is placed over his mouth and nose. He looks at her for a moment, then puts the bread and water on the small table and leaves. She makes a huge effort, and propping herself up on her elbow reaches for the water. Her hand shakes as she attempts to grasp the container and it slips through her hand and onto the floor. The water spills out of it. She is seized again by another wave of nausea and she retches up a small amount of bile onto the floor where it mixes with the water. Violent pains grip her and she crawls off the pallet to hover over the bucket. More stinking fluid streams out of her. It runs down her legs and onto the floor. She crawls back to the pallet where she tries again to clean herself with the discarded kirtle. She is hot, burning up and desperate for a drink. She falls back, licks her dry lips and slips into a heavy sleep.

Something is pulling from the deep place that her weakness has taken her to. It's a sound. She forces herself up to the surface and awareness. She hears her name. It comes again. It is her name. She opens her eyes. It is coming from on high somewhere – from the window. She slowly pulls herself up on one elbow. Her head starts to spin and she is still for a minute or two whilst it settles. Her name is called out again. Does she recognise the voice?

"Béatrice."

"Who's there?"

"Béatrice, oh Béatrice, thank God you're there, it's Pierre."

She sinks back. "Pierre?"

"Yes," he says, "it's me."

"Where are you?"

"I'm outside the loft on the ramparts where they pass by the Bishopric, near to your window. Listen to me

252

Béatrice, I've not got much time. I'm under house arrest at Mas-Saint-Antonin, but I can walk around on the ramparts and I bribed a guard to tell me where you are."

"Oh Pierre," she says, "I'm so ill, I think, I think… I will die," a sob escapes from her.

"Have you said anything about me – to the Bishop, I mean?"

"I… I was terrified..."

"Listen Béatrice, I must go in a minute. Jacques Fournier is trying to convict me of heresy and rampant sexual behaviour. He's after me. If you think you are dying, you could retract anything incriminating that you said about me and they will believe you. Please do this for me, otherwise I'll be burned alive. Béatrice, help me if you can. You were always the best." And he is gone. Béatrice slumps back on the bed. Her guts are rumbling into life again and she tries to get up but falls back. Did that happen or was it a dream? It would be just like Pierre, as outrageous as ever, finding a way to speak to her like that. She closes her eyes and falls straight back into a restless sleep. She dreams her children are in danger – her eldest son Bérenger is in grave danger, she must warn him… or is it Bérenger her husband? She must run but her legs won't move. She is hot, very hot. There is something blurred – an image – she can't quite focus on it, near her. The image shimmers and another blurred image moves – now another, and yet another are sharpening into focus. The first image is speaking.

"Madame, can you hear me?"

The image is clearing, it's familiar, the face and voice are the one she has been in the presence of so often recently and now he's here in the attic. Bishop Fournier is telling her something, showing her something. The words are falling into place.

"Brother Gaillard de Pomies, Brother Bernard Seguier, Bernard Gaubert, a jurist and Rainaud Jabbard, a clerk." A pause. "Madame, do you hear me?"

"Yes," she does, and she can see him now. She is looking at him.

"Madame," says the Bishop. "You are... you are gravely ill."

Her eyes move from one face to another. They are surrounding her. She sees that all of them, apart from the Bishop, have their hands over their faces.

"Your end may be close." He speaks carefully, slowly. "And because of that I now ask that if you have concealed anything regarding the heresy in the confessions you made to me, concerning yourself or others, or if you have accused anyone falsely, now is the time to reveal it and exonerate them. I ask you to do this Madame, or your very soul will be in peril."

She moves her head, still bursting with pain and looks at these men of God surrounding her. So they think that she's dying. Her head sinks down. She has a desperate thirst. She croaks out. "Water."

One of the Brothers goes to her and, holding her head, helps her to drink a few sips. The water tastes sweet and delicious and it has gone down without making her sick. She takes some more. She is becoming more aware of the situation. Her shift and the foul sacking that barely cover her are clinging to her and are saturated with sweat and filth. Oh to be washed, clean and fresh.

"Do you hear me, Madame?" says the Bishop. "Do you understand?"

She clears her throat. "Yes," she says. Her voice is shaky and weak but she focuses on the Bishop. What should she say? Should she say she told lies about

Pierre? That could put her in danger. It will probably make no difference now.

"Yes, I remember… it was Raymond Roussel, the steward at the Castle, who told me about God creating the spirits and the Devil directing the world. It was Raymond Roussel who told me that Christ did not descend from heaven and take flesh from Sainte Mary. Raymond told me the ways of the heresy. It was not Pierre Clergue who told me these things but Raymond. Everything else I told you about the priest, Pierre Clergue, and myself is true. I swear to you, upon my soul, that this is the truth."

She sinks back again onto the pallet exhausted by this extreme effort and aware that this is unlikely to make any difference to Pierre's outcome. It's all gone too far for that. And it was expected of her – she had to say something. Does she want to save him? She thinks that's not in her power, she wants to tell the truth and she thinks this is the truth, but her mind may be deceiving her, feeling as weak as she does. The same Brother comes to her and helps her to drink again. Bishop Fournier says, "Thank you, Madame. We will leave you now. We will pray for your soul.

"In Nomine Patris et Filii et Spiritus Sancti. Amen."

He makes the sign of the cross. As they walk away from her, she hears the Brother who gave her the water say, "Pardon me, my Lord Bishop, Madame de Lagleize needs more than prayer. She needs to be cleaned and given fluids. I… also… think she should see the physician we use when one of the Brothers is ill."

"Arrange for the physician to see her, and have both the Lady and the room cleaned and made comfortable," says the Bishop and leaves.

Jean Belmas arrives soon after with more fresh water and he helps her to sip it.

"A physician is to visit you, Madame. I believe he will be here soon," he says.

"Bring more water, please." Béatrice could drink a lake.

"Yes, Madame," says Jean.

There is a knock on the door and he goes to answer it. It's the physician brought up to the loft by the other guard. She watches him as he enters the room. By his appearance, he is not a priest or a monk, but he looks to be a nobleman, quite elderly, probably in his fifties. His face has a shocked expression on it as he glances around the loft. She follows his gaze and sees the filth, the evidence of her illness and the neglect she has suffered. He nods to Jean Belmas.

"Thank you." he says and turns his attention to her. She is aware of how she must look to him, her shaved head with the odd clump of matted hair on her head, the filthy rags that barely cover her. She must look like an old, sick animal whose fur is falling out.

"Madame, what has happened to you?"

He's one of her own kind. He's not a resentful guard, or a slow peasant, nor is he a smug churchman. He's a well-dressed nobleman, and his face and demeanour suggest that he's an intelligent and gentle man. Just to see him there beside her, just to look at his face which, though not conventionally handsome, is pleasant and thoughtful-looking, inspires her with hope. His alert eyes have an intelligent gleam in them and his expression is serious. He listens as she manages to croak out details of her illness.

"From what you have just told me," he says. "I think you will most likely recover now, as long as there is no more diarrhoea or vomiting. It seems that the

256

worst is over. You must drink plenty of water, small sips every half hour. That will replace the fluid that you have lost. After a day and night of fluids, you can progress onto soups and other easily digested food."

"Sire," she says, "the food here is dry bread and stale water, and the foulest of soups and stews..."

"How long have you been here, Madame?"

"I've lost count of time," she says. "Three or four weeks, I'm not sure."

"And you think your illness started two or three days ago?"

"I think so," she says.

"And no-one came to you until today?"

"No, they came so I could make a death-bed confession."

Just his presence and his understanding make her feel better. She'd forgotten that people like him existed.
"I will tell Bishop Fournier, puffed up in his fancy robes, in very strong terms that the lowest cur should not be kept in these conditions," he says. "In fact, no-one should be left in this state, not even the lowest cur. Whatever you have done to upset him, you are deserving of better treatment. From what you tell me of your illness and the neglect you have suffered at the hands of these men of God, I consider that you are fortunate to have survived, Madame."

She wonders whether she might yet live to regret her survival. But the physician gives her hope. Best of all, he is not frightened of the Bishop.

"These damn, pious churchmen," he says to her. "They're more concerned with souls than bodies. I shall tell them that a woman must be sent to wash you, to change your clothes and bedding, and to scrub and fumigate the room. Lavender must be hung around the

257

beams and scattered on the floor with rushes to sweeten the air. I'll remind the Bishop of what the Bible tells us, that 'cleanliness is next to godliness'." He grins at Béatrice. "I'll tell them that you need plenty of sweet, fresh water to replace the fluid you have lost from your body, followed by nourishing gruels and jellies for a few days after that, and then progressing onto more solid but easily digested food, such as fish and eggs for a week or two following that. If they can't prepare them here they must pay a woman to bring them in. There are plenty of good housewives in Pamiers who could do that for money. And then, when you are a little stronger, you must be taken out for short exercise breaks in the fresh air. What about your family, Madame?" he asks.

"I haven't seen or heard from them since I've been here," she tells him. "I have no idea whether they know I'm here or not. What I want most of all is to see my daughters."

"I'll make sure that you do."

And with a smile he leaves her. Béatrice lies back relieved. Just to have spoken to someone who seems to know exactly what to do, someone who is on her side, inspires her with hope. Not long after the physician leaves, a woman arrives with Monsieur Belmas. Béatrice recognises her, it's Alamande, who cut her hair. Alamande helps her to drink from the flask of fresh water she has brought with her.

"Oh my Lord!" says Alamande looking around the room. "This is disgraceful. Get Andre up here, Monsieur Belmas. He can make a start by moving that bucket. And tell him to bring up some hot water, a big jug full, and a bowl. We need brushes for sweeping and scrubbing the floor and walls, and clean fresh cloths and towels for washing my Lady here." She stands with her hands on her hips. "What a mess, Madame. But don't worry, I'll soon get you cleaned up and this place too." She shouts to Monsieur Belmas as he leaves. "This pallet bed needs completely refreshing. Everything must be burned."

Béatrice pulls herself up on her elbows, still weak and shaky, but so relieved to see this woman, with her sensible face and her strong, capable-looking arms. Alamande, although polite, wastes no time over niceties. As soon as the water arrives she sets to and washes Béatrice gently but firmly.

"I've got some soap here." She pulls a bar out of her pocket. "I got it from one of the Brothers. I knew we'd need some and I know they have it. They have all the best things, I can tell you. I clean their living quarters for them and they're not short of comfort, for all they say about leading simple lives. Can you sit up and move to the edge of the pallet, Madame? My, my, you're skinny," she says as she washes Béatrice's body and then rubs her down with a clean towel. "I've brought some old clothes of mine. This shift will be too big on you, but it is clean and will serve the purpose until you can wear your own clothes again. They'll need to feed you up, give you some proper food. I'll bet they've not fed you properly whilst you've been here, have they?"

"No, it's been… dreadful," says Béatrice.

"I'll send some food for you with Monsieur Belmas in a day or two." Alamande helps Béatrice to put on the shift she has brought with her. "He's not the brightest, but he's honest. At least he won't save it for himself. I bet you'd like a drop of homemade soup and bread wouldn't you?"

Alamande chatters on to Béatrice who basks in the luxury of being made clean and fresh by this motherly woman, who is younger than she is, but who is exactly what Béatrice needs. When Béatrice is washed and clothed in the clean shift, the young attendant is bossed around by Alamande, who oversees him, sweeping and scrubbing until all trace of Béatrice's illness has been cleaned away.

"Make sure you keep it like this, Andre," she tells him. "Or your father will know about it." She tells Béatrice, "His father's a real ruffian."

The room is now cleaner than it's ever been, the traces of Béatrice's illness have been scrubbed away, and the dust and cobwebs are gone. A new pallet bed replaces the old filthy one and soft, clean linen covers it. The scent of lavender freshens the air. There are rushes on the floor and Béatrice, freshly garbed in Alamande's old shift, lies on the clean pallet. There is plenty of fresh water to hand.

"Is there anything else I can do for you, Madame, before I go?"

"I can't thank you enough for what you have just done for me," says Béatrice. "I want to ask you…" It's an effort to speak.

"What is it?" says Alamande.

"Well," Béatrice licks her dry lips. "You work for them, yet…"

"You're wondering how I can work for them?" Béatrice nods.

"I'm a widow, Madame," says Alamande. "My husband died five years ago and left me with six children to bring up. He'd been a very fine weaver. The Bishop bought his cloth regularly and when he died they offered me work, which I badly needed. I work for them, that doesn't mean I agree with them."

Béatrice nods, she understands. "There is just one more thing. I think that the physician may have asked already on my behalf, but, more than anything else, I want to see my daughters. I want to know how they and my grandchildren are. Could you ask about this for me?" Alamande nods. Béatrice lies back and closes her eyes. She sleeps.

Chapter 16
Barthélemy

After the deaths of Othon and Béa, my life carried on without me. I was not present. I watched life continue but it all seemed so trivial and pointless. There were a few occasions when this strange detached feeling lifted for a while. Esclarmonde and Condors were wed within a year of each other and I was swept along by their and others' pleasure and excitement. Then it passed and I could not recapture it. In the years following these weddings, my grandsons were born. Their fresh, new beauty and innocence charmed me so completely that when I was with them, they helped me to feel real and alive for that moment. The rest of the time, I had a joyless existence. I was acutely aware of aging, of being in my forties, I felt I was an old woman. My sisters Gentille and Ava were aware of my melancholy and Gentille in particular watched over me, encouraging me to visit as often as possible. She would also continue to encourage me to attend church whenever I stayed with her.

"You know that Ava and Philippa will have a much better chance of making good marriages if you send them to church and to school for instruction," she said.

"Esclarmonde and Condors have both made good marriages without all that," I said.

"Nowadays, it's all the more important that they are seen to be good Roman Catholics. All the best families are strict Romans," said Gentille. "All young noblewomen these days learn literacy and know the Bible, and understand the mass. It's a sign of good breeding. Besides, I think they might want to go. Why don't you ask them, Béatrice?"

I had to acknowledge that there was some truth in this, so I asked Ava and Philippa about it.

"Oh yes, Maman! Can we go?" Philippa was excited. "Brunissende and Eglantine Faure go twice a week. We could go with them, couldn't we, Ava?"

Ava nodded and smiled. "Yes, I'd like to go too," she said.

"I'll go and see the priest and arrange it," I said. I saw that I'd been so bereft that I hadn't been thinking enough about those who were living. I must not let my grief prevent these younger daughters from doing what was normal for them.

I went to see the priest in charge. Guillaume de Montford was a thin, snooty, supercilious man of indeterminate age – he could have been forty or sixty. He looked down his long, rather purple, nose at me.

"Ah, Madame de Lagleize," he eyed me up and down, and his eyes lingered on my body for a moment too long. "We haven't seen much of you in church recently."

I bit my tongue, I didn't want to jeopardise my children's future.

"I know, that's true," I said. "That… well, that will change… I've come to see you about my two youngest children. They would like to attend the school for religious instruction and literacy."

"I'll speak to my assistant priest, Barthélemy Amilhat – he runs the school," he said. "But they must attend church at the same time and you should come with them every week to set a good example." He sniffed and looked contemptuously at me as he spoke. The familiar whiff of piousness wafted into my nostrils.

Ava and Philippa attended the school twice each week. I often walked with them to school and I noticed Barthélemy Amilhat's easy, friendly manner. He was a

263

pleasant man in his mid-twenties with dark brown, shining eyes. His hair was thick and black, his beard neat, and his even, facial features were good-looking. After a few weeks, I asked him how the girls were progressing.

"Very well, they're doing very well, Madame. They are good girls," he said. "I would like them to attend church every Sunday now they are learning so much about their religion. It would... it would be good to see you with them too. It would set a good example to your daughters." He smiled a shy smile at me. His teeth were even and white.

"Yes, I think you're right, I've been rather lax of late," I said. I knew that my eyes were shining back at his. It was time to make an effort and I decided that I would go to church to accompany the children. I could make some other changes too. I tidied my storage trunks and hunted out some clothes I hadn't worn for a while. They were too big for me as I'd lost weight and they looked old and worn. I decided to have some new clothes made. I gave away my old clothes and went to visit a woman in the village who sewed and professed to know what the nobility were wearing in Paris. I chose some fabric and looked forward to trying on my new clothes.

The first time I went to church with the children, I saw, when everyone went outside, that the two priests were talking together. They both looked up at me as I gazed at them and I had an uncomfortable feeling that they were talking about me. I looked around for the children who had run off somewhere. Barthélemy came over to me.

"We were just saying how good it was to see you at church with your daughters, Madame," he said. He looked back at the other priest who looked away.

"Oh, thank you," I said.

I felt sure that the old priest didn't like me for some reason and had said something derogatory about me to Barthélemy. It was kind of Barthélemy to come over; he had sensed my discomfort. I gave him a grateful smile. His dark eyes lit up as he smiled warmly back at me. Something passed between us in that moment. I felt as if deep inside me something that had lain dormant was flickering into life. It was like lighting a candle in a dark room. The world was suddenly illuminated.

I could not stop thinking about Barthélemy. A few weeks before I had been with some of my friends and neighbours to the home of a woman called Madame Gaillarde Cuq, who lived in Dalou. Madame Cuq was renowned for telling fortunes and offering folk remedies. Some said she could cast spells. It had been Madame Cuq's view that, as I had stopped bleeding a few months before, I would not have the sort of feelings and desires I was now experiencing about Barthélemy, ever again. Madame Cuq was wrong. I was strongly attracted to Barthélemy. I was uncannily tuned into him and his movements, and I would often encounter him as I walked around the village. Taking the girls backwards and forwards to school and going to church all gained a new significance for me. He was becoming an obsession and I was sure that he felt the same. He threw appreciative looks at me when we were in the crowd outside church and he always made his way over to talk to me. He smiled at me, his eyes sparkling, and I responded, smiling and laughing with him. I even began to wonder if he had cast some kind of spell on me, my feelings were so strong. My spirits, which had been so low over the last few years, lifted. I was thinking less of Othon, and Baby Béa, and a lot more about Barthélemy.

There was a spring in my step and a shine in my eyes. The world looked a better place. I found it difficult to contain my feelings, and was feeling more and more that I must speak to him, tell him.

But could I dare to do this? He was much younger than I was, and a priest, and although I knew, of course that priests were not immune from sexual feelings, I was a noblewoman, and I thought he would be too unsure as to my reaction to say anything to me. Of course I didn't know what his reaction would be either. I should remember that he was required to be celibate. I had had what I now saw as an ill-advised liaison with one priest – was I really thinking of embarking on such a thing again? On the other hand, it was not an uncommon situation. Everyone knew that and everyone accepted that these things happen. I must think carefully though about the whole thing before acting on my feelings. But I could hardly think of anything else, I could not get him out of my mind. I decided the only way was to do something about it, bring it in to the open somehow. And it was up to me to find a way to do this. I must take the lead. Planning how to make this move was a bittersweet pleasure. I could have misjudged the situation and he could be shocked and upset, and reject me. That was unthinkable and would be difficult to recover from. But more and more, I resolved I must take the risk. And an idea began to form in my mind.

I had long considered that I should learn to read and write. As a child, I had taken a few lessons with my brothers with the priest from Unac. This was the priest who remonstrated with my father about wearing the yellow crosses and I didn't like him. He favoured the boys and treated me with contempt, making it clear that he thought it unnecessary for a girl to read. I told my mother I didn't want to go and no-one encouraged me to stay. My lack of literacy had not really been a problem. Apart from the Bible and the Gospels, there was little to read, books were rare and expensive. The main reason I wished I could read and write was to send and receive written messages to and from my sons in Carcassonne, rather than verbal ones, which often became changed or forgotten on the way. Now it seemed like an opportunity to arrange something that I wanted very much indeed – time alone with Barthélemy.

I arranged for Ava and Philippa to stay with Condors for the night, making an excuse about some business I had to attend to which required an overnight stay in one of the other houses. I went down to church where the lessons were held. When the girls came out, I told them to go on alone and I would catch them up. I asked Barthélemy if he would call round to my house that evening, that there was something I wished to talk to him about. He agreed. I knew he understood what this was about.

That evening, when the house was empty apart from Sybille, I began to feel nervous as I waited for him to arrive. Suppose he didn't come? I would feel such a fool, a silly old fool. Then, when I had persuaded myself that he wouldn't come, that I was too old for him, that I was mad, that he would be outraged if I suggested anything to him other than literacy lessons, that he would push me away if I touched him, there was a knock on the door. It was Barthélemy.

"Good evening, Madame," he said. Even as I opened the door, I wondered if it would be someone else, not him.

"Good evening, come in," I said.

267

We stood together in the entrance hall of my house. There was a small silence.

He coughed and said, "You asked me to visit?"

"Yes," I said. "I have been thinking."

"Yes?" he said.

I had planned to ask for literacy lessons, but I stepped forward towards him and looked at him directly. I put out my hands for him to hold. He took them in his and looked at me. He stepped closer and very gently put his hands on my shoulders. I moved towards him and put my face up to his. He put his face down to mine and tentatively kissed me on the mouth. I responded to him and all the old feelings came flooding back through my body. I pulled away and said, "I want you to teach me to read and write."

"I think I can do that," he said.

I lifted my face to him again, we moved together at the same time to kiss and embrace. Our bodies were close.

"Well then, there's no need to say anything further. I thought we were of the same mind," I said, and, taking his hand, I led him up the stairs and into my bedroom.

"When can I come and see you again?" he said, as he prepared to leave.

"I'll try to arrange for the children to go to stay with Condors, or Esclarmonde, again as soon as I can," I said. "They mustn't know of this."

"And I must be careful with old Guillaume, the priest. He doesn't miss much and he's disapproving of such things," he said.

"I don't think he likes me," I said.

"Don't worry about him," he said. "We'll find a way."

268

I kissed him on the lips and he put his arms around me.

"I'm sure we will."

For the first time in a long time, I felt happiness. I had not realised what kind of a half-life I had been leading. It was the sudden contrast with my present happiness that made me see how I had been. I saw that I hadn't been living properly, merely existing. My instincts about Barthélemy had been right and the world was a different place. It was as if the sun shone twice as brightly and the sky was a deeper blue. The spring weather, with bright sunny days and the growth of lush foliage on the trees and plants, the wildflowers blooming, all mirrored my newfound delight in the world. The white scudding clouds on a windy day made me want to twirl around and laugh. I was a girl again, I had energy. Waking up in the morning, I smiled, and I schemed and planned so we could have time together. I brushed my hair and played around with it, plaiting it, tying it up or leaving it to flow down my back. I studied myself in the little mirror that I had owned since I was a girl. There were a few lines around my eyes but my hair was still the same chestnut colour overall in spite of one or two silver threads at the front. I had lost some of my back teeth but my front ones were all intact. My body, in spite of having borne seven children and being no longer fertile, was still shapely, my skin still smooth and soft. Barthélemy seemed to love me as I loved him, but I worried that he may grow tired of me or of the complicated arrangements we had to make to be discreet. We met as often as we could but it wasn't enough.

"I hate having to sneak about like this," he said, as we lay together in my bed one afternoon. "I want all the world to know how I feel about you."

"I know," I said. "I feel the same way, but what else can we do?"

"You know," he said. "Where I come from, Lladros in the Pallars, priests can marry in a civil ceremony, and they and their wives have the same rights as any other married couple. The Church allows it. For a small consideration, they turn a blind eye to it."

"I've heard of this before," I said. "It would be wonderful to live like that. But there are priests everywhere who have mistresses that they live with, or that they visit regularly. Many of those women who live with them as housekeepers are really living with them as wives."

"I know that, of course, but we can't do that," he said. "Until I have my own church, I must live with the priest here. I'm just starting out, so..." his words tailed off as he looked at me and saw me looking so despondent. "I love you, Béatrice, but we'll just have to carry on as we are. We are both in a situation that requires us to be discreet."

"I can't even visit you at your home because you are living with that miserable old priest," I said.

"He's old and difficult, I'll grant you that," he said.

"Difficult!" I said. "He's nasty. He looks down his nose at me, and I'm a noblewoman."

"Yes, he is supercilious," he said. "And he's nosy; he's always gossiping about the villagers."

"No wonder his nose is so long and purple if he's always looking down it and poking it in where it's not wanted. I'm surprised that no-one's squashed it for him. I bet he's said things about me." I looked hard at him. "He has, hasn't he?"

"No, well, not really."

"I can tell that he has! Come on, tell me, what did he say?" I persisted.

"He said... that you used to live in Montaillou."

"Yes, I did – what of it?"

"Well, it's notorious for having many heretics living there."

"He thinks I'm a heretic, does he?"

"Well, not quite that..." he laughed. "Anyway, let's forget about him and just enjoy the time we do have together."

"Yes, you're right, he's a bitter old man," I said. Condors and Esclarmonde arrived one afternoon at my home with their children. I had not expected them and I had arranged for Ava and Philippa to go to the home of their friends, Brunissende and Eglantyne, the daughters of the noble family from the next village. Barthélemy had been there with me for an hour or two and was just preparing to leave when Condors and Esclarmonde walked straight into the front hall. Barthélemy and I were embracing, saying good-bye; we immediately moved apart. Thank God I was dressed but my hair was tumbling down my back in disarray.

"Oh, I wasn't expecting you," I said as I tried to tidy my hair back from my face. I knew immediately that was the wrong thing to say.

"So I see," said Esclarmonde. There was a silence. Barthélemy looked embarrassed.

"Barthélemy is just leaving," I said. "He's been giving me lessons in literacy. I should have learned a long time ago, but I didn't, so I thought now that Ava and Philippa are learning, well, that I should learn as well so that I can write to your brothers." I stopped. I was gabbling and I was only making matters worse.

"Well then," said Barthélemy clearing his throat, "I'll take my leave, Madame." He raked his hand

271

through his hair which was also untidy and he left, bowing his head to them all. I had a sudden urge to burst into hysterical laughter but I managed to control it by kissing the head of my grandson who was in Condors' arms. Thank God for the children – they could be the focus of attention away from me.

"Please excuse me for a minute," I said.

I ran upstairs to my room and sat down on the tumbled bed. I sat still for a minute thinking and then stood up, looked in my mirror and rearranged my hair. I brushed it hard so that it looked calmer and put it up under a head-dress. I smoothed down my kirtle, straightened the bed covers and walked down to face my eldest daughters. I felt like a naughty child preparing to face an angry parent, not the other way round.

"Maman?" said Esclarmonde, looking serious. She was alone in the main reception room of the house.

"Yes?" I tried to smile naturally at her, but, try as I might, my face could not manage it. "Where are the children and Condors?"

"They've just gone out for a walk round the village. Condors has a headache and the children, well…" said Esclarmonde. "It's best they are not here, Maman, I cannot… I cannot just ignore this… I must ask you… what is going on?"

"Esclarmonde, really, there is nothing to say."

"I think there is," Esclarmonde looked flushed, her pretty face was serious and frowning. "The whole village is talking about you. I've… I've tried not to believe it, but now… having just seen him here, with you…"

"You must not pay attention to some gossiping peasants who have nothing better to do with their time."

I must remain composed. "Let me find some refreshment for us."

"Please, Maman, stop it." Esclarmonde looked close to tears.

"Esclarmonde, please, leave me be. I'm sure you can see how happy I am… just leave me…"

"Yes, I can see that, Maman, you have been much happier recently. But what about Ava and Philippa? It's not easy for me to talk of such things with you, Maman and…" Esclarmonde moved towards me and touched my arm. A tear rolled down her cheek. "Maman, he's a priest!"

"Priests are just men, Esclarmonde."

"Oh Maman, people are talking." She sniffed and withdrew her hand from my arm. "Suppose our uncles – your brothers – were to hear of this? They might try to stop him by… violence… they have a reputation for such things, I've heard you say so."

Tears of frustration prickled in my eyes. It was happening again, everyone wanting to control my life and tell me what to do. I took a deep breath to gain control whilst Esclarmonde just watched me.

"No, please, say no more, there's nothing to be done," I dabbed at my eyes with the back of my hand and searched about for a piece of cloth but couldn't find one. I sniffed and said, "I can't change how I feel."

"Maman, please," said Esclarmonde. "The children will be back with Condors in a minute. I'm sure you'll find a way to sort it out. You know it's because we love you… I can't bear to hear the gossip."

Esclarmonde put her arm round my shoulders. Seeing Esclarmonde's face looking so distraught, I said, "Don't worry, I'll… I'll think about what to do."

Late that evening, Barthélemy came back to see me. I let him in quietly as Ava and Philippa were asleep in bed. I knew he would come.

"How are you?" he asked. "I was so worried about leaving you, but I thought the only thing I could do was to go."

"My daughters are not happy with me," I said. "Esclarmonde talked to me after you left today. It seems the whole village is talking about us."

"Um," he said, stroking his beard, "I know, the Rector, de Montford, has spoken to me. He knows about it and he says it must stop."

"I don't want it to stop," I said, tears forming in my eyes.

"Neither do I," he said. He put his arms round me. "We will just have to be more careful."

"And how do you propose we do that?"

"Well, I don't know, perhaps if I just come in the evening, or late at night when it's dark." He looked helpless.

"You know that won't work, can't you think of anything else?"

"Can you?"

"We could leave this village and go somewhere else."

"Where could we go?" he said. "My work is here."

"Oh, I don't know – anywhere! We can't stay here and act as if nothing has happened. Let's just go away for a while, and then when things have settled down, we can decide what we want to do and where we want to be. Then you can find work somewhere else where we can be together."

"I can't stay now," he said. "I must go or de Montford will keep questioning me. I've told him I'll finish it. We must think about what to do for the best over the next few days. I'll come and see you when I can get away."

The next few days were a nightmare as he stayed away. I was thinking constantly about how we might work this out. I tried to continue in as normal a way as possible but I couldn't bear going into the village, so the children walked down to church for their lessons without me. I sent them to church on Sunday by themselves. I tried to do some household tasks but my heart wasn't in it. I spent a lot of time lying on my bed. It was a week later when Barthélemy appeared at my door late one night.

"I've decided," he said, as soon as I opened the door. "I can't stop seeing you, I love you too much. I think we should go to Lladros, if you are willing to go. I should be able to find work there." He embraced me. "I cannot live without you. I want to marry you, Béatrice. Will you come to Lladros with me and marry me there?"

He spoke quickly and he was breathless and red in the face when he stopped. A rush of feeling flooded through my body. It was as if I'd swallowed a large mouthful of strong spirits which caused my fingertips and feet to tingle and throb. I put my hands up to my face. I couldn't speak. He stared at me until I found the words.

"I've been so worried, I thought you had changed your mind about me, but to go to Lladros with you and marry you – that's what I want more than anything."

I kissed him on both cheeks and then all over his face. We both laughed.

"Oh, thank God," he said. "Thank God."

"I think that no-one must know of our plans," I said. "I don't even want to tell Condors and Esclarmonde because I know they'll try to persuade me otherwise. I've been thinking about what I can say if we decided to go away together. I thought I could tell them that I'm going to stay with Gentille in Limoux. Then later, I'll send a message to them to tell them where I am and what's happening. But I want Ava and Philippa to come with us, I can't leave them behind."

My mind was racing now with shock and excitement.

"You've made your mind up?" he said. "You've been thinking about it?"

"I've been unable to think of anything else since we last met and I had that conversation with Esclarmonde. I can't give you up. I knew that if you came to me and asked me, I would go with you wherever you wanted to go. I was just terrified that you would decide you didn't want me."

A day later I went to see Esclarmonde, taking Ava and Philippa with me. Condors was there with her children too, and I was worried they would see through my story and would try to stop me.

"I've decided to go away for a little while," I said. My voice sounded a falsely careless note.

"That's a good idea, Maman," said Esclarmonde, looking carefully at me. She was always the perceptive one. I could not meet her eyes. "I think a change will do you good."

"Where will you go?" asked Condors.

"I'm going to Limoux to stay with Gentille. I don't know how long I'll be there, but I'll send a message so you'll know what I'm doing." I looked at the two younger ones who were looking puzzled. It was the first they had heard about it.

"But Maman," said Ava, an anxious frown on her forehead. "I don't think I want to go to Limoux. Can I stay here?"

"Would you like to stay with me?" said Esclarmonde. "Just for a while until Maman has had a rest?"

"Yes, if Maman agrees." Ava looked at me and I nodded agreement. I saw Philippa frowning.

"What about you, Philippa?" I said. "Do you want to come with me to Limoux for a while?"

Philippa nodded. "Yes, I want to be with you, Maman." Philippa looked down and there was an uncomfortable moment of silence.

"Well then, that's all there is to say." Another strange, cheerful voice came out of me. "A little change… you will enjoy that, Philippa."

I struggled to hold back tears and I turned away from them all and walked out of the room mumbling, "Excuse me, I won't be a moment."

Facing the reality of what I was doing was forcing me to acknowledge the doubts that I had. It was only when I arrived back home that I remembered I hadn't given Condors the incense I had taken with me for her headaches.

In June 1316, Barthélemy gave up his employment as assistant priest at Dalou and I told my servants that I was going away for a while. I spoke to Sybille – I could be truthful with her. Sybille had some news of her own.

"I've been waiting for the right time to tell you, Madame," she said. "And I think this is it."

"What is it, Sybille?"

"I've… well, I've… someone has asked me to marry them, and I... I've accepted." She looked uncertain and embarrassed. "I don't want to leave you,

277

Madame, but, well, I'm not getting any younger and this might be the last chance I get."

"There's no need for apologies or explanations, Sybille," I said. I had been so wrapped up with Barthélemy that I hadn't noticed that Sybille had a suitor. "Who is he?"

"His name is Jean Cervel. He used to be a shepherd but he's given that up now he's in his fifties and he just keeps a few sheep of his own. He lives in Dalou, where he has a little house and some land with pigs and chickens. He is a good man, he was married but his wife died a year or two ago and his children are all grown up. He comes to help with the grape harvest at Crampagna and with the other harvests here. I've known him for some time."

"Oh Sybille, I am so pleased for you. I will miss you, but I want you to be happy and I wish you and Jean much happiness," I said. "I shall be away for a little while, there's a great deal I have to sort out. I don't know when I shall return. It all depends on how things work out."

I arranged for a mule and a muleteer to go with me and Philippa, to carry our belongings to Vicdessos, where we would be joined by Barthélemy two days later. Travelling separately like this we hoped no-one would suspect we were going away together.

Philippa and I stayed at the tavern in Vicdessos where Barthélemy and I had arranged to meet.. Whenever I had the chance to think, doubts about this whole venture came into my mind. I worried that Barthélemy might not arrive and part of me thought it might be better if he didn't. Then Philippa and I could just go to see Gentille and stay there for a while. But I was committed to him and this plan, so whilst we waited for him, I explained to Philippa that there had been a change of plan and that we were going south over the mountain passes to Lladros. It was difficult to know what to say to Philippa about Barthélemy, who had been her teacher and the village priest. I promised her that after we had stayed there for a while we could go to see Gentille, as I had told her we would. Philippa liked her Aunt Gentille and her cousins, and I suspected that this was the main reason why she had agreed to accompany me. I knew Philippa would feel let down by this change of plan, which wasn't a change of plan at all, and I suspected that Philippa would guess that too. Philippa became quiet and sulky after this news. She asked why this was happening now.

"It's become difficult for me to stay in Dalou," I said. "You will understand when you're older."

The same words my own mother had used when I asked difficult questions. I decided to break the news of our wedding at a later date, it would be better done a little at a time. Am I doing the right thing? This question kept forcing its way into my mind. I had a bad feeling about the whole venture. I had no idea what the future at Lladros would be like and dragging Philippa along felt wrong. But then again, I couldn't leave her behind.

When Barthélemy arrived he was in a subdued mood as we loaded up the mule with all our bags and bundles, and started out on our journey. The route took us high up in the mountains over steep and rocky passes. The small white clouds against the deep blue of the sky looked like puffs of freshly washed sheep's wool of fine quality. I took a breath of the pure mountain air and felt exhilarated, only to be downcast when I looked at Philippa, barely thirteen, who was walking alongside me. Questions about what I was taking her to and whether I had done the right thing continued to nag at me. I would miss my other daughters and grandchildren, and so would Philippa. I had friends and acquaintances, people who worked on the estate, jobs to do, responsibilities that I had left behind. What was I doing uprooting myself and Philippa from the comfortable life we knew? I should have thought more about it, given myself more time.

But I couldn't have stayed in Varilhes or Dalou, certainly not with Barthélemy. He would have had to move away, old purple nose would never have allowed him to stay as long as I was there and finding another position may have been difficult if the gossip had spread further. I could weather the talk about myself, but the impact on my daughters worried me. But to give Barthélemy up was unthinkable, so it seemed there was no other way – we had to continue with our plan. These thoughts crowded into my mind as we walked. I tried to dismiss them and concentrate on the fact that I could be with Barthélemy all the time. It was the only thing to do, to go away for a while. I was sure that once we arrived at Lladros and we were married, I wouldn't be plagued by these worries. Things would become clearer when we were there.

We climbed the first pass, the Saleix, with relative ease, but the pass from Couserans to the Pallars was rocky and steep, and made for difficult walking. The stony pathway disappeared altogether at one point and we stumbled and fell on the rocks. The ungainly, burdened mule slipped and skittered, and only just made it over the pass. We were all hot and out of breath when we got over the summit, and we stopped to rest and admire the view of the high peak, l'Artigue, which was close by for a while. The three of us and the mule plodded on towards the Vall de Cardós, an area of rich farmland in a verdant valley. The pleasant landscape uplifted me a little and even Philippa joined in when Barthélemy sang the Lord's Prayer and a tuneful version of Ave Maria as we walked on the track near the river.

We picked up pace, wanting to reach Lladros before evening. But when we rounded the bend in the track and got our first sight of Lladros, my heart sank. It looked such a dark and gloomy place, literally at the end of the road. There was no way through, the track ended there. I had a terrifying thought as I realised this – there was no way out the other side – the only way out would be to go back and I could not do that now. We had at least to stay here for a little while, but I knew immediately that I could not stay there for long. I comforted myself with the thought that this was only a temporary arrangement, we would not be there for long. Besides it was late and nearly dark when we arrived and I was sure that in the sun it would look more hospitable.

But Lladros seemed to be in shade most of the time and there was an oppressive feel to it. The buildings were small and squashed together, and the house that Barthélemy had arranged for us to stay in on the outskirts of the village was tiny and sparsely furnished. I couldn't help it, I began to cry when I saw it. I felt so confused about it all and I made an excuse to Barthélemy that I was very tired and not feeling well, but in truth I was aghast at what I had come to. The house was as small as the one in Prades. For the last fifteen years or so I had lived the life of a well-off noblewoman, so to come to this was distressing and humiliating. What on earth had I done? What had I brought myself and Philippa to? I tried to comfort myself with the thought that I would feel better after a good night's sleep.

There was some truth in that, and I did feel a little better after some rest, although I was restless and sleep did not come easily. The next day, Barthélemy said that he would visit his parents and see if he could find work. This was another concern as I had not met them yet and he had gone to pave the way. I had a suspicion that they knew nothing of Barthélemy's return to Lladros, and the reasons for that return. I knew that he would find it difficult to tell them about me. He was gone for the whole day and came back looking miserable. I knew that something was wrong.

"How are they?" I said.

"It was difficult," he said.

"Tell me."

"It's… well… it's everything," he said, sitting down and putting his head in his hands.

"It's me, isn't it?"

"No, no, it's not you," he said.

"Tell me the truth," I said. "It is me, I know it is."

"Well, yes, that's part of it."

"What else?"

"They were so proud of me becoming a priest. No-one in our family had ever been a priest. They aren't well off and they worked very hard to help and support me. They're strong Romans. They feel I've let them down, I feel I've let them down."

"Do you think that if I went to see them, I could change their minds?"

"No, no, that would make things worse," he slumped further down on the bench. "I feel so bad about this, I'm their only son, their only child and I've let them down."

"Did you even tell them about me?" I said.

"I… I… not in so many words," he said. "But they understood, I'm sure." He added this after seeing me looking at him in disbelief. He pulled me to him and kissed me. "It'll all work out, I'm sure."

I moved away from him. How could he be so weak?

"We should be married as soon as possible then your parents would see that we were committed and they would accept the situation more easily," I said.

"I'm not sure that it would make any difference. They don't understand..." His voice tailed off and I could see he was having trouble keeping back tears, and this made me cry. I'd hardly ever seen a man cry.

"Please don't cry, Maman," said Philippa who entered the room having heard the talking upstairs in the tiny house.

"No, I'm fine, Philippa, really," I said sniffing and wiping away my tears. "It's all so new and different for us here, but I'm sure we'll all settle in soon enough. Anyway we've really got something to look forward to soon haven't we, Barthélemy?"

"Have we? What's that?" he said without enthusiasm.

"Our wedding, of course." I tried to smile brightly at Philippa. "Yes, it's a surprise, we're going to get married!"

It sounded so hollow as I spoke, and as I forced my face into a false smile, I was covering up the fear that what I – what we – had done was wrong. Barthélemy was very quiet as we ate the fish and bread he had brought home for us. After Philippa had left us to go to bed, he told me that he had been to see the local priest.

"I went to see if he could give me some work," he said. "But he couldn't, there is an assistant priest already working here, and unless I wanted to work without pay, there is nothing for me."

"You'll have to earn some money," I said. "The money I've brought with me won't last long otherwise."

"I know that," he said. "So I've got a job as a farm labourer. I will receive food as well as money."

There was a silence. He looked so miserable and I felt so guilty about this whole situation. "Let's plan our wedding," I said in a bright voice.

"Béatrice, you must understand that it will only be a civil ceremony, a legality, to agree to us leaving our money to each other and so we can live here together. I spoke to the priest about that too –well in general terms – and he said that if I donate some money to him, the Church will allow us to have a spiritual blessing as well. But the wedding, well, it won't be like your previous weddings."

We arranged for our marriage to take place the following week. Barthélemy was right. It was a very small affair conducted by a notary at his home. We exchanged vows in front of witnesses, two people who we asked on the street, and little Philippa, who said she wished her sisters could be there. I knew as soon as the wedding was over that nothing had changed. Philippa was bored and lonely without the large group of friends and family and servants we had left behind.

On top of this, I looked at Philippa one day and noticed that she looked flushed. I asked her what was wrong and she told me that she was bleeding. This was her first bleeding and I remembered the words of a Jewess who I once met who had told me that if I were to save her first blood and give it to her husband or any other man, that he would never care for another woman. I explained this to Philippa.

"But I'm not betrothed yet, Maman," she said.

"I think next year or the year after you will be, so we must save your bleeding on a piece of linen and then we will have it for future use. I will keep it safe for you."

I cut a piece of my daughter's undergarment which was stained with blood. As there did not seem to be enough, I gave her another piece of linen so that she could save her menstrual blood on this material. This she did and I dried this fabric with the intention that, when her husband wed her, she would give it to him in a drink by expressing the cloths which I would soak.

"Will I be betrothed to someone here?" Philippa asked.

"No, of course not," I said. "There is no one suitable here, Philippa, we'll be going back soon."

This brought more doubts into my mind. Philippa deserved much better than this. She must be given the best opportunities to make a good marriage, like her sisters. I had been foolish and selfish, my head had been turned by a younger man who was now clearly plagued by doubts himself. But how could I go back on all this? I must decide what to do. But whilst I was still considering this, Philippa said what we were all thinking, "I want to go home, Maman."

"I'll talk to Barthélemy about it," I said. "I want to go back as well."

When Barthélemy came home, he was increasingly tired and uncommunicative. Talking about anything was not easy and when I tried to talk to him about our difficulties it developed into an argument.

"We've only been here five minutes," he said. "And now you want to go home."

"We're both unhappy, all three of us are unhappy, why can't we leave?"

285

"And do what? Have you any idea what I've given up for you? No you haven't. It will be very difficult for me now, having done what I've done, coming here with you, who many consider an old heretic. No-one will take me on as a priest."

"Oh, so I'm an old heretic, am I?"

"Yes, and worse, de Montford was right after all."

"What does that mean?"

"Do you really want to know?" he said. "Because you won't like it."

"Yes, tell me," I said.

"He called you an old heretical whore who would sleep with anyone who asked her."

"And that's what you think too, isn't it?"

He shrugged.

"I can tell you there are better men than you'll ever be who are heretics."

"You should know."

Philippa came downstairs crying. "Stop it, stop it, please don't argue," she said. "I can hear you."

I put my arms round her. "Oh Philippa," I said. "I'm so sorry."

"I don't like it here, Maman," said Philippa. "I miss Ava, and Esclarmonde and Condors, and the baby boys. Can't we go back to Dalou?"

"I know," I said, "I miss them all too. I think it's the only way, Barthélemy, we should go back. There's more chance of you finding work if we go back than if we stay here."

"Maybe you're right," said Barthélemy. "But we must decide soon because if we don't go before the autumn, it will mean staying until spring," said Barthélemy. "Once the weather changes, we won't get over the mountain passes. I will go with you, Béatrice, but I'll have to go wherever I can find work, we won't… we can't… be together."

"I know," I said. "I think I'll go to Limoux with Philippa, and stay with Gentille for a while before we go back to Dalou."

We were a quiet and sad little group as we walked back together over the passes. Barthélemy had sent the word out that he was returning and he was to go to Carcassonne where he heard there might be a position for him.

"It's the only way, Béatrice," he said as we parted. "We can't carry on like this, it's not right for any of us."

"I know," I said, "I just feel so bad about it all, I shouldn't have allowed my feelings to rule me."

"We made a mistake coming here, but we can still meet. I'll send a message when I'm settled."

"Yes, we'll meet soon," I said.

After staying in Limoux with Gentille for a week, Philippa and I went home. I took up my old life again, spending my time between the houses in Varilhes and Dalou. My family were glad to have me and Philippa back. There was gossip for a while afterwards as I knew there would be, but it faded in time. The old priest died soon after and thankfully a new rector was appointed. That made it easier to resume my life and try to put behind me the shameful mistake I had made.

Barthélemy sent messages telling me where he was, as he had promised. He was the assistant priest at the church of Saint Michel in Carcassonne for a year and I didn't see him at all until he moved to become the priest at Saint Cannelle, which was nearer to Dalou. We rarely saw each other as all the reasons which sent us to Lladros in the first place still prevailed. I did not want to upset my family by causing a scandal again and I knew that he wanted more than anything to work as a priest. I suppose that the interlude with me had clarified what was important for both of us. I knew we would never live together as man and wife again. I retained a strong affection for him and I think he did for me too.

In 1319, Barthélemy went to work at Mézerville, a place which was closer still to Dalou. This might have made it easier to meet, but in fact it didn't. I missed the intimacy and companionship of married life and there were times when I longed for him. We did meet a couple of times at a little secluded hostelry called Mas-Vieux, but we both knew that this would not be a regular occurrence. Most of the time, I was realistic and thankful for my family and my home. I resolved to make the most of my life. I had to apply myself to thinking about Ava and Philippa, and their futures. I made a point of attending church regularly, although my attendance did drop off after a while. But overall, I became busy and happy with family life once again.

It was 26th June 1320, when I received a visit from my notary, Pons Bole. The maid told me that Monsieur Bole was here on an urgent matter and was in the entrance hall. I went to meet him and he looked serious and worried.

"Madame," he said, "I must speak with you… an urgent and private matter."

"Monsieur Bole," I said and took him into a room where we would not be overheard by anyone. "What is the matter?" I asked, as soon as we were in the room and had closed the door. He frowned and wrung his hands.

"Madame, I'll not waste any time on small talk," he said. "My contacts in Foix tell me that the Bishop in Pamiers, Jacques Fournier, has been questioning witnesses about you and your... er, your... time in Montaillou and about people you may have known there." He stumbled over this phrase but cleared his throat and carried on. "I fear it is very likely that you are to be arrested on charges of heresy."

"Oh no, no, no." I held my head in my hands. At the back of my mind the ghost of this possibility had always lurked – now it was staring me in the face and it terrified me. "What should I do? I don't know what to do!"

"My advice is to go away as far as possible and lie low for a while to avoid the summons," he advised.

I just looked at him. I was so stunned that I was unable to think.

"I must leave you, Madame," he said, "Otherwise I risk arrest myself."

"Yes, yes, of course." I realised what he said was true. "And... thank you, for coming to warn me. I am extremely grateful to you."

I showed him out of the house and went back into the room where I sat and tried to think for a few minutes. It was difficult to think straight and I was unsure of what was the best course of action. I wasn't guilty of anything, was I? I didn't feel guilty, but my instinct was to flee. But if I left, then it may seem as if I was guilty. But just to sit and wait for the summons didn't seem right either. I must talk to someone. I couldn't involve my daughters, or my sons-in-law, and my friends and neighbours in Dalou and Varilhes, well... perhaps they couldn't be trusted, after all someone must have spoken out about me. There was

289

only one person I could talk to. Thank God, he was close by.

I paced around my bedroom until the early hours when I finally lay down and managed to sleep until dawn. The next morning, I sent one of the young farm labourers to Mézerville, with a message for Barthélemy, asking him to meet me. He sent a message back telling me to go to Mas-Vieux, the small hostelry just to the north of Rieux-de-Pelleport, where we had met once before when he had first moved to Mézerville. It was well off the beaten track and it was kept by an old monk who would give us food, and who could be trusted to be discreet.

The messenger also told me that Barthélemy could not get away on Sunday, and on Monday he had some other tasks to undertake, so it had to be Tuesday. That was the earliest time he could see me. So I had to wait until Tuesday. Those two days were an agony of waiting, but no-one came to arrest me and early on Tuesday morning I set off alone from Dalou. I was relieved that I was actually doing something. It had felt as if I was just waiting to be arrested. Now, I was taking action and I felt better. It was a morning's walk from Dalou to Mas-Vieux, and I made good speed. There, on the track leading to the hostelry, we had arranged to rendezvous. Barthélemy appeared from an overgrown tangle of bushes and brambles at the side of the track as I arrived at the spot. He came up to me and kissed me after looking around.

"Oh, Barthélemy," I said. "It's so good to see you."

"Let's make our way to the hostelry and see what Brother Michel has for us to eat," he said.

He took my hand and we walked on until we reached the hostelry. It had been part of a larger priory, but now the monks had a new building near Pamiers, Mas-Saint-Antonin. This place was maintained as an occasional stopping place for travellers, and for the vineyards which belonged to the monks. It was in a fertile valley and much of the food for the monks was grown there too. The building was old and dilapidated and sat in the midst of the vineyards, surrounded by outbuildings, where the business of wine-making took place. There was no-one else there at that time apart from Brother Michel, and a boy and a woman who helped him maintain the place. Brother Michel came out to welcome us as the big, old mountain dog that guarded the place barked on our approach.

"Hush, Chief." Brother Michel patted the dog. "Welcome to you both, have you had a good journey? You've timed it well – the meal is nearly ready." He showed us into the dining room.

The dining room was furnished with rustic, peasant furniture, a round table and chairs. A flask of water and some bread and wine was brought to us by the kitchen boy. We sat at the table opposite each other, and, catching each other's eyes, we both smiled. A door leading to the outside yard was wedged open with a flowerpot in which a red geranium bloomed. A big ginger cat lay sprawled in the sun in the doorway. It had opened its eyes and stretched as we entered the room. Sunlight poured through the open door and tiny specks and flecks of dust and pollen floated weightlessly in its rays. Mas-Vieux was a beautiful sanctuary, far away from anywhere else, on the plain near the river. It was like opening a door into another kingdom where the Inquisition didn't exist, and the Roman Church and its rules about celibacy didn't apply. I felt the magic of the place and I smiled at Barthélemy. I decided to prolong the illusion for as long as I could and Barthélemy didn't ask any questions.

Brother Michel appeared. "There's a stew of lamb to start with," he said. "It's flavoured with a cinnamon sauce, followed by trout, pork and crisp pancakes, with raisins and nuts to finish – and of course our wine."

"Are you settled at Mézerville now?" I asked Barthélemy when the monk had left us.

"Yes, I like it there, I think it's the best place I have been. The rector is a good man, but there is always a lot of work for me to do. He's getting old now, so I take on the majority of the work."

The stew in a pot was brought in by Brother Michel.

"It's hot," he said. "I've just lifted it out of the fire. It's this season's lamb. I hope you like it."

We both concentrated on eating our food. The lamb just dropped off the bone and each succulent bite melted in my mouth. After a few mouthfuls, I sat back for a moment.

"It seems a long time since we last met," I said.

"It must be about a year," he said. "How is everyone?"

"Ava will marry later this year," I told him. "And Philippa next year, she is betrothed. He's a young nobleman from Limoux. Gentille helped to arrange it."

After the meal we walked back to Rieux-de-Pelleport in the afternoon sun. After passing through the hamlet of Benagues, we walked along holding hands. It was very hot and the rhythmic sound of the cicadas was particularly loud. The vineyards on either side of the road stretched out in a long, hazy line to the mountains behind. There was not a soul about.

Barthélemy stopped and faced me with his hands on my shoulders.

"I miss you, Béatrice," he said and kissed me. "You taste of wine," he said, kissing me again.

"I think I'm a little drunk."

"Let's go off the road for a stroll. I want you so much," he whispered in my ear, as we picked our way hand-in-hand through the vines. "Let's sit down over there," he pointed to a spot on the far edge of the vineyard where a spreading fig tree cast some shade. I carefully followed him through the closely planted vines. In the shade of the fig tree and next to the vines, we lay down together on a sandy patch of earth. He removed his priest's tunic and made a little pillow with it for my head. The bunches of ripening grapes hanging close by exuded a juicy, honeyed scent which wafted over us as we lay together. I breathed in the familiar scent of him as I lay back and gave myself up to him. The noisy cicadas masked the soft sounds of our love-making.

We lay together for a short while afterwards, drowsy with wine, heat and sex. I felt so happy and at ease with him, I wished I could stay like that forever – but I had a sense of time running out – the past was catching up on me. I had to face it. So, when we roused ourselves and walked along the road together, I told him of Pons Bole's visit and his warning.

"Should I go and see the Bishop if he sends for me, or should I flee before he sends for me?"

"Are you guilty of anything that he might accuse you of?" he asked.

"No, I don't feel guilty of anything. I'm not a heretic, nor have I ever been," I said.

"Well then, go and see him. He is known to be an honourable man, completely incorruptible and rigorous. He would not do you an injustice."

The letter of citation from the Bishop came a day later. I was commanded to appear for questioning on Saturday 26th July 1320, at the Episcopal Palace in Pamiers. I consulted with my local rector, who gave the same advice as Barthélemy - to attend. He promised to accompany me along with the Archdeacon of Mallorca, who happened to be staying with him at that time. They promised to intercede on my behalf. I listened to their advice, the same as Barthélemy's, and, going against my own instincts, the three of us set off early on that morning of 26th July 1320.

Chapter 17
The Final Interrogation

Béatrice is regaining her health and strength through Alamande's nourishing food, fresh air and exercise, and the love and company of her family – all have played their part. She wears her own clothes and, although still thin, she fills them more than she did a month ago. Her hair has grown from spiky stubble into soft curls and with these changes a firmer sense of her old self is emerging. But hovering on the horizon is the ordeal of further interrogations to be faced. The Bishop will send for her again, but she doesn't know when. It is a desperate time for her knowing that sooner or later she will face him and he will decide what will happen to her. Will he find her guilty? And of what? She goes over in her mind what she has confessed to him. Surely he will see she was not and never has been a heretic. But she listened to them, and she associated with them, and she gave goods and money for their support. Others may have told him about her, others may have exaggerated or told lies to save themselves. The burden of guilt about what she told the Bishop of Pierre Clergue is still heavy. Even though he has done bad things, many bad things, she hates that she betrayed him. And Barthélemy, well, he would not have been taken if wasn't for her. She will have to say something about him and vows to make it clear that he was not involved in the heresy. She was desperate, she still is. She does not want to die, she has too much to do for her youngest daughters, and there's the grandchildren – and there will be more of them. Barthélemy will have been questioned and will have spoken, he must have spoken about her. They will have questioned him about her. Will he have blamed her for his actions? He must be very angry with her – if it wasn't for her, he would not be imprisoned. If she hadn't insisted that he walk with her…

Her patience and her hopes have been so tried over the past months that she lives now with very few expectations. The next interrogation will happen when the Bishop wants it to happen. And one day it does. Monsieur Belmas enters the loft and announces, "Madame, the Bishop will see you now."

Béatrice stands and looks at him. "I'm ready."

He takes her to the grand chamber, the place where she was first interrogated by the Bishop. There are a lot of people in the hall. The Bishop has the detestable Brother Gaillard de Pomies, looking fat and smug, sitting next to him at the same table. Béatrice walks to face them and bows her head. The Bishop gestures with his hand, sit. The crucifix is facing her just as she remembers from that first interrogation. She doesn't look up at it but glances at the two men facing her. Gaillard de Pomies is staring at her, his eyes travelling up and down her body with an expression of contempt on his overfed face as Bishop Fournier speaks.

"Madame, we are in the company of Guillaume Peyre-Barthe, my notary and Bernard Adalbert, notary for the Inquisition." He gestures in turn to each of the laymen sitting at either end of the table. She looks at each of the men as he introduces them. They are dressed in plain, well-cut tunics made of good-quality wool cloth. They are clearly noblemen and not clerics. This gives her some hope; maybe they will be more sympathetic to her plight than the clerics. They are both elderly but look alert and attentive, and very serious.

He does not introduce any of the others who are present. She identifies them by their virtue of their black-and-white habits to be monks and priests of the Dominican order, the founding order of the Inquisition. There must be about ten or so of them. They are standing to the side and at the back of her, on the periphery of the chamber. The Bishop, directly facing her, looks massive in his embroidered robes, but his eyes are fierce and intelligent looking in that plump, pasty face.

"Madame, as some time has passed since we last met, I require you to swear an oath to remind you of why you are here, and to remind you that you must speak the truth. Repeat after me." He says the words of the original oath that she swore and she repeats them.

"When you were ill and thought to be at the end of your life, I questioned you about your evidence. You then retracted parts of your statement. I ask you now if that retraction was the truth?"

"Yes, it is the truth, as is everything else I told you," she says.

"Why did you flee when I summoned you to appear here before me accused of heresy?"

"I fled out of fear, my Lord Bishop," she says. "And above all because, when I first appeared before my Lord Bishop, my father's name was mentioned, and my father was accused and convicted of the crime of heresy. I knew that I would be summoned, and I asked Barthélemy Amilhat, a priest, with whom I undertook a marriage ceremony in Lladros– " She looks at him for his reaction, aware that this is the first reference she has made to Barthélemy. The Bishop shows no reaction. Béatrice continues. "–I asked him what I should do if I were cited for heresy by my Lord Bishop. I asked him if I should flee and he asked me if I felt guilty. I told him that I did not. Besides which, he would have known if I was, because I would have spoken about this to someone I had been so close to and whom I had loved so much. Barthélemy told me that as I was not guilty, it would be better to appear before my Lord Bishop, as my Lord Bishop would not do me an injustice. Then, when I did appear, I was terrified by this mention of my father, fearing that because of him, you had already judged me guilty. Therefore, I decided on my return to Dalou, that I should leave the area. I collected my belongings together but I did not tell anyone about it. On the contrary, I told my daughter Esclarmonde that I would appear before my Lord Bishop on the appointed day."

Béatrice relates what happened between her and Barthélemy, how they met and stayed at Belpech, and how they arranged for her to stay at Mas-Saintes-Puelles until he could come and take her to Limoux to be with her sister, Gentille. She says that she insisted she could not come back and face the Bishop again, even though Barthélemy encouraged her to do so. She tells how they were arrested by the Bishop's men on their way there. He listens intently. She is loathe to do this, to speak of Barthélemy, but she cannot think how else to help him.

"Madame, when you were arrested, certain objects were found amongst your belongings. There were two umbilical cords of infants found in your purse, linens soaked with blood which seemed to be menstrual, in a bag of leather, together with a seed of colewort and seeds of incense slightly burned. There was also a mirror and a small knife wrapped in linen, the seeds of a certain plant wrapped in muslin, a dry piece of millet bread, written formulas and numerous morsels of linen. These objects are strongly suggestive of having been used by you to cast spells, which would therefore cause suspicion that you are a witch and familiar with casting spells. Can you explain for what purpose you carried these articles, Madame?"

"I have the cords of the eldest male children of my daughters and I preserve them because a Jewess, since baptised into the Roman Church, told me that I should carry them with me and if I were to have a lawsuit with anyone, I would win. I have not had the occasion to test this out." She pauses here for a moment and looks at him before telling him why she had the blood-soaked linens and the incense in her bag. "I did not intend to use it for casting spells. The mirror and the wrapped knife, no more than the morsels of linen, are not destined for casting spells. As for the seed wrapped in muslin, it was given to me by a pilgrim – it was for my grandson, Condor's son, who suffered from the falling sickness last year. I forgot to give it to her." She pauses, takes a breath and says, "I thought of these things as simple remedies and charms that are used by many people to deal with ailments and the difficulties of life."

"Have you cast any evil spells, taught them or learned them from anyone?"

"No, I have not, but I believed sometimes that Barthélemy, the priest, had cast some sort of spell on me because I loved him to distraction and I desired too much to be with him. I asked him several times about this but he always denied it." There, she's said it, it had to be said, she didn't want to say it but she could not be found guilty of witchcraft any more than she could of heresy. He nods and there is a short silence during which he looks steadily at her.

"Madame, I now require you to swear under oath that you repent and abjure all heresy against the Roman Church. Will you do this now, Madame?"

"I will, my Lord," she says and goes on to repeat after him. "I, Béatrice, appearing for questioning before you, Reverend Father in Christ, my Lord Jacques, by the grace of God, Lord Bishop of Pamiers, abjure entirely all heresy against the faith of our Lord Jesus Christ and the Holy Roman Church, and all beliefs of heretics, of whatever sect condemned by the Roman Church, and especially the sect to which I held, and all complicity, aid, defence and company of heretics, under pain of what is rightfully due in the case of a relapse into judicially abjured heresy. I swear and promise to pursue, according to my power, the heretics of any sect condemned by the Roman Church, and especially the sect to which I held, and the believers, deceivers, aiders and abetters of these heretics, including those I know or believe to be in flight for reasons of heresy. And to have them arrested and deported according to my power, to my Lord Bishop or to the Inquisitors of the heretical deviation at all times and in whatever places that I know the existence of the above said, or any one of them. I swear and promise to hold, preserve and defend the Catholic faith that the Holy Roman Church preaches and observes. I swear and promise to obey and to defer to the orders of the Church, of my Lord the Bishop and the Inquisitors and to appear on the day, or days fixed by them, or their replacements, at all times and in whatever place that I receive the order or request on their part, by messenger or by letter, or by other means. To never flee nor to absent myself knowingly, and to receive and accomplish, according to my power, the punishment and the penance, that they have judged fit to impose on me. And to this end I pledge my person and all my worldly goods."

The Bishop bows his head for a moment before speaking. "I shall keep you here until you are sentenced. You will be retained in the loft and you will be allowed certain privileges. You may continue to have visitors and to take exercise outdoors. I shall send for you when sentencing has been decided."

"When will that be, My Lord?" she asks.

"You will be sent for when we are ready," he says. "Now, let us pray for forgiveness for all our sins."

She bows her head and makes the sign of the cross. As she does so, she remembers what Guillaume Authier was supposed to have said about making the sign of the cross. If required to do this then you should say to yourself, 'This is my forehead and this is my beard, this is my left ear and this is my right ear.'

"In Nomine Patris et Filii et Spiritus Sancti" says the Bishop.

"Amen," she responds automatically. She cannot stop a small smile from passing momentarily across her lips. Even Bishop Fournier cannot control her thoughts.

Chapter 18
Sentencing

Béatrice waits for sentencing. She looks at her reflection in the mirror which has been returned to her in her bag. Her hair is growing, the rich chestnut has faded and there are white streaks in it now. The short, loose curls frame her pale face. There are lines around her face and mouth, and her cheekbones are prominent as flesh has dropped off her face. Her teeth are still strong at the front but she has lost some at the side and back. She looks older, her time in the loft and her illness have aged her. It has been seven long months since she was arrested with Barthélemy and the world has changed. As she awaits her fate, she has little to occupy her time apart from some needlework brought in by her daughters, and her own thoughts. The visits from her family are regular now and she is brought fresh, wholesome food: fish, cold meat, cheese and fruit.

The attic, although still shabby, is now kept clean. A clean pallet has fresh linen on it which is changed regularly. The layers of cobwebs and filth have been swept away and a rough wooden screen hides the bucket in the corner which now has a cover on it. It's winter and very cold. Béatrice spends much of her time wrapped up in her old fur-lined mantle. She is allowed the freedom of a daily walk around the ramparts accompanied by a guard. She often wonders if she will meet Pierre or Barthélemy, but she never does. She looks down at the street scene in Pamiers as she meanders around the ramparts. People walk, talk to each other, carry baskets and babies, lead donkeys and mules. Old people, bent over, move slowly; children skip and run. No-one looks up and sees her as she walks, accompanied by a guard and occasionally by one

302

of her daughters. She ponders on the lives of the people she sees below. They are busy with their ordinary daily activities.

These weeks are tedious, but in her mind she confirms what is important to her and what will continue to be, if her life is spared, as she expects that it will. The ghosts of the past flit around her room during these weeks. She sees them out of the corner of her eye. Some of them hover for a long time until she faces them. Her parents, dead for some time, her mother's advice – that long ago conversation they had – 'you must be careful... the penalties are too severe,' she said. Just this, all she has been through in this familiar place, this is enough of a penalty. Surely the Bishop will see that.

A yellow spectre looms large for a while, in her dreams, animated and forever behind her, chasing her. It's the yellow crosses. She can never leave them behind, there has been no escape from them, they have always been there. They are indelibly etched on her mind. The ghosts of her childhood, her brothers and sisters, friends, neighbours, they are there too. Now, she sees other routes she could have taken – if she hadn't married Bérenger and gone to Montaillou... if she hadn't allowed Pierre into her life... if she hadn't married Barthélemy. Men told her what to do – her father, her brothers, Pierre – she was expected to comply. She sees the men who desired her. The château of Montaillou looms before her on its rocky plateau, surrounded by mist and mountains.

It has always been a case of dealing with the next thing that fell in her path. There are few regrets. Happiness? Yes, there has been happiness. She thinks of Pierre and their times together, arguing about and discussing religion – they shared some happiness, but it was wrong, sinful and, since then, he has descended into a degenerate way of life. He has done some truly bad things. She laughed with Bérenger, argued with Barthélemy. There were good times with Othon too, her memories of him are generally good. Her two sons now living far away and brought up by the de Rocquefort family, they have wives and children of their own now but she doesn't know them. She recalls the joy of her first-born son, her daughters, and now her grandsons. Bringers of joy and sorrow all of them, but mostly of immeasurable love and joy. Thoughts of her losses, her parents, two husbands and a beloved daughter, bring tears to her eyes. But she does not dwell on this. Some women lose many children; she has been fortunate in this respect. These thoughts lead onto the same vexed questions of God's existence and the purpose of life. Will God save her, or will He be angry with her for her doubts and questions? She cannot hide her doubts and lies from herself or God, she can only be true to herself in her own mind. If there is a God, this most blasphemous of all thoughts worries her, can He see into her heart? Does He even care about her? Above all, she wants to live, to be with her family. Simple things: the countryside, meadows, vivid blue sky behind snowy, white mountains. Good food and wine, the children. Béatrice vows again and again that she will behave like a good Roman in future, going to church, crossing herself, staying out of trouble, whatever she believes inside – she could never, and will never, blindly have faith.

It is the fifth of March 1321 when Béatrice next appears before the Bishop, and Brother Jean de Beaune, Inquisitor. The Palace, the procedure, the people are all so familiar to her now. This time she is taken to the small room that she went to previously, where the large crucifix bears down on them. If it had been a figure of the Virgin, another woman, would that have made any difference?

The Bishop is alone on this occasion. He seems bigger and fatter than ever, his face pasty and bloated. He must eat and drink a lot, and spend a lot of time sitting on his backside. He doesn't have to harvest and thresh the grains for his daily bread, or pick and prepare the grapes for his wine. Women will clean his rooms and wash his linen. He will snap his fingers and people will attend to him. He doesn't have far to walk to church. If he is ill, he will receive the best of attention.

He speaks. "Madame, I have the evidence and the confessions you have made concerning yourself and others, and the oaths you have sworn in regard to the Church, and in the matters of heresy and heretics. Is there anything that you would add to this?"

"No," she says. "Except that I have spoken the truth and told you all I know, and I ask only for judgement to be passed according to these facts and, and…" here she stumbles. "And that I be shown mercy." She looks up at the figure of Christ as she says this and then closes her eyes. A tear runs down her face. After all she has been through, surely He will be merciful. If He exists.

"I have assigned to you a day when your sentence will be passed." The Bishop is speaking again. "It is Sunday 8th March. You will be taken to the Dominican friary here in Pamiers. From there, you and others will be taken to the cemetery of Saint Jean, Martyr of Pamiers, where sentence will be passed in public. In the meantime you will remain in my custody, here in the loft of the Bishopric."

This is the usual procedure and now there are only a few days until she knows her fate. She is strangely calm and resigned during this time. She has survived thus far and knows it is unlikely she will lose her life. That is reserved for Perfects and those who are impenitent. She has sworn her penitence.

Sunday morning arrives, 8th March, 1321. Béatrice is taken down early in the morning through the Palace to walk the short distance to the Dominican friary accompanied by two guards. They walk through the quiet streets of Pamiers. There is no-one about at this hour. She is calm and composed. It is a cold and misty day for the time of year and she is wrapped in her fur-lined mantle. It is old, worn and moth-eaten now and she thinks she will have a new one after this. When this is over.

As they approach the cemetery, they meet the other prisoners who are to be sentenced too. Amongst them is Barthélemy Amilhat. They see each other simultaneously. Their eyes meet. The shock of this hits her like a punch in the guts and takes her breath away for a moment. Her heart thumps hard in her chest and a flush rises from deep inside and suffuses her face. So many feelings are entangled together, like several strands of wool, so impossibly intertwined and knotted that they can't be teased apart. Tears start in her eyes. She sees through her tears that he turns away.

They turn a corner and amongst the crowd of prisoners she sees another familiar form and face, limping and struggling to keep up. It's Alazaïs Azema, her friend from Montaillou. From the glimpse she has of her, Alazaïs looks a lot older, her face thin, pale and lined. She must have been in prison too.

The Bishop, the Inquisitor and other churchmen, many Dominicans wearing the familiar black-and-white robes, now lead the procession. The embroidered banner of Saint Dominic, the founder of the Dominicans and the originator of the Inquisition, is in front. The banner carries the words "Justice and Mercy" under a depiction of Saint Dominic, carrying a sword in one hand and an olive branch in the other. Behind this banner is a large crucifix carried on high. They are compelled to walk on with the guards to the cemetery of Saint Jean, next to the friary, where a large crowd awaits the spectacle of sentencing, hoping for blood, no doubt.

The sentences are passed, Béatrice de Lagleize – condemned to the Wall of Carcassonne, the prison, in perpetuity. Barthélemy Amilhat, priest and husband, also condemned to the Wall of Carcassonne in perpetuity. Alazaïs Azema condemned to the Wall in perpetuity.

The words hang in the air. Condemned. To the Wall. In Perpetuity.

They fly at her and cling to her. They are around her neck, strangling her. They are pressing on her head, causing it to ache so fiercely that her eyes cannot see. They are on her arms and legs, paralysing her. She folds under the impact of them.

She comes to, shaken awake by the rattle of her bones as her body is flung around roughly. This movement is all she can feel for a minute, she lifts her head and looks around. She's in a large cart – in the bottom of the cart – surrounded by feet. The feet belong to others who are sitting along the sides of the cart. Her hands are tied behind her back and she struggles to change her position. Somehow she raises herself up, helped by someone's feet until she is leaning against the legs that are near her. She looks at the others and sees that Barthélemy is one of them. He doesn't speak to her, he turns his head away from her. He must bitterly resent his involvement with her. The others look like hard-working peasants, their faces browned and lined by the sun. Their hands roughened by their work. Men and women dressed in peasants' working clothes. Alazaïs is amongst them. Alazaïs has an empty look on her face, eyes looking far away into the distance. One of the men speaks to no-one in particular.

"Well, that's it now. We might as well be dead. Life in prison isn't any life – maybe burning would be better than this."

She remembers now what she heard in the cemetery and she closes her eyes.

Chapter 19
Inside Alleman's

"I thought we were going to Carcassonne, to the Wall," says a man.

"We are, aren't we?" replies another.

"No, Carcassonne is that way." He gesticulates with his head, "We're going in the opposite direction. Look at the sun." They all look up towards the sun in a sideways glance as it is shining high in the sky as midday approaches. "See, the sun is high, I know, but I can tell which way we're going," the man says.

"I recognise this road," says another man.

"Where are we going then?" Says an old woman.

"To Alleman's Gaol, south of Pamiers, I think," says the first man.

"Why are they doing that?"

"I don't know, but I've heard that Alleman's is not as bad as the Wall."

"Perhaps it means they're not going to keep us for long," says another.

"How do you work that out?"

The discussion continues, but Béatrice hasn't the strength to join in. She listens but she knows it may not mean anything, this ride to Alleman's. It just means we are going to Alleman's. They can do whatever they want with us. We will find out what they want us to know, if and when they want us to know. We can only accept what is given to us. The words of the sentence have defeated her. She is light-headed as if she may swoon again. She concentrates on her head, trying to keep it still.

Alleman's Gaol, just outside Pamiers, is a tall, looming stone château with high window openings covered by bars. It is a dark and forbidding place. They are taken through an entrance, guarded on each side by a sentry in a small stone building. Immediately in front is a huge portcullis, which is raised to allow them entry into an inner court. The cart rumbles through as the iron grid is raised. The grid cranks back down behind them slowly, but with relentless certainty as to where it is going. There is a terrible finality to it, the falling back of that grid as it grinds and clinks into place. She is a prisoner again. Guards appear and shout at them.

"Out, you lot, come on, look sharp – you too."

She is pulled up roughly by a guard as the other prisoners jump and stumble out of the cart. Her legs are weak and will not support her as she is pulled down from the cart. She ends up on the ground. Barthélemy, held by a guard, sees her fall and starts to struggle. Another guard moves over to help restrain him.

"No point in struggling," says the guard.

A guard grabs Béatrice's arm and pulls her up again to a standing position. This time her wobbly legs support her. She looks at Barthélemy helplessly. He looks away.

"Men over here with me," shouts a guard.

"Women with me," says another.

Each group is pushed and pulled towards a narrow door in a corner of the courtyard. Men to one, women to another. The doors each lead to a steep stone staircase. Béatrice, Alazaïs and two other women are herded down until they reach the bottom level, the dungeons, where an iron door leads into a large square room with doors to the cells all around it. As they descend the stairs a foul stench hits them. It is the stink of urine, human excrement and dirty bodies, merged with the rancid odours of rotting food, and the vermin that infest the place. One of the women stops and

310

retches. She is pushed on. They halt. Béatrice's hands are untied and a double door to one of the cells is unlocked by the guard. Béatrice is flung into the cell and the doors slam closed behind her. She lands on the stone floor where she remains for a moment. She hears a voice from within the dark recesses of the cell.

"Madame?"

She lifts her head. Her eyes take a minute or two to adjust to the darkness of the cell. She blinks and sees the figure of a young woman sitting on a pallet, which is against the back wall of the small cell. As she becomes more accustomed to the darkness, she can see that the young woman's head has been shaved and there is a fine growth of wispy hair on her scalp. She has a pale face and her big dark eyes are fringed with long, dark eyelashes which gives her a bovine, passive look. She would be pretty without the dark circles under her eyes and with her hair grown. Her skin is ghastly pale, almost grey. She is wearing a grubby kirtle made of rough-looking linen.

"Who are you?" says Béatrice.

"Grazide," says the young woman.

"Grazide?" says Béatrice.

"Yes, Grazide Lizier, I think we are to share this cell, Madame."

Béatrice can feel her mind working slowly, slotting together what the young woman has told her, making sense of it, trying each piece of information until a picture begins to form. It was like doing a wooden puzzle that Raymond Roussel helped one of her sons make once, long ago. The painted pieces all fitted together to make a picture. Now she has it.

"Grazide, Fabrisse's daughter?"

"Yes, that's right," says the young woman. "I know who you are, they told me this morning you were coming. You're Madame de Lagleize, my mother's friend."

Béatrice pulls herself up, she is trembling. Grazide moves over to her and, taking her arm, she helps Béatrice to stand.

"Come and rest here," says Grazide. "You look exhausted. We must share this pallet, there's only one."

Béatrice moves slowly across the small space and obediently lies down. "I think I will rest for a while," she says. "I feel so tired." She closes her eyes and falls into a deep sleep.

She is woken up by someone gently shaking her. It's Grazide. "Madame," she says. "You have slept for several hours and we have been brought some refreshment. It's not much, just bread and water, but it's all we will get for today, so I thought I'd wake you so could refresh yourself."

Béatrice slowly sits up and takes the water that Grazide offers her. "Thank you," she says.

"You must keep your strength up as best you can in this place," says Grazide. "You never know when you might need it."

Béatrice gives her a questioning look. "For what?" She says.

"They might just fling open the door one day and say, you're free." Grazide laughs.

"Not for me, they won't," says Béatrice. "I'll never be free, my sentence is imprisonment in perpetuity." She speaks quietly.

"You must never give up hope, Madame," Grazide says. "Hope keeps me going, it helps me to sleep at night and to wake up in the morning. It helps me to eat and drink, and to walk and talk with the others here. People do leave here all the time. If you have family and friends working for you outside then

312

it's possible they may secure your release. There are prisoners in here that have better treatment than others, and it's because they or someone they know outside has bribed the warden, or someone else with power and authority. Bernard Clergue is here and he's forever wandering around trying to get people to change their testaments about himself and his brother, Pierre. They say he bribes the warden, that's how he has such freedom. You will learn how things work in here and one day, well, you never know what could happen. You are a noblewoman with more influence than us peasants, so don't give up hope, Madame." Grazide sits down next to her. "It's not so bad you know, we can walk around in the main hall there." She points to the inner hall. "There are many people you will know here from Montaillou."

Grazide is probably right to say she must not give up, though at the moment she does not have it in her to feel any hope. The shock of the sentence has overwhelmed her and she needs time to recover from that. She must rest some more. She settles down on the shared pallet with Grazide, and the young woman's warm body comforts her and she sleeps again.

The following morning after more bread and water, they are required to empty their bucket, which she notes at least has a cover over it, and they are expected to sweep and wash the cell floor. They are given water but no soap to wash themselves and the cell. They are given a candle which will be lit for them later. They are allowed out into the inner courtyard for exercise and there they mingle with the other women prisoners. This is the regular routine of the day.

That first morning, after they are served their ration of bread and water, the gaoler's wife, Madame Garnot, appears, to shave Béatrice's head. This time

Béatrice puts up no resistance and her hair, grown over the months since it was first shaved, soon lies in soft clumps all over the cell floor. Madame Garnot works in silence and Béatrice says nothing. This procedure, so humiliating the first time, means nothing to her now. Grazide chatters constantly to Béatrice and to the other prisoners when she has the opportunity. What might once have irritated Béatrice now sooths and sustains her, as well as informing her of all that goes on inside and outside Alleman's. It is Grazide's presence which helps Béatrice to recover from the shock of her sentence. She cannot help but be interested in what Grazide has to say about the inmates of Alleman's. There is a great deal of contact with other prisoners, the women mainly, although, as Grazide has told her, Bernard Clergue has the run of most of the prison at times, and is constantly trying to make contact with various women who have implicated him and his family, to ask them to retract their testimonies. He frequently tries to pass messages to Béatrice through the other women and becomes angry, and shouts oaths and curses at those who will have nothing to do with him. He cannot enter the women's area, but he talks or shouts through the grating of the double door which guards the entrance to the women's quarters.

"He is asking for you to speak to him and for me to withdraw what I said about Pierre Clergue," says Grazide.

"I will never speak to him and I will never change my story, and nor should you, Grazide." She is firm. "You told the truth didn't you?" Grazide nods. "Well then, unless you want to be burned instead of Pierre or Bernard Clergue, you must remain quiet. Don't speak to Bernard. Ignore him when he shouts for you. He will soon grow tired and give up."

"No-one wants anything to do with them now, the Clergues. It was Pierre who betrayed the Cathars of Montaillou, well mainly him, there were others as well I believe, not from Montaillou, from elsewhere. Can you believe it? They were the strongest Cathar family in Montaillou." Béatrice winces as she listens to Grazide. "I told Jacques Fournier what Pierre told me, that it wasn't a sin in God's eyes for him to know me carnally as long as we both enjoyed it. I told him about Mengarde Clergue as well. She's dead now, consoled by the Good Men, I heard, but no-one witnessed it. Pierre buried her under the altar in Sainte Marie de Carnesses. People said she was a bad bitch who'd raised a bad brood. You should have seen the funeral they had for his father, Madame. Alazaïs helped to lay his body out, and they cut off his hair and fingernails to keep in the house to ensure that the luck of the family would carry on. Many came from miles around to pay their respects, but people said they were frightened that Bernard would take more land from them or more money if they didn't come, either that or else Pathau Clergue, their cousin, would beat them."

Béatrice lets Grazide's chatter wash over her. She learns that Raymonde Guilhou, the Clergues' servant girl, has talked and is here in Alleman's, along with the Maurs brothers, the two remaining sons of poor, mutilated Madame Maurs. Alazaïs, she learns, is on bread and water rations for her part in supporting the Good Men. The sad, bereft Guilabert family, whose young son, the shepherd boy, received the *consolamentum*, are here too. Alamande Guilabert and Guillemette Benet are here on bread and water rations, and shackled in their cells. Fortunately, no-one seems to know about or recall Béatrice's own father's *consolamentum*, otherwise Béatrice, too, could be shackled and be on bread and water only. Guillaume Fort, whose house in Montaillou was torched by the Inquisition and turned into a dung heap, is imprisoned here, also on the strictest of regimes. What tragedy is here in this foul place. These people who helped their loved ones or followed their hearts, and now they are here. The old questions about God run around her mind. Is this God's way? She is interested and saddened, but resigned. Nothing can harm her now. The worst has happened, she has lost her freedom.

At night she sleeps well, her body next to the warmth and comfort of Grazide's body, whilst cockroaches roam around the cell, climbing the walls and scuttling away into unseen cracks when a thin finger of light points its way into the cell in the early morning. Rats regularly creep in and lurk there, sniffing the air and circling the cell, then out again. They leave her alone, these loathsome creatures, and she is not afraid of them.

In August, when the one thing to be said about Alleman's is, that although it is a stinking and festering hell-hole, it is relatively cool, Grazide and Béatrice hear a small commotion as the great doors to the women's quarters open, and a line of women prisoners is pushed and pulled and shouted down the stairs. Their cell door opens and a woman is shoved in. They both recognise their new companion. She is the mother of one and the friend of the other. It's Fabrisse.

"Maman!" says Grazide.

"Fabrisse!" says Béatrice.

Fabrisse stares at them. She's unsure, puzzled. Then her pale, drawn face breaks into a toothless smile.

"You both look so different," she says. "Your hair, what's happened?" She moves to Grazide and touches her scalp.

"Why are you here? What's happened?" says Béatrice.

The three of them move to sit on the pallet and Fabrisse, squashed between them, tells them. "I told Jacques Fournier that I saw Guillaume Authier at the Clergues' house all those years ago, and… well, it seems that Bernard Clergue has told many lies about me saying that I was a supporter of the Cathars. He seems to be telling lies about everyone and everything to try and save himself." Fabrisse pauses and sighs. "They said I was consorting with heretics and supporting them and that I hadn't told the truth. I'll have to be questioned again some time soon. That's why I'm here. I never would have thought that we would be together like this."

Grazide starts to cry. Her mother puts her arm around her. "This place, it must wear you down."

"We've got each other," says Béatrice. "That's the only good thing about it. Grazide told me never to lose hope when I first came here and she's right, we must not give up."

Grazide nods. "We must help each other."

Together the three of them, Béatrice, Grazide and Fabrisse live through each day in their tiny cell. At night, they lie together, their bodies curled around each other on the shared pallet and they sleep well. Life in Alleman's is bearable because of this closeness. Béatrice tells them, piece by piece, of her capture and interrogations, and they in turn tell their stories.

In August 1321, they learn of the death of Guillaume Fort of Montaillou. He has been burned at the stake in the cemetery of Saint Jean. His crime was that he could not bring himself to say that he believed in the transubstantiation of bread and wine into the body and blood of Christ at the altar, and for this he lost his life. In September of that year they hear a great wailing and shouting. It's Bernard Clergue screaming out all over the prison.

"My God is dead, what shall I do now? How can I live without my God?"

They learn that the God he refers to is his brother, Pierre Clergue, who was under house arrest at Mas-Saint-Antonin. Pierre Clergue has died there. Bernard's loud weeping and wailing only stops when the wife of the master of the prison Madame Rival comes down and threatens to chain him if he won't stop his weeping.

"You must grieve quietly as others grieve," she tells him.

There are rumours that Pierre Clergue was tortured and that he died from his injuries. They hear that as Pierre lay dying he did not renounce his Cathar beliefs. Bernard Clergue now complains constantly about his cell-mate, Barthélemy Amilhat, who recites his canonical hours every day, the eight offices of Matins, Lauds, Prime, Terce, Sext, None, Vespers and Compline, day in and day out. This demonstration of Roman steadfastness irritates Bernard. In November, Bernard is questioned by the Bishop and allowed his freedom on condition that he attends for further questioning in December. Bernard gleefully proclaims this to the inmates as he leaves his cell. The talk around Alleman's is that Barthélemy has information for the Bishop about Bernard Clergue, who has incriminated himself by refusing to cross himself and pray as a good Roman should. Bernard has been so full of his own concerns that he has not thought that Jacques Fournier could be as devious as himself.

Béatrice, Fabrisse and Grazide remind each other of the ways of good and faithful Romans. They pray and cross themselves and they ask for a priest to confess to. They will do whatever is necessary to help themselves. They hear in the spring that their friend Alazaïs Azema has died in her cell.

It is the following year, on 4th July 1322, that the warden of the prison appears at their cell door. He clanks his keys and opens the doors.

"Béatrice de Lagleize, Fabrisse Rives, Grazide Lizier, come with me."

They follow obediently. They ask no questions but along with some others are herded into the courtyard of the prison. The master of Alleman's is there in the company of an Inquisitor, who reads from a scroll the names of those who are to be released or given further penances.

"Barthélemy Amilhat, for release today, and required to do further penance through prayer. Fabrisse Rives for release today and required to wear double yellow crosses in perpetuity. Grazide Rives for release today and required to wear double yellow crosses in perpetuity. Béatrice de Lagleize for release today, and required to wear double yellow crosses in perpetuity."

She shivers. She had expected penances, a pilgrimage, prayers perhaps but not the yellow crosses. She can never leave them behind now. They've clung to her all her life. She smiles to herself, how could she have ever thought she could escape them? But she takes a deep breath, she has the strength to bear these pieces of cloth, that's all they are, pieces of cloth. They will not destroy her. She has much to be grateful for, her life, her family, her homes, her money. She will not let the yellow crosses contaminate the life she has left. She will wear them in public, she will go to church and appear to be a good Roman. No-one will know her innermost thoughts, except perhaps God – that is if he exists.

Aftermath

Bishop Fournier continued to interrogate Bernard Clergue over the next three years, sending for him from Montaillou. There were many witnesses whose testimonies incriminated him and, finally, Bernard, who became ill at home in Montaillou, was sentenced to imprisonment at Carcassonne in August 1324. By the September, he was dead.

Those consoled by Cathar Perfects, Bernadette Benet, Na Roqua and the young shepherd boy, Guillaume Guilabert, were amongst the many whose graves were desecrated by the Inquisition. Their remains were dug up and the piles of muddy bones were paraded through the streets of Pamiers on carts, then ceremoniously burned until they were reduced to ashes. Even dead believers were not left to rest in peace. The very last Cathar Perfect, Guillaume Belibaste, was burnt alive in 1322, at Villerouge-Termènes.

It was in the January of 1329 that Pierre Clergue's remains were also exhumed and posthumously burned because he died without renouncing his Cathar beliefs. But Mengarde Clergue, Pierre Clergue's mother, as far as anyone knows, remains buried near the altar in the church of Sainte Marie de Carnesses in Montaillou. There were no witnesses to her *consolamentum*, and there was no evidence to show that she had been consoled.

The last vestiges of Catharism were totally and utterly erased by the end of the second decade of the fourteenth century.

Bishop Jacques Fournier had an illustrious career on the strength of his work as Inquisitor in Pamiers. In 1327, he became a cardinal, and, in 1333, he was elected Pope Benoit XII, at Avignon. He commissioned the building of a great Palace in Avignon, where the Papacy was situated, which took seven years to build. He died in 1342 and his remains are in the church at Avignon.

Acknowledgements

Thanks are due to many people who enabled me to complete this book. The list starts with Jean Duvernoy, a French historian and translator, who first translated and published in 1965 the remarkable records of the Inquisition on which this book is based. The records had been kept in the Vatican archives for nearly 700 years until they were released into the public domain in the 20th Century. Bishop Jacques Fournier and the people he interrogated spoke Occitan. The records were written in Latin, Jean Duvernoy translated them into French. In 1978, Emmanuel Le Roy, Professor of the History of Modern Civilisation at the College de France, Paris, analysed the records and published his book, *Montaillou.* The book became a best seller and was further translated into English by Barbara Bray. Nancy P Stork, Professor of English and Comparative Literature at San Jose State University, California has since translated many more of the records into English.

In 2000, Rene Weis, Professor of English Literature at University College, London published *The Yellow Cross*. It was this wonderful book which first drew my attention to the story of the last Cathars, and I am eternally grateful to Rene Weis for his accessible and absorbing account of what happened in and around the village of Montaillou, at the end of the 13th Century and in the early years of the 14th Century. Those events still have the power to fascinate and resonate strongly with us today.

I owe thanks to the friends and family who read early drafts and editions of this book, to Debi Alper, who understood what I wanted to do, to Sarah-Clare Conlon for her editorial skills (and her friendship), to

David for accompanying me on many trips to the Pyrenees and for giving me space to write.

I wish I could also thank the people of the Langudoc, whose voices can be heard so clearly in Jacque Fournier's records. They describe not only their religious beliefs but also many details of their daily lives, giving us a unique source of such information. In the pages of the literature the people of the Languedoc come to life and show their humour, their intelligence, their strengths and their weaknesses, their humanity.

For them the driving force behind the final revival was the belief in Catharism as the only way to salvation. The self-indulgent, vow-breaking behaviour of some Catholic priests and the universal dislike of the extortionate taxes demanded by the Church added weight to the Cathar cause. But there was perhaps also a deeper motive and more generalised motive, a hatred and fear of the power and control that the Roman Church exercised over the peoples' lives. Viewed in this context the final attempt at a revival of Catharism can be seen as a bid for freedom, a deeply felt cry from the hearts of people who felt strongly enough to risk their lives for their beliefs.

I believe that the story of these courageous people and the wrongs that were perpetrated against them should never be forgotten.

Susan E Kaberry

Jan 2018